AISHA TRITLE

NOUMENA

Black Rose Writing | Texas

ISBN: 978-1-68513-172-2
PUBLISHED BY BLACK ROSE WRITING
www.blackrosewriting.com

Printed in the United States of America
Suggested Retail Price (SRP) $21.95

Noumena is printed in Adobe Garamond Pro

*As a planet-friendly publisher, Black Rose Writing does its best to eliminate unnecessary waste to reduce paper usage and energy costs, while never compromising the reading experience. As a result, the final word count vs. page count may not meet common expectations.

Dedicated to Mom & Dad, Miranda for being a stalwart pillar gem, Frankie my tango partner, Ruhi and Sam for keeping me going with our food diaries, Laura for being a wise glam inspiration, Roger the life sherpa, Tommy for putting up with me at my most emo, and Vidhya the wonderful pal and neighbor.

NOUMENA

Your past goes away when the Renewers bring you back. Sometimes all of it, sometimes just a little, but it's never completely there.

I remember that I loved once. He stayed behind when I decided I wanted the future and now, I don't know where he is. We were both burned out, our faces marked by lines we'd acquired by living as best we could. We had children once, but they were killed by the Infirmum.

And that is why the world is what it is. The sickness rampaged across the Earth. Then, suddenly, all the children were gone without the chance of there ever being any more, leaving behind a brokenhearted population who might as well have been dead themselves. Tears filled the streets that soon became empty because no one wanted to stay.

I'm here because I'm selfish. All of humankind was in ruins and I decided there was still more to see. The world was dying, but I didn't want to. We were given the chance to witness a better world but he didn't take that chance, so we were separated.

I might've lost my heart the day I said goodbye, or at least half of it, but is that bad? Self-preservation: I chose that. Maybe I have less of a soul than I did, but I don't need the entirety of my soul to live.

I look around at the rest of us. Those who fall short have been disposed of by those who wield authority, leaving faces lit with youth, bodies examples of perfect health. The world is now a secure urban jungle of steel and cement. Its occupants are beautiful, and I am one of them.

The countless tests I went through to get here, the analyses, the sacrifices—they were all worth it. I have everything I ever wanted, except him. And the details of the face that I once loved are leaving my mind, replaced with the sight of another.

Michael's was the first face that I saw in this life. His clear blue eyes and golden hair reminiscent of an angel as he looked down on me. That thought of him is clearest in my mind. Everything from before is a blur. There are things I think I remember, but they don't make me feel. Almost nothing from my past life makes me feel.

Except, I still get chills when I remember the mist, the glass in front of my face, and my awareness slipping into blackness. But then I woke up.

My name is Astrid Rayner. I chose self-preservation, and I got a new world.

CHAPTER 1

The sharp click of my heels is drowned out by the dutiful bustle of the city. Beautiful faces flock past, sometimes illuminated by a flash of light that outlines a part of the hex grid that forms our sky. The seal protects us from ever being subject to a terror like the Infirmum again.

Our souls—or whatever we have left of them—are much older. But we aren't scarred by the difficulties of the past. We focus on the present. The new life we've been given, free of sicknesses like the Infirmum, has renewed us. There is still suffering. But only for those who are unworthy.

I pull the collar of my coat up and focus on my destination: The Office of Regulation – known as "OR" - a mirrored dome that stretches up 34 levels. Only a select few are allowed to pass through its doors, and I am one of them.

I hear the buzz of a Regulator's gun and turn my head. You'd think the sight of an unworthy being taken away would have lost its novelty by now. But there's something about the process that fascinates me.

The widening of the eyes in shock, then the limpness of limb, followed by two Regulators carting them off. There's no chance for a fight. The one they're taking today looks like all the others. He's young and attractive. There's hardly any way to discern an unworthy by their appearance. The Renewers are careful. But sometimes they bring back someone who disrupts the balance.

There are many ways to disrupt the balance. Sometimes when people are brought back, their mind changes. My mind probably changed. The psych evaluations from a past life don't always carry through. After all, if a person doesn't have their memories, who *are* they? So, someone will do something. Or sometimes, a person just doesn't fit or offer anything we need: human surplus. No one chooses who is brought back or what their occupation is, that's left to the Intelligent System.

But sometimes the System makes mistakes.

I don't have to worry about being an unworthy. The reason my job exists is because of them. I'm not a Regulator either. Well, I'm a regulator of sorts. But the Regulators carry out their jobs in public. There are no witnesses to what I do.

I grab the handle of the door and it opens. Heartbeat signature recognition via electrical activity. We can't have just anyone coming inside.

The lighting in the building is garish, a stark contrast with the refined interior. Smooth gray furniture, opaque glass walls. Everything in this city is sleek.

There's only one person on the first floor: David. He's of an unassuming appearance. Blond hair, pale skin, light brown eyes. He's always here when I visit, even in the ungodly hours of the early morning. It's nine p.m. now and I wonder if he ever sleeps.

"Astrid." He nods.

I nod back and feel his eyes on me as I walk towards the elevator. Part of me wonders if I'm the only one he watches so closely, and if I'm the only one, then why? But David is unimportant. He is just the face people see when they visit the OR, and there are only a few of us.

The elevator feels like it's barely moving. The doors open on the tenth floor. *Mr. Winters' Floor.* No one knows him by any other name.

My footsteps resound loudly down the cold hallway. His office is at the end. I pause in front of the steel doors and knock twice. Silence follows, as it usually does with Mr. Winters. I rub my hands together while I wait. The OR is always kept at a cold temperature consistent with its sleek aesthetic. I hear the lock of the steel doors click open and push my way in.

Mr. Winters: a name befitting a middle-aged, silver man. But we don't have any of those now. He sits on a leather chair: the only sign of comfort and domesticity in a cold, dead room. Olive-skinned, black hair, aquiline nose, and brows that sit heavy upon green eyes that seem much older than the body that possesses them.

"Astrid."

"Mr. Winters."

Silence follows again.

He lifts a thin hand and touches the glass table in front of him. It lights up and green text flows rapidly across the surface. He says nothing. He only speaks when he has to, and I'm loath to start a conversation he doesn't want.

He sprawls out two fingers and stops the flow of text. A picture appears, next to the usual list: name, occupation, address, personality profile, where to find them, and relevant details as to why exactly they're on Mr. Winters' smart glass. I fix my eyes on the picture. It's a man, aged twenty-five, as all are. Cropped brown hair, brown eyes, wide grin. He looks far happier than most of the occupants of this world.

I look at his occupation. "Network Architect?"

Mr. Winters clears his throat. "A Network Architect guilty of misusing his knowledge. He manipulated the System and brought back an unworthy."

I feel a slight wave of disgust and confusion. "Why would he do that?"

Mr. Winters waves a hand towards my coat pocket. I pull out a small sheet of glass—a 4-inch display version of what he uses as a table—and lay it on top of the picture. Immediately, it absorbs all the information and glows with a blue light. I slip it back into my coat.

"It really doesn't matter why he did it," says Mr. Winters. "What matters is that he disrupted the balance."

I run a finger across the warm glass in my pocket, and I know disrupting the balance is an unforgivable sin.

"What happened to the unworthy?" I ask.

"The unworthy will be taken care of shortly."

I fix my gaze on the glass table again. The green text above the picture reads, "Damon Roberts." There is still something about his expression that strikes me, maybe a certain purity that the rest of us are missing.

"He can't be returned," says Mr. Winters. "You know what to do." He leans back and crosses his hands neatly in his lap. "We'll send someone after you're done."

It's the usual process; I eliminate the problem, somebody else cleans up. With a wave of my hand, I turn and stride out of the room. Soon, I'm back out in the street. Everyone is still out. The city never sleeps. If the streets were ever empty, it'd be like it was before. The past that everyone wants to forget. The past that's slowly turning into a haze.

My occupation makes it impossible for me to take public transportation. So, I shun the rail and turn down a side street close to the OR. Despite the lack of any seemingly worthwhile places to visit on this street, the crowded sidewalk forces me onto the road.

I walk for a few minutes before I find it: the warehouse. The streetlight in front of it has given out, or maybe it was put out. I cross the sidewalk and push my hand onto the steel door of the warehouse. Again, heartbeat recognition. The door gives way. I quickly slip into the darkness and let the door click shut behind me.

As soon as it shuts, the warehouse fills with garish light similar to the lighting in the OR. But inside of here, everything is at my disposal. The sleek occupants of the space are automobiles and motorcycles, along with a few tanks and small aerial pods left over from the last life. Another benefit of the seal is that we never need to blaze through the streets in a tank or shoot through the sky in an aerial anymore - but for some reason, they're still maintained.

I pull the glass out of my pocket and check Damon Roberts' location again. He lives close, about fifteen minutes away. I walk past rows upon rows of dark cars – all autonomous, some 4-seater capsules between giant wheels, some sleek two-seaters with bodies that seem to glide. My favorite is a two-seater in the back; I leave all my tools in it. Its rich, black exterior comes into view. I open the trunk and unzip a duffle bag. Gleams of silver greet my eyes; the bag has everything I need. But I've already decided what I'm going to use.

I wrap my hand around a small roll of wire and close the trunk. It's simple, but it always gets the job done. I settle into the car and the windshield lights up. I input the address. A door in the back of the warehouse slides open, and I'm off.

I settle back into my seat and slip the roll of wire into my coat pocket. The purity of Damon Roberts' expression is stuck in my mind. He was smiling. No one before him had ever smiled in any of the photos that I'd been given. What did it *mean*? I try to think, but my thoughts can only get so far. Recently it seems like there's a wall. A wall that hasn't been there in the past.

But things change when you're brought back. Everybody knows that. The streetlights glow outside the window. Light sparks in a honeycomb pattern again; a side effect of the weather control. Soon, I enter the more exclusive section of the city: Oriel, somewhere I know well. Maybe living in such brilliance gives them the courage—the *ego*—to disrupt the balance.

Fools. Who else would risk the chance of never returning? The buildings in Oriel stretch far into the sky. Shining masses of glass and steel and gold. But unlike the paved jungle I've just come from, Oriel has greenery: trees, flowers, parks with fountains. There is even Oriel Lake in the center. It's a pond, really, but Oriel is too magnificent to have a mere pond.

I settle further back into my seat. Golden light from Oriel's lamps filter through the window. I've seen the scenery outside so many times it holds no excitement for me anymore. Damon Roberts' grin is searing into my mind, but I can't make any sense of it. Then again, he lives in Oriel. Why wouldn't he be smiling?

I relax the muscles in my body one by one, they'll be working hard soon enough. The car glides along with a low hum.

I run my fingers along the coil of wire in my pocket. I've always been confident of never being an unworthy, though a machine could do my job. It really could. But technology could render any job done by a human moot. That's why those at the top have instated limits. Limits keep our society functional.

I draw air deep into my lungs. I'm safe. I will *never* be an unworthy. I pull the mirror down and turn the light on. I smile and stare at my face. I look innocent, pleasant. There should be no problems. Things will happen as they usually do.

The car stops in front of one of the shorter buildings in the city. What it lacks in height, it makes up for with its structure: curved gold, rose-tinted glass. I touch the left corner of the glass windshield and a blue set of zeroes appear on the screen. I set the timer to exactly twenty minutes. As soon as I step out of the car, it glides away.

I enter the lobby. No one's there. Most of the residential buildings in Oriel don't hire front-desk staff anymore; they rely on welcome screens. It lights up as I walk past, ready to help me with whatever information I need for my visit. But I already know where I'm going, and I have the key to get there.

I pull my glass out of my pocket and slide it across the entry sensor for the elevator. The doors open. I press the button for the third floor. Damon Roberts occupies the entirety of it. The doors slide open, revealing a room furnished with the most expensive pieces of furniture and art. There are some Grecian sculptures, some paintings by…I can't remember. But what a waste.

I step out and look around. I don't see Damon anywhere so I call out. "Hello?" The sound of rushed footsteps meets my ears. He comes through a door on my right, his face contorted with confusion. I try to look apologetic. "So sorry," I say. "I think my glass malfunctioned. I can't get back to my place."

The confusion leaves his face, and he smiles. A chill runs down my spine. There's something about the smile that strikes me. *Is* it purity? Maybe it's kindness.

He fixes his brown eyes on me. "What's your name?"

"Astrid."

He holds out his hand, I take it. Another chill runs down my spine.

"I'm Damon, nice to meet you."

I bring my hand back down, still feeling the warmth of his grasp.

He crosses the room. I see his smart glass laid across the kitchen counter. "I guess we'll have to call maintenance," he says.

I unfurl the wire in my pocket. "Yes, I suppose we'll have to."

"But first, let me get you something to drink." He smiles again.

I stare. I can't help it. "Water would be great, thank you."

He nods. "Coming right up."

I cast my eyes around the apartment. It's perfectly furnished in shades of cream and black. But the only signs of life —*real* life —are the pictures on the far wall. They're pictures of him and a woman. I study the apartment again. Nothing indicative of a woman's presence.

Then, it clicks in my mind. The unworthy. I turn my head to the pictures and focus. Who was she? Red hair, brown eyes, another kind face.

Damon's voice interrupts my studies. "Here you go," he says, handing me a glass of water.

I take a sip. "Thanks."

"Now, to call maintenance," he mutters, crossing back to the kitchen counter.

I quietly set the drink down. The wire is around his neck before he can touch his glass. It cuts into his skin, then deeper into his flesh. There's blood dripping down his shirt. He struggles. His hands try to pull at the wire. But I can handle him. I've done this many times.

He makes the sound that they all do: that pitiful gurgle. He tries to live, but he won't. His legs give way and he collapses. I kneel with him. His arms fall limply at his sides. I remove the wire from his neck. I steady my breathing, then throw the wire into the trash and wash the blood off my hands.

But blood can be hard to get off sometimes. I grab the kitchen towel and scrub at what's left sticking to my skin. There's some on my coat sleeves, but that's why I wear black. I throw the towel in the trash. Then, I gaze upon my work.

Whatever it was that struck me about his face is gone. His eyes are soulless, face and limbs frozen. I pull my smart glass out of my pocket and notify Mr. Winters. The cleaner never takes more than five minutes to show up. There's no need for me to stay around. They're all the same in the end. Why did I think he was different?

CHAPTER 2

I huddle in my chair and pull my coat around me. It's cold. But doctor's offices normally are, and the exclusively white interior adds to the chilly feeling. The other ten people in the room all look cold as well. A tan, green-eyed man stares at me. There's a slight smirk on his face. He looks familiar.

It takes me a minute to realize that I've seen him at the OR. It makes sense. We're grouped together and assigned to different doctor's offices based on occupation. This is the first time I've ever seen anyone else from the OR here, though. I look at all the others in the waiting room. What do they do? The man who's staring at me nods. I nod back.

A blonde woman comes through the door to my right. She seems stiffer than usual.

"Astrid Rayner," her voice booms as she fixes me with hazel eyes that always seem colder than this office.

I stand up and follow her through the door. She leads me down a hallway that has exactly five doors on each side. I feel my heartbeat quicken. As much as it bothers me to admit, these weekly visits are the highlight of my life. The woman ushers me through the last door on the left, and my heart pauses.

"Hello, Astrid," says Michael.

His white coat hugs his broad shoulders. Bright eyes, brilliant smile, husky voice…everything about him is perfect. I've spent the last six visits trying to find a flaw, and I can't. It takes me a moment to find my voice. "Hello."

"And how are you today?"

"I'm doing well, thank you. How are you?"

I hang my coat up on the hook next to the door. Michael crosses over to the gray leather chair in the middle of the room and waves me over to it.

"Things are busy, per usual. It's good to see you."

I know he probably speaks out of polite formality, but I feel my cheeks flush. I lean back in the chair and try to bring my heart rate down to normal. He walks to the wall of smart glass on the opposite side of the room.

"Have you ever been to Caron Park?"

My attempt to slow my heart rate fails. Why is he asking me this?

"No, I haven't. I've heard good things though."

"They're shutting it down in a week. It's going to be replaced with a new community called Chrysos," he scoffs. "It's supposed to be the next Oriel."

The disdain in his voice resonates with me. I shake my head. As if we need another place filled with people who disrupt the balance. The wall of glass illuminates, covered with all my vital statistics. Michael runs his hand through his hair and studies the screen.

"Well," he says. "It would seem you're a victim of the white coat effect again."

I see the numbers on the glass climb up even more. The last time I managed a normal heart or blood pressure rate was probably two months ago.

"Oh, there it goes," says Michael, with a little laugh.

I try to keep the color out of my cheeks, but the warmth I feel tells me I haven't succeeded. He turns back to me.

"There's really no need to be nervous, Astrid."

If he only knew. "Sorry."

"You're fine." He smiles and grabs a small vial of blue liquid, piercing the seal with a small syringe. The blue liquid has everything I need; it's everyone's weekly routine. It's why we'll all be forever young. I barely feel the needle as it pushes through the skin on my arm.

"What are you doing tonight?"

I turn my head. "What?"

Michael's blue eyes seem brighter than usual. "What are you doing tonight?" he repeats.

I've received no notification to go to the OR, but you never know. "Nothing."

Michael is silent for a few moments as he disposes of the needle and bandages my arm. The room is too quiet. My breath and heartbeat seem to ring out deafeningly.

Finally, he speaks again. "Would you like to come to Caron Park with me?"

I stare, hardly believing my ears. "Yes, I'd like to go to Caron Park with you."

His expression doesn't change after my answer, much to my disappointment. It's hard for me to gauge what he's thinking. "How about I meet you there at seven p.m.?"

"That works."

His face shows that he's definitely not as nervous I am. I doubt his heart is even going at half the rate of mine.

Michael goes to the Smart glass to type up a few notes. I gaze at the back of his head, trying to organize my thoughts. Why does he want to go to Caron Park? There's nothing much to do in Caron Park, I think. I didn't realize anyone still went there, much less people like Michael. It has none of the excitement that the modern parks have. There are no cutting-edge amusements or restaurants buried within.

He turns back to me, and I try to pretend like I haven't been staring at him for the past minute and a half.

The corner of his mouth goes up into a half smile as we lock eyes. I cast my thoughts back to when I first met him six months ago. He's maintained the same, aloof composure since then. *Why is he asking me to go to Caron Park with him now?*

"You look well today," he says. "Black suits you."

I know black suits me. It suits everyone. That's why I always wear it. But his words still make me nervous. "Thank you."

"Do you feel you've adjusted completely?"

I start to feel more relaxed at his clinical question. "Yes, I do."

His gaze bores into me, and I almost feel as if I've said the wrong thing. "Interesting," he says.

His reaction puzzles me. "Is six months too soon?" I ask.

Michael's blue eyes widen at my question. "Everyone is different." He shrugs. "Some adjust within a month, others take years."

The tone of his voice is strange, as if he's trying too hard to sound like he doesn't care. He clears his throat. "So, I'll see you tonight at Caron Park? Seven p.m.?"

I wonder if he does this to a lot of his patients. Does it matter if he does? "Yes," I say. "I'll see you there."

He extends a hand and helps me out of the gray chair. Our hands stay together a little longer than they should. I hear his voice call out right before the door closes behind me. "It was lovely seeing you, Astrid."

CHAPTER 3

100 years ago. That's the last time I was in a place like this. And he was with me, along with our children. 100 years isn't that long when you've been asleep for most of it. But there are some who have been awake the entire time.

Granted, there have been plenty of advancements. This is supposedly the city where I spent most of my past life, but it looks nothing like it. I've taken the bandage off my arm; it's already completely healed. *Curat*— that's what they give us. They pump you full of it when you're renewed until you're reanimated with peak health, and then they give you small doses every week to maintain your regenerative abilities.

They'd just begun to come out with early versions of Curat when I was put under. From what I've been told, the creators of Curat survived on rudimentary versions of the drug until it was refined and deemed suitable for widespread use. I wonder about Michael. Has he been here the whole time? I know next to nothing about him, and I don't know what to make of the little I do know.

He was a Renewer six months ago. He renewed me. But now he's my doctor. Renewers hardly ever go back to being doctors because being a Renewer comes with prestige, money, and the ability to afford a beautiful place in Oriel. I smooth my dress. Why did he switch? Was he forced to because of a mistake? No, Michael doesn't seem the type to make mistakes. He's too in control, too self-possessed.

"Hello, Astrid."

I turn my head and look at the man who occupies most of my thoughts. It's the first time I've seen him out of his white coat. He's wearing a white button-down shirt, black denim pants, and polished oxfords. A black leather jacket hangs over his right arm.

"Hello," I say.

He steps closer, and I resist the urge to completely close the gap. "You look nice," he replies.

I try to keep my cheeks from turning as red as my dress. "So do you."

Michael laughs. His laugh is one of my favorite sounds. He waves towards a path on our left. "Shall we?" We walk down the trail, flanked by trees, flowers. Sometimes I think I hear the scurrying of a small animal, but I'm not entirely sure small animals exist anymore. "Such a shame this will all soon be gone," says Michael, with something that's somewhere between disbelief and hate.

"It *is* a shame," I say. But I lie. I don't care. I just want him to win him over. I feel his eyes on me and wonder if he knows that I'm lying.

"You don't have to pretend, Astrid." So he knows. My cheeks flush. He laughs again. "I'm glad you came with me tonight," he says.

There's no one else nearby. The only sound is the crush of gravel beneath our feet. "Of course," I reply. *Why am I here?*

His feet stop on the gravel path, and mine follow suit. He smiles. "I really appreciate you coming. It means a lot that you're here."

I don't know what to say. We start walking again, our path illuminated by the soft golden glow from the occasional lamp. There are so many questions I want to ask him. So many things about him that I want to know.

"So, Astrid. How do you fill your days?"

He has my file. He brought me back and evaluated me. Surely, he must know. "I work at the OR."

"People who work there have a lot of spare time on their hands. What else do you do?"

I stare at him, at a loss. *What do I do?* I think of the past few days. I train for an hour in the mornings and afternoons, I eat, I sleep. "I suppose I do what everyone else does."

"I see," says Michael. He's not convinced this time either.

I decide to shoot back, eager to deflect the spotlight. "What about you? How do you fill your days?"

"I spend most of my time at the practice." We've reached a part of Caron Park that holds an old fountain. It sprawls up about thirty feet and doesn't look like it should still be standing. Light flashes across the sky again. A chill runs down my spine. I can feel Michael looking at me again. I turn my head to meet his gaze. The expression on his face is different this time. He's intensely focused. His eyes shift back and forth, studying.

"What?" I ask.

"Have you been here before?"

"No, I haven't."

He doesn't reply; he just stares. Then I feel the warmth of his hand slipping into mine. He leads me past the fountain and down an avenue of trees. My heart is beating even faster than it was in his office. My courage picks up as we go down the shadowy lane. "Michael."

He stops, and his warm grasp moves up my arm. I wonder if he can hear my heartbeat. There are so many things I want to ask. Where do I start?

"What do you want to know?" he asks.

"Everything," I say, voice barely above a whisper.

He smiles but shakes his head. "I can't tell you everything."

I feel a slight pang in my chest. "But you know everything about me. You have a file."

"I don't know *everything* about you, Astrid," he says. We stare at each other for another silent moment. I think he's getting closer. I can't tell. The chills I feel are too distracting. He pulls me into him and whispers, "But I'd like to."

CHAPTER 4

High ceiling, silk sheets, the most comfortable bed I've ever been in. I stretch my arm out and run my hand across the smooth fabric. Suddenly, I'm enveloped in a warm embrace.

"Good morning," Michael says.

He kisses the side of my head, and I turn to look at him. "Good morning."

The sun is just starting to filter through the windows. The clock on the far wall reads six a.m. His blue eyes are locked onto mine and show no signs of leaving. How can so much change in less than twelve hours?

"Are you hungry?" he asks.

"Yes."

"What do you want for breakfast?"

This all feels foreign to me. Yet, I feel strangely relaxed. "What are my options?"

"Just tell me whatever you want," he says. "I'll put a request in to the Server."

I think of the bland breakfast I eat everyday: oatmeal, fruit, bread. I can't ask for that. I don't know what to ask for. I scan the bedroom I'm in; it's so refined. I run my hand through his hair. "How about you surprise me?"

It works. He smiles. "Okay." He kisses my forehead and gets up, pulling a gray robe across his shoulders as he exits the room.

I rub my hands down my face. *Why me?* Why would he pick me? But again, I hit the wall that's recently appeared in my thoughts. I'd told him I'd adjusted completely; and I have. Enough. It no longer feels like I'm floating in a dream. I know this world is mine. But this room that I'm in is filled with things that show Michael has *lived.* Art covers the walls. Sculptures, books, and trinkets are spread about. Everything in this room makes me feel plain and unworthy. My breath stops. I'll never be an unworthy. I bring balance. This world *needs* me.

Michael strides back into the room and hands me a robe. "Breakfast is ready," he winks.

I follow him through the door and into a wide, open space. It's rare that any interior in this city be anything but white or gray, but the walls of Michael's apartment are a comforting shade of blue. He leads me to a weathered wood table. Plates are laid across it and heaped high with salmon, omelets, crepes, whipped cream, and berries. I must look stunned because he lets out a laugh.

"Come on," he grins as he sits down. I watch him dig into the food with abandon before I start. He's used to nice things. Is he used to having nice breakfast companions?

"I haven't seen so many beautiful things in one place since I came back," I mumble, and his eyes lock onto mine. My cheeks flush because he's the most beautiful thing in here.

"Before the Infirmum, I collected many things worth keeping," he pauses and the smile leaves. "Back when we could explore, and see and feel things that expanded our minds."

He stares at something unseen and for a moment, I feel forgotten. Then, he's back.

"Do you remember what it was like outside of this city, Astrid?"

No images stir in my mind, much to my frustration. Does he find me boring? I shake my head. Michael reaches over and gently brushes a strand of hair from my face.

"That's fine," he whispers. "Hardly anyone does."

His hand slides down to the nape of my neck. I want him to keep it there but he turns his attention back to his breakfast. I should do the same.

"I have to go to work in a little bit," he says, between bites. "But you are more than welcome to stay here all day."

His pleasantness is pushed out of my mind by the realization that I haven't checked my Smart glass this morning. I don't even know if I can accept his offer until I check it. Mr. Winters might need me.

The corner of his mouth goes up and his blue eyes glow. He leans forward. "If you have to go to the OR, how about you just come back here after?"

I stifle a smile. "That sounds good."

I don't know what else to say, but he looks happy.

A shrill beep rings through the air. Michael pushes his plate away. "That's my cue."

He kisses my head again before going back into the bedroom. I get up and walk over to the coat rack by the front door. As I near it, I hear a muffled buzzing noise from the pocket of my coat.

I sigh. I'm being called in. Not that I mind. I pull out my Smart glass. It seems they want me in as soon as possible. I need to stop by my place for fresh clothes. I check the time again: it's 6:15 a.m. Usually when they call me in this early, it means one thing: *a full day.*

Michael shoots out of the bedroom impeccably dressed, hair perfectly styled. "Astrid, give me your glass."

I comply, almost without thinking. *Why do I trust him so much?* He puts it on the screen by the door, and both illuminate with a green glow.

"There you go," he smiles, handing it back to me. "Now you can get in without me." And just like that, he's given me a key. My own smart glass is advanced enough that I could've gotten in anyway, but he *gave* me a key. I stare at the warm glass in my hand. Why does he trust *me*?

He gently lifts my chin and kisses me. "I'll see you later?"

"Yes."

And he's gone.

CHAPTER 5

I stretch my arms to the side and roll my neck. Mr. Winters pays no mind to my movements as he pulls up the file on the smart glass. I've disposed of two disrupters today. It's only three p.m. Normally, I'd have no physical pain or fatigue at this point of the day. But the last two jobs were particularly strenuous.

Blood. There'd been so much blood. I bring my arms down and check my wrist: the victim of a mishap on a job today. I look at the hydrogel I've set around it; it's wrapped up pretty well. It feels like it's already healing. I suppose I could have Michael look at it.

Mr. Winters clears his throat. I switch my attention to the smart glass. This time, it's a woman. I step closer to the glass. It's hardly ever a woman. For some reason, most of the disrupters are men. Women hardly ever attempt to skew the balance; because they're intelligent enough to understand the risks. She looks strangely familiar. Red hair, brown eyes, kind face. My breath stops for a moment. It's the woman from the pictures in Damon Roberts' home.

Mr. Winters' voice cuts into my thoughts. "You look perplexed."

I shrug. "I'm just surprised that it's a woman."

I never share my thoughts with Mr. Winters. He doesn't reply. The name above the picture reads, "Christina Blythe." Occupation? Security Analyst. And she lives on the opposite side of Oriel. Interesting. I want to ask if she also brought back an unworthy – or if she *is* the unworthy he mentioned yesterday, but Mr. Winters's stoic face makes me feel that he's not in the mood to divulge…

"She's a Security Analyst," I say.

Mr. Winters fixes his green eyes on me and says nothing. But I decide to ask my question.

"Did she hack into the System as well?"

"More knowledge misuse," grumbles Mr. Winters. And he won't say anything else.

I set my smart glass on the table to get the info, then I head out of the room. I rarely care about my jobs. I'm never really interested in the people. But there's something about this situation that intrigues me. Once I'm in the warehouse, I go through the options in my bag. A part of me wants to use the wire again. But I've gotten enough blood on me today, and I'm tired.

I pull out a pistol and load it. It's plain, time-tested, and the most convenient tool right now. I grab a silencer and slide into the front seat. After I input the address, the car speeds out of the warehouse. Soon, the golden lights of Oriel are shining through the window. Questions fill my mind. Who is this Christina Blythe? And how exactly is she affiliated with Damon Roberts?

I think back to the photos on Damon's wall. Were they lovers? Family? The photos were filled with smiles. Genuine happiness. True happiness seems to be lacking in Oriel. *True love.* Did it even exist anymore?

The divorce rate in Oriel is 79%. When you're young, rich, and basically immortal—and surrounded by the young, rich, and basically immortal—I guess things don't last long. But then why is Christina on the opposite side of Oriel when photos of her were in Damon's house? I don't know.

The car stops in front one of the tallest buildings in Oriel. It's familiar to me; I had two jobs here last month. I screw the silencer onto the pistol, set the timer to twenty minutes, and get out.

I pull my glass out and use it to enter the lobby door. There are a few people in the lobby by the welcome screen, but nobody pays attention to me. My access gets me into the elevator, and I press the button for the twenty-second floor. My shoulders ache, as does my wrist. As soon as I'm done here, I get to go back to Michael and his beautiful eyes, his smile, his voice...

The elevator doors slide open and I step out. Then, I see her. She's pushing clothes into a bag and freezes. I can tell by her face that she knows why I'm here. I freeze as well. *Nobody* ever realizes what I am so quickly. We stand there; looking at each other. She should be dead by now. Why haven't I killed her yet?

She slowly raises her hands. There's something about her face that keeps me from moving: a lack of fear. Once people realize what I am, they're usually scared. But she isn't.

"Please don't," she says, voice calm.

I know what I have to do, so I don't know why the pistol is still in my pocket.

"You can let me finish packing," she says. "And I'll go. You'll never see me in this city again."

Obviously, I can't let her get away even if I want to. The cleanup crew would have no body to clean up, and Mr. Winters would return me, or worse.

"Why'd you do it?" I ask.

"Wouldn't you go to the ends of the earth for your family?"

I stare. She seems to be getting calmer, if that's possible.

"You and Damon..." My voice drifts off. Why am I so curious? Confusion crosses her face. She thought I knew everything.

We stand there for a few, silent moments. Her eyes shift back and forth, and I can tell her thoughts are running a thousand miles per hour.

She breaks the silence. "Just do it."

No one ever tells me to kill them. Her peaceful demeanor is making this difficult. It's never difficult for me, it's *always* easy. A chill runs down my spine. But I lift the pistol and she nods.

She lowers her eyes and steps forward, pushing her forehead into the silencer. I still don't pull the trigger. She just stays there, eyes lowered, silent. I want to know what she's done. Who did she bring back? *Who is she?* I'm taking too long to do this. The timer on my car is running down, and the cleaners are waiting.

I pull the trigger. She's too close. Blood splatters all over me. I stumble back and rush to the kitchen sink. I splash water on my face and rub it vigorously with a towel. I've been covered in blood many, many times, but it's never bothered me before. The hair on the back of my neck stands up. *There's someone else here.* I grab my pistol from the counter where I set it down. Then, I turn around.

Everything makes sense. A young man is staring at Christina's body: eyes wide, brow furrowed, hands pulling at his red hair. He turns to look at me, and I see the same purity that I saw in Damon Roberts' face. There are no tears in his eyes, just utter bewilderment. And I know why. I killed his mother *and* father. He's the unworthy they brought back.

I lift my pistol. He stares at me silently, then starts backing away. He knows what I did, and he's an unworthy. There's only one option. I pull the trigger.

CHAPTER 6

I set my glass on the screen next to the door and let myself into Michael's apartment. My body hurts even more than it did earlier, and my wrist is throbbing. I can't remember the last time I felt like this. Do I need more Curat? My next appointment isn't for another five days. The lights in the apartment illuminate as soon as I step inside. Michael isn't back, which is no surprise; it's only 4:30 p.m.

There's a smart glass pillar—the Server, able to fulfill almost any request—in the middle of the room, which doubles as a mirror when you're not using it. I take off my jacket and check my reflection. There's blood on my collar. There's also blood on my sleeve. I feel like an idiot.

Why didn't I stop by my place to change my shirt? *What would Michael think?* But Michael knows I work at the OR. He must know what I do. He's the physician for everyone who works at the OR. If he hasn't been told, he must have formed some sort of educated guess. I quickly slip off my shirt and tap the Server. The mirror's gone, now replaced with a set of options. I scroll through and find the wash option. The pillar splits in half and I insert my shirt in the gap. The pillar closes over the shirt, and I step back.

I'm such a fool. I should've stopped by my place to pick up extra clothes. Because he might ask me to spend the night again, I think. Or not. I don't know what's going on. This whole situation is foreign to me.

Within a minute, my shirt is done. I pull it out of the server and put it on. I check my reflection again. I look fine. My hair is smooth. The pain that my body feels isn't showing through in my face. I'm bright-eyed, rosy-cheeked.

The door opens. I turn around and our eyes meet. We stand there for a silent minute, just taking each other in. Why do I trust him so much? Because he's my doctor? He's the first face I saw, maybe that's why. Or it could be something else entirely.

He smiles. I don't think I've ever seen anyone more beautiful than him. He crosses over to me. The nearer he gets, the warmer my cheeks become. His hands gently hold my face and his lips press into mine. I don't think there's anything I want more in the world than him.

He pulls back and kisses my forehead. "I'm glad to see you," he says.

"I'm glad to see you, too."

He slides his arms down my back and brings me into him. We stand there for a while, not saying anything. I run my hands across his shoulders. There's no better feeling than being close to him.

Finally, he breaks the silence. "How are you?"

"I'm doing well. It's been a busy day—an interesting day."

The pain I feel seems to be going away.

"Interesting?" he asks. "How so?"

I take a while to reply. I trust him, but how much should I tell him? Those who work at the OR are not allowed to speak of their work. I shouldn't tell him anything. I pull back and look at his face. "What do you think of unworthies?"

He raises his eyebrows at my question. "I don't think the name is fitting."

"Why not?"

"Well, they're just like us, aren't they?"

He looks completely sincere. A wave of confusion sweeps over me. I'm *not* the same as an unworthy. Unworthies are low, unneeded, pointless. I have a point. I serve a purpose, and so does Michael.

"They're *not* like us," I say.

He sighs and narrows his eyes. I can tell he expected my answer. "How are they not like us?"

How can he not see? "You and I serve a purpose," I reply. "Unworthies don't have a purpose, or they disrupt the balance. Both are unacceptable. They're low."

"You believe balance is the most important thing in the world?"

"Balance is how we survive."

"How do you define balance?"

I can tell there's a deeper inquiry within his simple question.

"You can only have balance—perfect harmony—when you have the right amount of all the components. Unworthies shouldn't even be a component. Thus, even one unworthy will ruin the—"

I stop. Michael is shaking his head.

"What?"

"What's an unworthy, Astrid?"

I stare. "You know what an unworthy is."

"Just tell me," he replies. "In your own words, tell me what an unworthy is."

I take my time before speaking. I don't know what to make of his questions. "An unworthy can be one of two things: they can be a person who commits violent or disruptive acts, or they're pointless—human surplus."

I know he finds my answer unsatisfactory, but I can't tell what he wants. He backs away from me.

"You're just repeating what everyone's told," he says, disappointed.

"And what's wrong with that?"

"Think for yourself, Astrid!"

His voice is just short of a yell. I feel numb for a moment.

"We're all human," he says. "You say unworthies are low. What makes you or I better?"

A sinking feeling invades my chest. How did this turn into a battle? "We serve a purpose," I protest.

Michael leans forward. "Unworthies can serve a purpose, but they're robbed of that chance. Because someone—*something*— is deciding who lives and who doesn't."

A chill runs down my spine. What's happening right now? The eagerness that was on Michael's face when he entered is gone now. His eyes are narrow, brow furrowed, voice low and intense. I don't know what I did. And I don't know what to do.

"Do you feel, Astrid?"

His words hit me like a knife in the chest. "Of course I feel."

"Do you *really* feel?"

My voice fails me. Does he think that I don't feel? Then what was last night? He doesn't know what he's done to me.

"What do you feel when you rob people of their lives, Astrid?"

He *does* know what I do. I don't know whether to be relieved or scared. I still can't speak. His eyes bore into me, and I can tell he's becoming more frustrated.

"Do you feel any shame?" he asks. "Any regret?" I certainly feel shame now. I might feel regret soon. We stand there in silence. But the silence hurts this time. He crosses his arms. "Are you going to address any of this?"

I step further away from him. I don't want to be here anymore. He just stands there, studying me. "I feel," I say, my voice little more than a whisper.

Suddenly, there's regret in his face. Our eyes are locked to each other as I keep backing away. He rushes toward me. "I'm so sorry." But I have to leave. I can't stay here right now. He grabs my wrist and notices the hydrogel around it. He puts a hand on my shoulder to keep me from leaving. "Astrid, what happened?" I push his hand off my shoulder. "You're injured," he gasps. "Let me look at it."

But I don't even feel the pain from my wrist. The pain I felt earlier is gone, replaced with something that hurts far more. He follows me to the door. I can hear him begging me to stay, but I can't. I open the door and step out.

CHAPTER 7

The elevator doors slide open. I head down the hallway to Mr. Winters' office. The OR is unbearably cold, and it's been pouring rain outside. My hair is damp, so is my coat. I can't remember the last time I felt this cold.

I knock twice on the steel doors. It takes about a minute before the lock clicks open. The time between knocking and unlocking seems to extend more every time I visit. I push my way in and am greeted by the sight of Mr. Winters. He isn't in his usual chair. He's standing, arms crossed. My feet stop. He usually looks cold, but he's downright menacing today.

"Astrid."

"Mr. Winters."

Silence follows, per usual. He touches the table of smart glass and brings up a file. The man today seems different; shaved head, heavy brows, piercing gray eyes. I look up at Mr. Winters. His face now holds the same expression as usual: indifference. I turn my attention back to the glass.

The name reads, "Maksim Smith." There are fewer details than usual. His occupation isn't listed. Occupations are *always* listed.

"Who is he?" I ask.

"Everything you need to know is in the file," replies Mr. Winters. I run through the file again. It tells me hardly anything about him.

"All this tells me is his name and where he lives."

"That's all you need to know."

Every muscle in my body tenses up. I could swear that someone told me that being given harder jobs, or jobs that require more discretion, is a sign that you're working your way up at the OR. But I can't remember who that someone was…

Mr. Winters is sitting in his chair now, looking at me expectantly. I set my smart glass on the table to get the file, then I leave.

The rain isn't so bad when I step outside. I guess they've manipulated it to make it less severe, though I don't know why they would give us such heavy rain in the first place…

The streets show that everyone who can has stayed inside. I pull my hood up and head to the warehouse. There's a sinking feeling in the pit of my stomach. I'm not usually *this* nervous. But today feels different.

The way to the warehouse is clear except for a few people. I reach it much faster than I expected. As I walk to the car, I bring the file up on my glass. The faces of most people in this world hold a certain coldness, but there's something about Maksim's face that surpasses that. I open my black bag and think about what to use. I stare at the contents for a minute, lost in thought. Then, I pull out a knife and strap it to my thigh: my coat will cover it.

I pull out the pistol I used the other day, load it, and pull out a silencer. I continue to rifle through the bag. There *must* be something else. *Overkill.* Why do I feel the need for all this? I close the trunk and straighten my back. I've done this hundreds of times before. Everything will be fine. I slide into the front seat and input the address. He lives just down the street from my place. Mr. Winters has never given me a job so close to home.

Not that my apartment feels like home. The car speeds out of the warehouse and I settle back into my seat. Home is in the past. Home is where *he* was. But the other morning when I woke up in Michael's bed, that felt like home for a moment. It's been three days since I saw Michael, and he hasn't been out of my thoughts. *"Do you feel, Astrid?"* His question has been ringing through my mind. It bothers me to no end. Of course I feel. *Everyone* feels.

I look down at the file on my glass again. Maksim's harsh expression shoots back at me. *Everybody* feels, except maybe Maksim. I slip the glass back into my pocket. The file is making me uneasy. I turn around and look out the back window. Should I have gotten something else from my black bag? My breath isn't steady; I'm too nervous. As a trained killer, I shouldn't feel this way. I've never been this nervous on a job; not even the first. When I started, it felt like I was made for this job. With minimal training, I was set: always on top of my game, everything executed with no problems. But today feels different.

It's the lack of details in the file. What is his occupation? Is he like me? I push myself back into my seat. *What if he's like me?* My hands feel like they're being pricked by a million pins. I shake them out. I'll be fine. The car stops in front of a building that looks an awful lot like mine: tall, opaque glass. I set the timer on my car to fifteen minutes; five minutes less than usual. I want to get in and get out as quickly as possible.

I push my pistol into the pocket of my coat and step out. The rain has gotten heavier again. It pours down on my head as I enter the building. I wipe the water off my face with my sleeve. There's a couple in the lobby. The way they look at each other digs into my mind. Is it love or is it just lust? I don't think love exists in this city. I rub my face with my cold hands. I'll be fine.

I press the button for the tenth floor. The elevator doors slide open. *Darkness.* I stand there, puzzled. Is he not here? Even if he isn't, apartment lights usually illuminate whenever someone enters. I step out of the elevator. The lights still don't turn on. I switch my smart glass into flashlight mode.

My breath is short, and my hands are still tingling. I pan the light around the room. The apartment is strangely bare. It's not that it's empty; there's a decent amount of furniture. It just doesn't look like anyone *lives* here. There have been a few jobs in the past where I've had to ask Mr. Winters to ping me the target's exact location, because apparently the OR can't be bothered to give me live updates. It looks like I might have to do that today. I'm starting to feel more and more uncomfortable. I switch the light off on my smart glass and look at the file again.

Should I call Mr. Winters? My hands continue to tingle. I shake them out one by one. Suddenly, I feel the collar of my coat pulled back and a hand swings into the side of my face. I reach for my pistol, but that's quickly knocked out of my hand. My smart glass is on the floor now. The faint glow from its screen is the only illumination in the room.

I see Maksim's face: frozen, empty.

He reaches for my throat; I dodge his hands and strike his chest. He steps back. I try to kick his knee and miss.

It's so dark…I can barely see. I feel my feet knocked out from under me and fall on my back. I get up as quickly as I can. My hand reaches for the knife I strapped to my thigh: it's gone. I see a flash of steel coming towards my face and block it. A scream of pain escapes from me as the knife cuts straight through my right palm.

I put my left hand on the handle of the knife and fight Maksim for it. The darkness is causing him to stumble as well. I manage to kick his knee, and his grip on the handle loosens. The pain in my hand is almost unbearable, and it gets worse as I slide it off the knife. Two hands close around my throat; I blindly thrust the knife in front of me. I can feel it dig through bone, then there's blood. The handle leaves my hand as Maksim falls away from me.

I see the outline of his body on the floor and my breath stops. My muscles are tense, ready for him to come back at me. But he doesn't move.

I don't know how long I stand there. Blood from my wounded palm flows in rivulets down my fingers. Finally, my breath comes back. I reach for my glass and turn it back into flashlight mode. Maksim is dead. The knife went through his forehead. I kneel to get a closer look. In the past, when I've killed, I've noticed that people's faces change drastically as soon as the life leaves them. The face becomes empty; a shell. But this man's face looks the same.

Was he even alive before? I feel sick. I frantically pan the light around the room. The layout of this place is strange. I stumble through the nearest door and into a bathroom. The lights inside of the room illuminate as I turn the sink faucet. Chills run through my body as I catch sight of myself in the mirror. Is this what I always look like after I kill someone?

I thought I always looked fine. I *should* be fine right now. But I'm not. I back into the wall and fall to the ground, my body trembling.

For the first time since I was brought back, I cry.

CHAPTER 8

"Astrid, what happened?" Michael studies me. I turn my head away. It's been two days since the incident with Maksim. I'm at my weekly Curat appointment. My neck and cheeks feel warm. Michael gently holds my hand. It's a mess of colors. "Why didn't you come in earlier?"

I still don't look at him. I can't tell him what happened. I can't tell him I've been crying in my apartment for the past two days. There's been a pain. A pain that digs into my chest, my brain, everywhere. I'd almost forgotten about my hand. Michael's focus doesn't leave my face. I can feel those blue eyes boring into me. His hands leave mine and settle on my shoulders.

"Astrid," he says.

I can't avoid looking at him now. "What?"

"Why didn't you come in earlier?"

I shrug. He stares at me in disbelief. I don't have to tell him everything. A part of me wants to, but I shouldn't. "Curat fixes everything, doesn't it?" I ask.

He crosses the room and picks up a syringe and the usual vial of blue liquid. Perfect golden hair, broad shoulders. Looking at him hurts more than my hand does right now. He fills the syringe with the liquid and crosses back to me. I don't feel the needle as it pierces my skin. All I feel is pain and desire, and all I see is his face.

He looks like he might be hurting, too—or maybe that's just what I want. I want him to regret what he did. He's not looking at me right now, so I study him. I still can't find any flaws.

"Astrid," he says, voice low.

"Yes?"

A moment passes before he replies. "What are you doing tonight?" This again. I stifle a scoff. He looks eager, and it bothers me to admit that my heart is beating much faster than it should. "What are you doing tonight?" he asks, again.

"Why do you want to know?"

"Because I'd like to see you," he says.

My heart starts to race even faster. I shouldn't want to see him, but I do. "I'm busy."

"No, you're not."

"How do you know?"

He steps forward. "Don't lie to me, Astrid."

We stand there for a minute. Silent. Eyes locked onto each other. I want to get closer to him. Close the gap that separates me and him. I can tell he does, too. *"Do you feel, Astrid?"* His question rings through my head again.

"Sir, your next appointment is waiting," says a shrill voice. It's that blonde woman who ushers everyone in.

Michael's eyes narrow. "Thank you." The woman's face doesn't change as she looks from me to Michael, then back again. "Thank you," repeats Michael.

The woman stiffly shuffles out. Everything in this city happens with precision. Nothing is ever late. The rail's longest delay is six seconds. My appointment was supposed to end five minutes ago.

"You should probably get on to your next appointment," I mutter.

Michael leans down and puts his hands on the armrests of my chair. He's blocking me. He doesn't want me to leave.

But I should. "You'll probably get in trouble if you get off schedule."

"I'll be fine."

My heart and breath are far too fast, and my cheeks are blazing. I try to act like I don't care. I try to act like he doesn't affect me so much. "You get off schedule often?"

"No."

Should I push him away? There's something about his voice and the way he looks at me that keeps me from moving.

"You should see me tonight," he says.

It feels like my heart has leapt into my throat. "Why? Why should I see you?"

His face is getting closer. I turn away. He stops. "I'm sorry, Astrid."

I can feel myself already starting to give in. *Why am I so weak?* "I should see you because you're sorry?"

"Please, let me see you." His eyes are pleading, begging. This is what I've wanted for the past six months. I've wanted him to want me.

"I don't know," I whisper.

Michael's cheeks are starting to flush as well. He's frustrated, angry. But I don't think he's angry with *me*. He stands up and buries his face in his hands. "I'm such an idiot," he mumbles. I resist the urge to pull him back to me. We stand there in silence; I'm not sure for how long. I'm surprised the blonde woman hasn't checked in on us again. Finally, he brings his hands down from his face.

"Astrid…"

"Yes?"

I stand up. He sets a hand on the back of my head and pulls me into him. I remember there's no better feeling than being close to him. *Why have I already given in?* "Will you come over tonight?"

The desperation in his voice is compelling. I nod.

"Do you promise?"

He presses his lips into mine. I return his kiss. "I promise."

CHAPTER 9

I turn my smart glass into mirror mode and check my reflection before stepping into the elevator. I think I look fine. I've made an effort. A part of me is embarrassed by just how much of an effort I made. The elevator doors slide open. The skyscraper where Michael lives is structured differently from many in this city: it's twice the size of most apartment buildings, with each floor divided into two residences.

I head down a short hall to my left and stop in front of his door. I take a moment to steady myself. I can handle this. My heartbeat rings in my ears as I set my glass on the screen next to the door. The door clicks open. So, he never deactivated my key.

"You came."

Michael's blue eyes are wide, lips parted.

"I told you I would," I reply.

He looks like he can't quite believe his good luck. We stand there, gazes locked. I'm not sure if I should push my way in or just stay here. He takes my arm and pulls me into the apartment. "Are you healing up well?"

I steal a glance at my bandaged hand. It only hurts a little now. "Yeah, it's healing up well. No pain."

The corner of Michael's mouth goes up in a half-smile. "Good."

I look around the apartment, stunned. It's obvious I'm not the only one who put in an effort. Lit candles are spread around, soft music is playing, and there's a bouquet of crimson roses in a vase on the table. There's something about the roses that holds my attention. I don't know what it is. They're beautiful, but there's something about them – about all of this, actually - that just seems so *familiar.*

"Would you like some champagne?" Michael walks over to the Server in the middle of the room and looks at me expectantly.

"Champagne?" I ask. "What are we celebrating?"

"Your presence is just cause for celebration."

I smile. I can't help it. He smiles back. The two halves of the pillar separate, and he pulls out two glasses of champagne. He hands me a glass and his fingertips touch mine.

He waits a bit before letting go of the glass. "Cheers."

"Cheers," I say. He downs his glass. I follow suit.

"Have you eaten?"

I shake my head. His hand slips into mine. "Come here," he whispers. He leads me to the Server. "Alright, what do you want?"

I can't think right now. I want him. But I won't say that. "I don't know. How about you decide?"

He brings up the culinary options on the pillar. I'm not sure what he chooses; I'm too busy looking at him. I've never seen anyone so *perfect.* He turns away from the pillar and his hands slide down my back. "It'll be a minute or two."

"Okay."

Michael's getting closer. I know I shouldn't give in so easily. I turn my face away. He stops.

"Would you like some more champagne?"

I hand my empty glass back to him. "I'd love some, thank you."

A panel of the pillar lifts and he puts the glasses in. Within seconds, they're filled again. He hands me my glass. The pillar beeps and opens to reveal a feast: grilled white fish, steamed vegetables, French bread, and even some things that I don't recognize.

"Ah, perfect." Michael sets his glass down. I try to help him carry the food to the table, but he brushes me off. "Please," he says. "Sit."

I hesitate before settling down at the table. He's being so *nice*. I'm not used to it. No one's been this nice to me since I came back.

Michael sits down across from me. A huge smile lights up his face.

"What?" I ask.

"I'm just happy that you're here."

It's getting harder to breathe. He heaps food on my plate.

"Please, dig in."

But I'm nervous. I drink some more champagne.

"Astrid," says Michael, in between bites. "What's your favorite part of this new world?"

My eyes widen at his question. My favorite part of this new world is him. But again, I can't tell him that. It takes me a while to formulate an answer. "There's less pain here," I say.

A few seconds of silence follow. "Did you lose your children to the Infirmum?" Michael asks, voice hoarse.

A chill runs down my spine. *Why did I bring pain up?* I've ruined the mood. "Yes, I did."

"Me, too." We sit there for a few minutes, trying to find the right words. Neither of us succeeds. Michael clears his throat. "You haven't touched the food."

"Ah, sorry." I pick at my plate.

Michael downs his glass of champagne and leans forward. "Do you like living alone?"

I accidentally drop my fork. "Um, no, not really." Memories from the past two days flood my mind; crying in solitude.

"Neither do I," says Michael. He gets up and goes to the pillar to refill his glass. He's normally so calm, cool. But he's fidgeting, tugging at his collar. Is *he* nervous? He returns to the table with a full glass. His eyes are lowered, cheeks flushed.

"Are you alright?" I ask.

"Yeah, yeah, I'm fine." He stares at the glass of champagne for a minute before downing it. I stop eating and study him. He's definitely nervous; more nervous than me. He leans over the table to take my hand.

Chills run through my body when he touches me. "Astrid, will you move in with me?"

My heart stops. He sits there: staring, holding my hand, waiting for an answer; and I can't bring myself to speak. Suddenly, I feel a buzzing in my pocket. It's my smart glass. I'm being called in to the OR. I look back at Michael. Disappointment covers his face, but there's still a glimmer of hope in his eyes. His hand caresses mine. He wants an answer. But I can't give one to him right now. I pull my hand away and start to get up.

"I have to go."

He grabs my arm. I lean down and run my hand through his hair. He sighs. "Should we discuss this when you get back?"

I know what I want to say, but something holds me back. "Yeah, let's talk about it later."

He nods and kisses my forehead. "Just be safe, Astrid."

CHAPTER 10

The golden lights of Oriel are shining through the window of my car once again. But I'm not stopping in Oriel today. I'm heading past it, to the other side called Lutum. Despite the city's best efforts, Lutum seems to be perpetually dirty. It's where the lower-class citizens live. Not by designation, but they all seem to end up there. I don't get sent on many jobs in Lutum. The people there keep to themselves. The only reason I can think of for the residents of Lutum to not all be classified as unworthy is to keep a functioning hierarchy. Perhaps they *are* essential in a way. After all, someone has to be at the bottom. And from what I've seen, only people from Oriel and other affluent communities can cause the real damage; they have the resources and the influence.

But I don't know.

Havoc. That's what comes to mind as the car speeds outside of Oriel and into Lutum. The inhabitants always seem to be making some sort of pitiful stand against the order that permeates the rest of the city. Trash litters the streets. People wander around disheveled, with looks of disillusionment. Some of the streetlights are out, but I can't tell if they've been put out intentionally or if the city just hasn't bothered to maintain them.

People turn to stare at my car as it goes past. It's attracting far too much attention. If I get out in front of the building I'm heading to, I'm bound to be followed inside. I look out the window and scour for side streets and alleys. I hear something hit the side of my car, followed by a yell. Liquid drips down the side window.

Idiots. I let the car take me into the middle of Lutum, then have it pull into an empty side street. I set the timer to thirty minutes and get out. I hear another person yell at the car as it rolls away. The people in Lutum are the worst. I pull up the collar of my coat and try to adopt the same broken demeanor they all seem to have. The person I'm supposed to eliminate lives about a block away. I brace myself for the journey. Thankfully, no one looks at me as I tread the dark sidewalk…

My shoulder's bumped. The hairs on the back of my neck stand up. How did I not see them coming? I look back. A flash of sleek dark hair dressed in a coat far too nice for a Lutum native disappears around the corner. Something about the walk seems familiar. Is it someone else who works at the OR? Strange. For as long as I've been doing this, I haven't ever crossed paths with another while out on a job.

But it doesn't matter. I continue on my path.

I've only ever been to Lutum once before. The last job here was a man who killed his wife. Today's job is a little more interesting. My target is a woman who's refused to go to her weekly Curat appointments for a year. I have no idea why anyone would refuse. It would seem, however, that Lutum is filled with people who are all manners of stupid.

"Astrid, will you move in with me?" Michael's question hasn't left my mind. And his face so full of hope, eagerness. I want to take him up on his offer, but it's so soon. Why is he so bold?

I've reached the address. It's a cold, gray building composed mostly of steel. There are a few windows here and there. It looks absolutely miserable. I enter the dimly lit lobby. It's empty. The furniture is torn up as if someone dug a knife into it a few times. I feel the pistol holstered at my hip. In a place like Lutum, it's best to have the fastest and most convenient weapon on you. Otherwise, you might end up dead.

I set my glass on the screen next to the elevator and the doors creak as they slide open. I step in somewhat reluctantly. It looks like it might fall apart at any time. The woman lives on the tenth floor on the building, and it seems to take an eternity to get there. The doors slide open again to reveal a surprisingly homey apartment. I step out. The apartment is decorated minimally, but tastefully. Most of the furniture is simple gray plush, a few cheap prints line the walls, and curtains have been spread across the back wall to give the impression of there being a window. Whoever lives here has made more of an effort than I have.

I look around. No one's come out to check who's entered the apartment. Is she not here? I wonder what kind of person refuses to go their Curat appointments. The photo in her file showed a person who seemed normal enough: round face, dark skin, full lips. Further info in her file showed that she'd been captured by the authorities a few times and forced to comply with the mandatory Curat injection. But, the effort they'd made to keep her on track just wasn't worth the time and money. So, they've sent me.

Why on earth would she decide to rebel in this way? Idiot. The apartment is tiny. If she's here, there are only two other rooms she could be in. I check both. They're similarly decorated: homey, tasteful. But, she's not in either of them. I could tell Mr. Winters and have him ping me her exact location, or I could wait for a bit. I settle down on the plush gray sofa. Might as well wait. I have to think.

"Astrid, will you move in with me?" I smile as I think of his question. I want to say, "Yes." I've only been back for six months, so I have little knowledge about how relationships go in this new world. It feels like everything is moving really fast...but I don't know why that would be bad. I would love to rid myself of the solitude that I go home to every night; I've hated it these past six months. But why does *he* want things to move so fast? He's probably been awake this whole time. He's used to solitude. Or he's used to other women.

I hear a creak from the elevator. My hand slips down to the pistol in my pocket. I get up and cross the room to make sure that I can't be seen from the entrance. The doors slide open. She steps out. I bring my pistol up and she sees me. *Her hair is gray.* My finger doesn't pull on the trigger like it should. *Why is her hair gray?*

A look of fear crosses her face, but she doesn't run away like the rest of them usually do. "You look surprised." Her voice is deep, leathery.

"Your hair…" It hits me. *The Curat.* Can avoiding Curat for a year really do that to you?

"I don't use that bullshit," she says, her dark eyes piercing into mine. I see shallow wrinkles around her eyes and mouth. It's been so long since I've seen someone who wasn't young, I can't help but stare.

"Why wouldn't you use it?" I ask.

I want to know. Why would she *choose* this?

"Because look at you," she scoffs. "Look at what you're doing right now. Would you have done this before?" Her words seem to fall heavier than they should. I'm not sure why.

"What do you—"

"You wouldn't have done this before. I can tell you that."

What is she talking about? The gun in my hands?

We stand there in silence. I keep running my eyes over her. How could this happen? We're not told about this. Curat is supposed to give you a faster healing rate, and keep you young, healthy, *immortal.* It's not supposed to propel you into old age if you don't take it. The fear is still in the woman's eyes. I can see every muscle in her body tense up, prepared for flight.

"I didn't think they would take it this far," she says, voice strong. But instead of running away, she charges towards me.

I pull the trigger.

CHAPTER 11

The wind bites into my face as I walk down the street. It's raining now. I welcome the coolness. Too many thoughts are running through my head faster than they should. There's a queasiness in the pit of my stomach. I can't shake the feeling that there's something I'm missing. A pattern? Maybe.

Damon, Christina, Maksim, and the woman I just killed. *What is it?* Lightning cracks the sky as the rain begins to pour heavier. I stop walking and lift my face. The silver hex pattern lingers for a few extra moments before leaving.

The woman's hair was gray. She looked as if she were aged fifty, if not older. Everyone in this city is biologically twenty-five. She aged that much in one year? I shudder. I never realized that Curat wore off that quickly.

I look down at my hand and unwrap the bandage. The stab wound has almost completely healed. My hand would probably have become infected if I hadn't taken Curat, then I would've lost it or my life entirely. I throw myself into situations that I never would have touched in the past because I know an injection can fix everything. Maybe that *is* wrong.

I slip my hand into my pocket and continue walking down the street. It isn't wrong. There's nothing wrong with wanting to be young and beautiful forever. Immortality is a beautiful thing. Michael's face floods my mind. What if forever is too much for him? He could tire of me. People hardly ever stay with each other in this city.

The rain is soaking through my coat, but I know I won't get sick: I have Curat. A slight wave of disgust comes over me. Everything is so easy for us in this city. I'm almost to the building where Michael lives. I have to decide what I'm going to do. I want to say yes. I want him, but there are risks. I thought I left pain behind in the past. But he could hurt me. I enter the lobby of his building. There are a few people milling about - all beautiful, sleek, empty-faced. They look at me when I enter. I wonder if my dilemma is obvious to them. Pity suddenly fills their faces, or maybe I just imagine it.

I set my glass on the screen next to the elevator. The doors open. I hesitate before stepping in. Maybe I need more time. It's late, almost 11:30 p.m. He might be sleeping. I could come back tomorrow morning.

A dark-haired man brushes past my shoulder and enters the elevator. "Going up?" He asks. I step in. The elevator hits his floor first. He turns around to scan me from head to foot with eyes that are a strange mix of black and deep blue. "Have a good evening," he says.

The elevator doors close and re-open on the floor where Michael lives. *"A good evening."* If the man only knew. I walk up to Michael's door and pull my smart glass out of my pocket. He gave me a key with such ease. Does he give a key to everybody? I stand there for a minute, running my finger over the glass. Insecurity seems to fall upon me as the rain did outside, and I'm nervous. But, I'm already here. I set my glass on the screen next to the door. It clicks open. I push my way inside.

Michael jumps up from the sofa as soon as he sees me. For once, he looks a little haggard. "You came back."

We stand there: eyes locked, taking each other in.

"Of course I did," I say.

It looks like these past few hours have been hell for him. His hair is mussed as if he's being pulling at it. His collar is unbuttoned.

"I thought I scared you off," he says, his voice hoarse. He steps forward, frantically running a hand through his hair as if trying to make himself look more presentable. "I'm glad you came back."

"I'm glad I came back, too," I reply. And I mean it. Now that I'm here with him, I know that I never want to leave.

He walks toward me carefully, as if he's afraid that I might run away. My heart beats faster with every step he takes. I reach out and pull him in. He kisses me. "Will you do it?" he asks.

I smile. "Yes, I will."

CHAPTER 12

I'm not sure what I'm looking at. Hope? Fear? Desperation? A strand of gray hair falls across his face. I guess this form of rebellion is more common than I thought. He hasn't put up a fight. He's just surrendered, standing there with hands up in the air. There are too many things I don't understand, but if I let what I don't understand get in the way of my job, I'll be dead. And I have so much to live for. I have Michael now.

This man doesn't live in Lutum. He lives in one of the more upscale neighborhoods. Maybe that's why they're getting rid of him faster. He has more resources and influence. *He's more of a problem.* I still haven't pulled the trigger. I'm not sure why. Maybe because I'm intrigued. This man looks like he's forty-five at most. He's still attractive, fit. He looks like he takes care of himself, yet he's stopped taking Curat. *Why?*

I still can't quite tell what lies in his eyes, but he's not like the woman. He won't run. His gaze is steady—I just wish I knew what it meant. He looks just as resigned to his death as I am to killing him. I would never have thought that people could be resigned to death. I haven't seen him blink or move, aside from his chest. His breaths have shortened. So, he *is* nervous. He looks like he's about to say something now. I catch my breath.

Why do I care so much? Why am I so interested in him? I've never cared before. I've never tried to know people before I killed them.

"Why haven't you done it?"

His question hits me like a brick in the face. *Why* haven't I done it? I don't know.

"Why'd you stop?" I ask.

"What?"

"Why did you stop taking Curat?" He says nothing. My arm is getting tired from holding my pistol up. I've been stalling for so long. But he hasn't replied, and I want to know. "Why did you stop taking Curat?" I repeat.

"Wouldn't you like to know," he sighs. "Wouldn't you like to know *everything*."

Chills fly under my skin. "Everything? What do you mean?"

He just looks at me, silent, and I figure out nothing from his eyes.

"Just tell me," I mutter, trying to keep the desperation out of my voice. He looks like he pities me now. Rage stirs inside of me. He's not saying anything. He's silent; *challenging* me. I walk forward and put the barrel to his head. He still looks like he pities me. "Tell me."

Still nothing except pity. I step back and pull the trigger. A wave of disappointment sweeps over me as I look at his body on the floor. I wanted to know him. I wanted to know why he did what he did. I step back and look around his apartment. Art, fine furniture, trinkets. This man *lived*. And yet, he stopped taking Curat. He chose to die. I slip my pistol into my coat pocket and walk to the elevator. As I head down to the lobby, I pull out my smart glass and notify the cleaners.

I step out into the street. It's not raining today. The sky is clear, and the weather is too balmy to wear a coat. But alas, I have to keep it on. My car is back in the warehouse. The job today was close enough to my place I decided to walk. I've enjoyed walking recently—much more than I ever have. I've enjoyed everything a lot more recently. I wonder if it's because of Michael. It feels like there's something inside of me that's waking up.

I keep pushing my way through the crowd. The enjoyment that I was feeling is dissipating: the back of my neck is getting hot. I look back over my shoulder. It's hard to distinguish anything or anyone in the sea of people. I turn around and start walking down the street again. But, the back of my neck is still hot. There's a building a little way down with a mirrored exterior that expands across the whole block. I'll use that.

I pull my collar up and slow my pace a bit. Someone bumps into my shoulder and steps on my foot. There's no "excuse me" or "I'm sorry." I scoff. *People these days.* I turn my head slightly as I reach the building. There's nothing. No one. Maybe I'm just imagining it. I rub my forehead and turn my head again. Still, no one. Then—

Tan skin, green eyes. He looks terribly familiar. He wears a black coat that's like mine. His shoulders are hunched forward, and he lets a few dark curls stray into his face as if he's trying to hide it. A memory from Michael's office floods my mind. He's the man who smirked. The one who works at the OR. *And he's following me.* A sinking feeling appears in the pit of my stomach. *What do I do?*

I'm about two blocks from my place now. I finger the smart glass in my pocket. His glass has the same advancements. He could easily follow me into my apartment whether I want him to or not. The building I live in comes into view. It's a little different from most buildings in this city. It's constructed entirely of glass that's opaque to the outside. *No one will see him when he kills me.*

I feel sick. The mirror's gone. I can't check to see if he's still behind me, but I know he is. I enter my building, walk over to the elevator, swipe my glass, and head up to my apartment. I could've gone somewhere else or tried to trap him. But it wouldn't have been of any use because he's like me, but bigger and stronger.

I pull my pistol out of my pocket and slip off my coat. I can hardly hear for the pounding of my heart in my ears. I stare at the elevator doors, but he doesn't come. Maybe he's waiting until later. I walk over to the window and look out. He's not in the streets. I wait a while before setting my gun down. The honeycomb light glares in the sky for a few moments and makes everything around me far too bright.

Maybe he just happened to be there on the street, just happened to notice me, *just happened to follow me.* But I don't think so.

CHAPTER 13

I step back and survey the last of my unpacking. The corners of my mouth have been turning up into smiles all day. All my clothes are in Michael's closet now. I can't tear my eyes away from the sight. My clothes are next to his clothes. My books are next to his books. There's something in the simple domesticity of it all that just seems right.

Michael wraps his arms around me from behind. "Need help with anything?"

I turn around and run my hand through his hair. "No, that was the last of it."

"Just books and clothes?"

"Just books and clothes."

Michael raises his eyebrows. "Really."

"Is that bad?" I feel a slight tinge of nervousness.

He kisses me. "No, it's attractive."

"How so?

"Priorities. You keep what you need, no clutter."

I laugh. I definitely don't have enough things of importance to clutter up his apartment. The only books I've brought along are history books detailing the time since the Infirmum to help fill the gaps in my memory, and to help me learn about the time when I wasn't here. Although, I suppose I don't need them since I have Michael. I suspect he's been here the whole time.

He tightens his hold on me. I don't want him to ever let me go.

"You're beautiful."

I lean back and study his face. He's different. There's a certain warmth—a certain *life*—there that seems to be missing in everyone else.

"What are you thinking?" he whispers.

"You're different." My words fall heavier than I expected. The smile leaves his face. "Did I say something wrong?" I ask.

He tightens his hold on me even more. "No, no," he says. "I was just thinking."

"What were you thinking?"

He answers with a kiss and pulls me onto the bed. Chills run through my body, but I want my answer. I push him away. He laughs.

I shoot him a smile. "What were you thinking?"

He leans back. "Do you feel you're different too, Astrid?"

I don't know what to say. It takes me a while to reply to his question. "I don't feel like I'm different. But I don't really feel like I belong here."

Michael's face is hard to read. Maybe I sound like an idiot. "Do *you* think I'm different?" I ask.

He's staring at the ceiling, deep in thought. When he finally answers, it's with a question. "What were you like in the past, Astrid?"

I wonder what's going on in his mind. "I don't know. Probably very similar to the way I am now."

"Are you sure?" He sounds unconvinced and takes my hand in his. "Tell me about your past."

I feel uneasy. That wall in my thoughts always seems to appear before I can remember anything important. I could tell Michael about my husband. But does he even matter anymore? Michael seems to read my mind.

"Were you married back then?" He's looking at me earnestly; there's almost something pleading in his face. Was *he* married? I don't doubt it. How do I compare to that love from his past? Do I even compare?

"Yes," I admit.

"Tell me about him."

I try to remember what I can. More and more of my memories seem to turn into a haze every day. "He loved me very much. I don't remember what he did. There's a lot I don't remember, actually. I remember he loved our children very much, and they loved him, too. He was a perfect father. Really, just a perfect man. I don't remember ever being unhappy or frustrated. We used to go to the parks on the weekend. He loved parks."

"Did you love him?"

Michael's question hits me like a pin prick. I don't know why. "What?"

"You say he loved you, he loved the children, the children loved him. Did *you* love *him*?"

"Of course I did."

"Of course you did?" he asks, eyes narrow.

I feel strange. Chills are running through my body again. "I think I did."

We sit there in silence for a few moments. I wish I knew what Michael was thinking.

"What did he look like?" he asks.

There's the wall. "I don't remember," I breathe. The flat expression on his face doesn't change. My curiosity and unease get the best of me. "What are you thinking?"

"You would've remembered."

"I would've remembered what?"

Michael rubs his eyes. "Nothing," he mutters. "Don't listen to me."

Chills are still running through my body. I don't know why I feel so strange. I want to stay in silence for a little while, but he asks another question.

"Would you bring your family back if you could?"

"Of course I would," slips out. I could kick myself.

"*Of course?*" He's annoyed again.

"I'd bring back my children," I reply. Michael lies there staring at me, and I can't read him.

"What about your husband?" he asks, voice low.

I can't bring myself to say I'd want to bring him back, because it'd be a lie. If my husband was here, then I wouldn't have Michael. Or I'd have Michael, but he'd be something else entirely when I'd want him to be more.

"You don't know," says Michael. He sounds disappointed in me. Would he bring back the love he had in the past?

I don't doubt it.

"How far would you go to bring back your children?" he asks.

My chest suddenly feels like it's caving in. "Please don't ask me questions like that."

"Why not?"

"Because thinking like that gives me hope when I know there is none."

Regret crosses his face, but he doesn't apologize. We lie there in silence – him probably sifting through a rich collection of memories, while I try to remember anything at all.

"Tell me about your past," I say, though part of me doesn't want to know. I can't measure up to the love that was there, but the quiet sits heavier than it should right now. And I should want to know him.

"My past is long," he says. "I don't know where to start."

"How about from the beginning?"

Michael's brow furrows. "There's too much pain, Astrid."

I feel guilty for asking the question. But he's such an enigma. A part of me might not want to know about his past, but I *should* know at least a little more. "You could tell me the important things."

He doesn't reply for a while, and I wonder if I've said the wrong thing again.

"I was married," he says.

I catch my breath. This is it. The ghost I could only ever hope to measure up to. He takes a few seconds before continuing.

"She was the most beautiful woman I'd ever seen, with one of the most compelling minds I'd ever met. She loved our children but there was always a certain harshness there, no matter how hard I tried to help her. She had this energy, this *desire* to explore things unknown, and it affected people deeply," he takes a deep breath like this is taking too much. "But she had too much power. She could talk to someone for a few minutes – a *minute* - and have them wrapped around her finger, and it led her into a job that gave her far too many liberties. Far too many lives to play with…"

His voice drifts off and there he is again, staring at something unseen. My heart sinks. "You make her sound extraordinary."

"I'll always love her."

The silence comes back, but no one breaks it this time. We just lie there. He stares at the ceiling. I bury my face in my hands. A shrill beep rings through the air. Michael groans and gets up.

"That's my cue," he sighs. "You alright?"

I lift my face to look at him. "Yeah, I'm fine."

He kisses my forehead. "I'll see you later."

He heads out of the room, leaving me alone with my thoughts. He'll never love me as much as he loved her—*still loves her*—and that kills me.

CHAPTER 14

Michael pierces the top of the vial with the syringe and fills it with Curat. The former pale blue tint of the liquid has changed into a deep aquamarine. No surprise. I know they have a team constantly working to improve the formulation. *Or do they?*

The needle pierces my arm. Why do we have to come in every week? Wouldn't they have made a version by now that didn't have to be injected so frequently? Memories from the other day fill my mind: the woman's gray hair, her leathery voice. She was only a *year* off Curat. Michael disposes of the needle and bandages my arm. I could ask him. He's been here the whole time. He was a Renewer. He should know. But I'm a little scared of how much Michael might know.

"Someone's deep in thought," he says, smiling.

"Sorry."

"Why would you apologize?"

He doesn't give me a chance to answer. He lifts my chin and kisses me, then pulls back and looks at me. I can never tell what he's thinking. I want to ask, but I know I should leave. Nothing in this city ever runs late or behind schedule except our appointments, apparently. I give him one last kiss and stand up.

"Do you *have* to go?" he sighs.

I hold back a smile. "You have other patients to see."

He shakes his head. "But none of them are as interesting as you."

I don't know how to react when he compliments me. Surely, I can't be deserving of his words. He's so much better than me. He could have anyone he wanted. *Why me?* I slip my hand into his for a moment. "I'll see you when you get home."

He kisses me on the forehead. "Alright, I'll see you later."

I head out of the room and into the hallway. I can feel the blonde woman's cold eyes on me as I exit through the lobby. What does she think of us? Her face is so blank, though, that sometimes I wonder if the thoughts that pass through her mind are few and far between. The sun falls warmly on my face as I step outside. I haven't received a notification to go into the OR today and for some reason, I feel relieved. Before, I wouldn't have cared. At least the OR would give me something to do with my day. But now I realize that there are so many ways to fill my day. The sky is beautiful today; free of clouds and a crisp shade of blue – though the flashes of light that remind us this sky isn't real are growing more frequent. The sun is warm. It's the perfect weather for walking. I wonder if the park Michael and I went to is gone yet. Perhaps I'll go check.

The streets are crowded, but I don't mind. I shoulder my way through the throng. I wonder if they're enjoying the weather as much as I am. Everyone's faces hold the same blankness. *I wonder if they feel.* I keep moving through the crowd, studying everyone around me. Then, I feel it again: that heat on the back of my neck. I turn around. It's hard to distinguish anything in the crowd, but I know he's there. I feel different from the way I felt last time. I'm not scared today; I'm angry. *Why is he following me?* I continue making my way through the crowd. He can follow me for the time being. I'll get him.

It's about a fifteen-minute walk from Michael's office to Caron Park. The heat on the back of my neck grows stronger, encouraging my rage. I catch glimpses of him from time to time in the reflective surfaces of buildings. He's trying to hide his face again. I clench my fists. I'm almost to Caron Park. I don't care how, but I will make him face me. My palms are sweaty. I'm nervous, but it doesn't matter. I can handle him.

I'm at the park now. It's still open, despite the construction vehicles that have moved in. My breath quickens as I walk through the arched wrought-iron gates. I head down a gravel path to the right that's lined by trees. A couple minutes pass before I hear the faint sound of him walking behind me.

I quiet my footsteps and listen. He sounds reluctant, nervous. He probably knows he's heading into a trap. I scan the landscape in front of me: more path, but then a copse of trees. *Perfect.* I heard towards them. I know I'm being reckless, but I'm angry. It's dark in the copse. I don't think there's anyone else in here with us. There are plenty of good places to hide and wait. I know he's closer now, though I can't hear his footsteps anymore.

I dash towards a small open space on the left and hide. There's a little dip in the ground between two trees. I bend down and wait. He walks into the space, unsuspecting. I grab the back of his neck by the pressure points, and he's on the ground before he can fight. I settle on top of him, pin his arms behind his back, and wait a few seconds for him to regain consciousness.

"No! Let me go!" he mutters when he wakes. Useless. I don't think there's any fear in his voice…*yet.* Just annoyance. I tighten my grasp on him. He winces.

"Why are you following me?" I ask. A moment of silence follows, then a bitter laugh. I twist his arms behind him even more. He groans. "Answer the question," I hiss.

He takes a deep breath. "Maybe I'm just a fan."

His humor is so misguided. I dig my nails into his arms and push my knee into his lower back.

He yelps. "You should let me go."

"Why?"

"Because I know his secret."

The confusion I feel causes me to loosen my grasp on him, but he doesn't try to fight me. He just laughs.

"That's what I thought," he smiles.

"You thought what?" *His secret? Could he mean Michael?*

"Your weak spot," he replies, his voice emphasizing each word.

He's definitely talking about Michael. I tighten my grasp on the man. He laughs while wincing. I feel sick. "What do you want?" He doesn't respond for a moment. I dig my knee into his back again. He just keeps laughing. I repeat my question. "What do you want?"

"Just let me keep watching you, Astrid."

The way he says my name sends chills under my skin, and I know he's not being honest. "Tell me the truth."

"I just find you fascinating," he says. "Really." I twist his arm far enough for him to be in severe pain. "Astrid," he says, his breathing strained. "I'm being honest."

"Liar."

"Just let me watch you."

I don't know what to do.

"We don't need to do any of this," he says. "None of this *aggressive* business."

He spits the words out with distaste. I stifle a laugh. As if he doesn't go about being aggressive every day. Same goes for me though. We're identical, he and I. Or are we?

"Why do you want to watch me?" I ask.

"Because, like I said, I find you fascinating."

I dig my nails into his arms. "You're going to have to do better than that."

"It's the truth," he gasps.

I can't hurt him. Mr. Winters would find out and I would be punished. Is he *really* telling the truth? We sit there in silence. No one else comes into the copse. I don't think anyone else is in the park, despite its vastness.

He speaks up. "Are you going to let me go?" His behavior bewilders me. I haven't been this confused in a long time. I know I'll have to let him up soon. I can't hurt him. "Astrid, come on." His voice is sly, warm. He's mocking me. He knows I can't do anything.

I stay on top of him for a minute, nails digging into his arms. I wish I could hurt him. I wish I could make him tell me everything I want to know. He laughs again, and I know I've kept him in this position for longer than I should.

I let go of him and get up. He rolls over and stares at me before rising to his feet. I study him. It's hard to keep my perception of him from being skewed by rage. Dark curly hair, tan skin. He's dressed simply but fashionably: tight black shirt, denim jeans, boots. Perhaps he just makes everything look fashionable.

A glimmer of amusement creeps into his green eyes. He brushes himself off and holds out his hand. "Crispin," he says. I don't want to take his hand. I don't want to know him. The corner of his mouth quirks up into a smile. He grabs my hand and pushes it into his. "It's nice to meet you officially," he smirks.

I'm not sure what it is about him, but I can't stand him. The longer I touch him, the sicker I feel. I pull my hand away. "I don't bite," he says. "I'm not going to hurt you." But I don't trust his voice. He laughs again, like he's entertained. He watches me for a minute before speaking. "Well, Astrid, I'll be seeing you around." He backs up, smirk still on his face. Then, he's gone.

I don't know what it is about him, but I feel so sick. I fall to the ground hyperventilating. My cheeks are warm, and so is my neck. I run my fingers through the grass. *Why does he affect me so much?*

CHAPTER 15

The streetlamps have just lit and the silver grid outline is there, gleaming in the sky. It's beautiful, but it's been there far too long. I want it gone so I can pretend that this sky is the one we used to have in the past; the one I used to look up at from home…

I haven't gone home at all since I met Crispin. *Home.* My home is with Michael now. It's only been a few days, but I can't imagine home being anywhere else in the world. I'm not sure how long I laid in the park. Nobody came to bother me. I don't know if anyone else came to the park at all. A pity, really. It'll be gone soon. Destroyed to make room for Chrysos.

I push my way through the crowd on the sidewalk, stepping onto the street sometimes to get around them. The green eyes and tan skin keep flashing through my mind. *Who is Crispin?* The weather is temperate tonight, but I'm shivering. I rub my arms, but that doesn't help. I'm almost home. I don't think Michael will be there yet. He worked late last night. It wasn't until I moved in with him that I realized how strenuous and erratic his schedule can be.

It's been three days since I was called into the OR. I wonder if Crispin is feeding them information. Did they tell Crispin to follow me? *"Just let me watch you,"* he said. He's interested in me. *Is it that simple?* I rack my brain and delve into my thoughts. I try to go back and figure out what I've done to spark interest. But I can't remember.

I can't remember anything nowadays. I still remember *him*, but I can't remember his face. What kind of wife forgets her husband's face? Two men pause their conversation as I enter the lobby. I can feel their eyes on me as I cross to the elevator. It would seem everyone wants to watch me nowadays, or perhaps it's just my imagination.

I walk out of the elevator and down the hall. I set my glass on the screen next to the door and push my way into the apartment. My breath stops. Candlelight, all sorts of savory smells, another bouquet of crimson roses. I can't tear my gaze from the roses.

"Astrid!"

Michael enters from the bedroom, a big smile on his face. He's dressed impeccably; completely in black. Suddenly, I remember I laid on the ground for hours. I quickly smooth my hair. I must look a mess. I expect him to wrap his arms around me and kiss me, like he usually does. But, he stops before he reaches me. There's a strange glow in his blue eyes.

"What are you doing?" I ask.

His smile returns. "I'm just looking at you."

"Why?"

"Because I want to remember this. I want to remember you, just as you are, in this moment." Something about this—about his words— seems so familiar. *But it can't be familiar if it's never happened before.* He walks forward and takes my hand. Chills run across my skin. I don't deserve him.

"Come on," he says. He leads me to the table. It's covered with everything you could want from a feast. I don't know if I'll be able to eat. I feel so comfortable around him most of the time, but right now I feel nervous. I sit down across from him. He's smiling again. "Go ahead." I timidly dig into a steak. He enthusiastically fills his plate. "How was your day?" he asks.

I can't tell him about Crispin. Or maybe I *shouldn't*. I don't know. I'm slowly remembering how to be with someone and it's hard.

"It was good," I reply. "Nothing too exciting. How was yours?"

"I don't believe you."

My heart drops. Does he know? He lets out a little laugh. "Everything about you is exciting, Astrid."

I feel the blood rush to my cheeks. Sometimes I feel like Michael knows me better than I know myself, and yet sometimes I wonder if he knows me at all.

"My day was good," he says. "The same as usual. Patients in, patients out. There was one patient in particular who I found very intriguing."

"Who?" I ask.

"I'll just say that whenever she's in the room, our appointments run late." He smiles again. It's the most beautiful thing in the world. "You've barely touched your food," he says.

I glance down at my plate. "I'm, uh, not very hungry right now."

Michael sets his fork down and pushes his plate away. "Well then, let's do something else." He leans over the table and folds his hands beneath his chin.

I feel a slight tinge of guilt. "You can eat if you want."

He shakes his head. "No, no, we'll come back to it later." He reaches his hand out, I take it. "Come on," he whispers, leading me away from the table.

"What are we doing?" I ask.

He presses something on the pillar and music starts to play. It's a low, piano-driven piece. There's something eerie about it. *Why does everything feel so familiar?*

He puts my arms around his neck and slips his hands around my waist. "Dance with me."

I smile at him. "I always feel like smiling when I look at you," I whisper.

He kisses me. I want more, but he stops.

"What is it?" I ask.

His face is an inch away from mine. I can feel his breath, and it gets faster. "I have to tell you something," he says.

My heart seems to stop again. Maybe he's figured out that he doesn't want me. I never deserved him anyway.

"I love you." I can't believe my ears. I try to say something, but no words come. He says it again. "I love you, Astrid."

I have to say it back. "I love you, too." I mean it. I could've said the same words six months ago and meant them as much. Did it start six months ago for him, too? He slips his hands into mine and kisses me again. And I know: I'll always love him.

CHAPTER 16

I don't favor variety nowadays. Not when it comes to my job. I run my finger across the pistol in my pocket. I'm not sure why I ever favored variety in this job. Strangling, poison, stabbing—all too messy. *All too close.* I can keep my distance with a gun. I don't have to sully myself with their blood or feel the life leave their bones. I can kill them and walk away without having to feel anything; without having to wash anything off me.

And I so desperately want to be clean.

I've been sent into Oriel again. No surprise. The car speeds quietly along the street. I'm about two minutes away. The target today is boring. The details in his profile left me disappointed: he simply pissed off the wrong person. The hierarchy in this city is hard to understand completely. I know the people in Oriel are rich and powerful, and this man lives in Oriel. So, who is the person he pissed off? And how is this person more powerful than a resident of Oriel?

The more I learn about the people I kill, the more I realize how little I know about our hierarchy. We have an official government. I am, technically, part of the government. But the top of our government is veiled…and I wonder…

The car stops in front of an intimidating skyscraper; gold, glass, twisted beams. I remember gasping at the beauty of the buildings of Oriel when I first saw them. Nothing here impresses me now. I set the timer to twenty minutes and get out.

I set my smart glass on the screen and step into the elevator. It whirs and ascends a little slower than usual. Or maybe it just seems slower because I'm eager to get home. The elevator doors open. I step out.

He's sitting at the table; clad in a sweater, hair tousled, bowl of pasta in front of him. A picture of comfortable domesticity. He looks up at me, innocent. He doesn't know why I'm here. I should probably just shoot him, but I don't. I've been taking my time recently.

He doesn't look scared or uncomfortable. A few moments of silence go by before he speaks. "What's your name?" His reaction intrigues me. He hardly looks bothered by the fact that a stranger is in his apartment. I thought he was going to be boring, but maybe I was wrong.

"Astrid," I say.

He'll soon be gone. Might as well try and make interesting conversation.

"Would you like to sit down?"

An interesting question. I sit down across from him.

His small eyes light up as they give me the once-over. He holds out his hand. "I'm Arthur, by the way."

I shake his hand. "Yes, I know."

"Of course you do." His behavior bewilders me. He gets up and walks to the kitchen. "Would you like anything?"

I shake my head. "No, thanks."

He trots back to the table and sits down. "Yes, of course not," he says with a chuckle. I don't know what to say or think. Does he know who I am? He can't. How would he? "You're actually much earlier than I expected." His eyes keep running up and down, appraising me. There must be a misunderstanding.

I put my hands in my coat pockets. "Am I?"

He nods. "You also look a little different from what I expected."

"Are you disappointed?"

"No, not at all. Pleased, really."

I think I know what the misunderstanding is, but I'm not sure. I've never come across any whispers of prostitution in this city. But the high divorce rate, the lack of people in monogamous relationships…it makes sense.

Arthur's cheeks flush a deep shade of red. "It's been a while," he says, voice quiet.

At last, he looks uncomfortable. So, my guess is right. Pity comes over me as I look at him. I feel sympathy for him. He looks so shy, so insecure. I want to comfort him.

"It's okay," I say.

He shoots me a grateful smile. "I've never, uh…"

His voice drifts off. I want to know what he's thinking.

"You've never what?"

"I've actually never done this before."

"You've never hired someone like me?"

His eyes widen. "No, I've actually never…*you know*."

I stare at him. He looks to be the same age as the rest of the men in Oriel: mid-twenties. Could he be almost as young as he looks? I never stopped to consider that the residents of this city could actually be *young*. I assumed the youthful façades belonged to people who were once tired and old, like me. But why would I assume that? I was of the older generation, there were plenty of people younger than me when I went under. Approval to be frozen in a cryo tube could happen anytime, provided that you passed the tests. They rolled the program out five years after the children…

Arthur clears his throat. Suddenly, the gun in my coat pocket seems to sear into my skin. "Could you, uh, could you undress, please?" he asks.

A lump appears in my throat. "I can't do that for you."

"Oh, I'm sorry."

"Don't apologize."

He looks apologetic and holds up his hands. "I really don't know what I—"

And that's it. He falls back onto the ground, blood pooling around his head. There's so much blood. I set the gun down on the table. I kneel next to him, his blood covering my fingertips.

What have I done?

CHAPTER 17

I reach out and feel nothing but the silk sheets. My eyes flutter open. It's dark, and Michael isn't here. I sit up. It must be the middle of the night. I look around the room. The clock on the wall reads, "3:27 a.m." in red. The house is dead quiet. I hear no footsteps, no doors opening or closing. I rise to my feet and walk into the living room. The lights don't turn on. They usually turn on if I walk in. Have they been adjusted to stay dark if someone leaves?

Or maybe I'm wrong. Maybe he's here, and the lights are glitching. I walk to the pillar and tap the option to turn the lights on. The living room, dining room, and rest of the open space illuminate. He's not here. I check the bathroom. He's not there either. Where could he be? I go back to the bedroom and pull out my smart glass. I want to call him. I want to find out where he is and ask him to come back. But something makes me put the glass down: *"I know his secret."* Crispin's words shoot through my mind. I've tried not to think too much about it. I don't trust Crispin.

But it's 3:28 a.m. and Michael isn't here. He is a doctor, though. I know his schedule can be irregular, but he never gets called out around this time. I walk back out into the living room. Maybe I should try going back to sleep, but I don't know if I can. I don't like being home alone. I go to the pillar and request a cup of tea. It's steaming in my hand within a minute. I sit down at the table and wait for it to cool. *Does* Michael have a secret? We all have secrets. But which secret was Crispin talking about? Silver light from the sky gleams through the window.

I scan the bright room, my eyes pausing on the bookshelves. My books only take up one shelf. The rest of them are filled with Michael's books and journals. There are *so* many journals. I could read them. I could find out the secrets of the man I love so much. But maybe the secrets he has are not ones he'd write, because he can't risk them falling into the wrong hands.

The silver light goes as quickly as it came. I sigh and sip my tea. There are so many things I don't know, even things about myself. Why did Crispin affect me so much the other day? I have a feeling that I knew him in the past, but I don't know if I can trust that feeling. He made me sick. Why? *"I know his secret."* I set my mug down roughly and some of the hot liquid sloshes out onto my hand. I wince and shake it out. Why would Crispin know Michael's secret? The tan skin, green eyes, slick hair, smirk: he looks like someone who knows secrets. *Does he know any of mine?* I hardly feel like I know my own secrets nowadays.

The journals on the shelf seem to call to me, tempting me. I know I shouldn't look at them, but I walk over to the shelf. They aren't labeled by year. The age of the book itself is the only exterior clue as to when it was filled. There's one journal that's obviously the oldest. I run my finger along the binding. I want to know all about Michael.

Secrets are a dangerous thing.

I pull the journal off the shelf and dare to crack it open to the first page. It isn't dated, and is slightly yellow. His handwriting is beautiful, almost like calligraphy.

"I miss her more and more every day. This life is even more unbearable without her. But I won't stop looking. I don't care what I have to do."

I hear the door opening and push the journal back onto the shelf. My chest feels heavy, wracked with guilt. I step back from the bookshelf.

Michael's blue eyes widen. "You're up?"

"I realized you were gone, and I couldn't go back to sleep."

"Oh, I'm sorry," he mutters.

He's dressed in a black turtleneck and black jeans. I can't tell where he's been. He's lingering right inside the door, as if reluctant to come forward.

"What have you been up to?" he asks.

"I had some tea."

"Nice."

He clears his throat. A few seconds of silence follow.

"Where have you been?" I ask.

At last, he steps closer. "I just went on a walk."

"Where'd you go?"

"I actually went to Caron Park. Felt the urge to see it one more time before it's gone."

"At this time of night?"

We stare at each other for a moment. He opens his mouth as if to say something, then closes it.

"It's an odd time to go to Caron Park," I say.

He laughs and shrugs. "For some reason, I couldn't sleep. That walk tired me out though."

He walks over to me and kisses me on the forehead. "I'll see you in bed," he winks.

I stand still for a while after he leaves me. I don't believe him.

CHAPTER 18

"Hello, Astrid."

His voice makes me recoil. I could sense him watching me, but I didn't think he'd be this bold. I should've been more careful. I should've lost him. He sidles up next to me. I try to walk faster than him, but he's not letting me get away. I want to run but I shouldn't, because I'm not a coward.

"You miss me?" Crispin smirks.

"You know I don't," I mutter.

He laughs, and I hate the sound of it. "I told you I'd be seeing you around."

"Yeah, I was hoping you were lying."

He lets out a low whistle. "Why the hate?"

The street we're on is crowded. I scan the sides, wondering if I can slip into an alley. A familiar flash of dark hair slips past in a coat…I stop for a moment. Could it be the same person I saw in Lutum? *Who is that?* But they're gone, swallowed by the crowd.

Crispin's stare pierces me as I start down the street again. "I don't know what you want," I huff.

He sighs, but the smile that follows tells me he's only feigning frustration. "I already told you: I just want to watch you."

"You say you just want to watch me," I reply. "And yet, here you are *talking* to me."

"You got me."

I shoot him a glance. He's like me. He always wears black. He looks sleeker today than the last time, I'm not sure how.

"What do you think, Astrid? Do I look good today?"

Almost every word out of his mouth has a tone of teasing defiance. I don't dignify his question with an answer.

"I guess there are some things I shouldn't ask. Don't blush, dear."

"Could you go away, please?"

"And end our fun?" He laughs. "No, I can't do that."

I wonder if I should go home. Maybe I shouldn't. I suspect he knows where I live, since he followed me. But I won't lead him to my door. I didn't really have an idea in mind of where I wanted to go today. I just wanted to walk and think. But here is Crispin: intruding on my thoughts.

"You should leave me alone," I say.

"Why? What are you going to do?"

A wave of frustration sweeps over me. I want to push him away. He smirks again.

"You know you can't do anything to me," he says. "The powers that be would find out, and you'd be screwed."

I try to walk away from him again, but he seems determined to stay with me.

"Just give in, Astrid. Walk with me. You won't be able to lose me anytime soon."

I slow my pace. He's right, it's probably impossible to lose him. Perhaps if I talk to him for a little, he'll be satisfied and go away. If I could just figure out what he *wants*. "So, Crispin."

Confusion crosses his face before his eyes widen. He gasps. "At last, you say my name."

His insolence rubs me like sandpaper. "So, Crispin. Why are you interested in me?"

"Great question," he replies. "I just find you so *fascinating*."

I wait a few seconds before responding. "That's your answer?"

He nods sweetly. It's sickening.

"Why do you find me fascinating?"

"It's personal."

His attitude bewilders me. I haven't met anyone like him in this city. Granted, I don't meet many people…outside of work. "How do I get you to leave me alone?" I ask.

He shoves his hands in his pockets. "See, here's the thing: you can't."

I growl in frustration. "Are you serious?"

Judging by Crispin's face, my annoyance entertains him. "I'll never leave you alone," he says. "Whether you like it or not."

My heart drops. I desperately want to be rid of him.

"So, Astrid, where are you walking to on this fine day?"

I wish I could choose a place where I know he wouldn't want to go, but I don't know him. I shrug. "Haven't decided."

"How adventurous."

"But wherever I'm going is definitely somewhere you won't be."

"I'm everywhere. Didn't you know?"

I want to slap his smug face. Since he insists on staying around, I'd like to at least walk in silence so I won't have to listen to him. But it's obvious that Crispin does not favor silence.

"We should hang out sometime," he says.

"Isn't that what we're doing?"

He chuckles. "I suppose, but I mean a proper hangout. Let's go out to dinner. Or grab some coffee. Whatever it is that friends do."

I feel queasy. "You want to be my *friend?*"

"I'll be anything you want me to be, Astrid."

"Do you just go around bothering people for your own entertainment?"

He raises his hand to his face in mock shock. "Am I bothering you? That hurts. That really does."

"Really."

"I want you to like me, Astrid."

"Well, you're going about it in the wrong way."

"What can I do?"

"I'd like you much better if you weren't here."

He bursts into laughter. "Your sense of humor just kills me."

"I wish it *would* kill you," I hiss.

The laughter stops. "Now, now, be nice," he says. "After all, I know things."

His words freeze me. We stand there in the street, the crowd milling past on either side.

"Aw poor Astrid. You look worried."

I don't know what to say to him. Does he really know things? Or is he just switching tactics to get under my skin?

"You're worried because I know your weak spot, aren't you?" He squeezes my shoulder. I swat his hand away. He clicks his tongue and shakes his head. "Sensitive, aren't we?"

I still don't know what to say. He looks amused. I can tell he likes to see people flounder.

"Have you figured out his secret?" he asks.

My palms are sweating. I stick my hands in my pockets.

He arches a brow. "You don't know, do you?"

I want to know the secret he's talking about, but it scares me. "You could be lying right now," I say.

"You don't know."

"Why are you being like this?"

"Do I intrigue you, Astrid?"

I glare at him. My patience is gone, if it ever existed. But I don't walk away. There's something in his voice—*in his face*—that's keeping me from leaving.

"You want to know what I know, don't you?" Crispin gets closer. Does he expect me to back up? I stand my ground.

"If you meet up with me," he says, his face inches away from mine. "I might tell you."

He repulses me, but I stare into his eyes and he enjoys it. He enjoys the closeness. I want to know what he knows. But secrets are dangerous, and so is he. Suddenly, a buzzing meets my ears. I reach for my smart glass, but it's his that's vibrating. For the first time since I've seen him, the brashness leaves his face. He looks genuinely disappointed.

"I guess our time together is being cut short," he sighs.

I resist the temptation to shoot back a cutting reply. He smiles, but his eyes are sad. I don't know what to make of him. All I know is that I hate him.

He turns back to wave as he walks away. "I'll see you soon, Astrid."

CHAPTER 19

I reach out for Michael and feel nothing. His side of the bed is empty again. I walk out into the living room, and the lights stay off again. I go to the pillar and switch them on. I know he lied to me the other night. The fact that he didn't *tell* me his secret doesn't bother me as much as the feeling of not knowing what this secret is.

I don't know what to make of it. It's getting bigger in my mind, even though I haven't furnished this unknown secret with any possible details. Is he trying to protect me? Or maybe he just doesn't want to tell me; the thought of that stings a little. I want to trust Michael, but does he trust me?

He gave me a key to his place right away, asked me to move in so quickly. He must trust me. But trust is a funny, complicated thing. I read the time on the pillar. It's just past two a.m. I don't think he leaves every night, but perhaps I just sleep through his absence. I don't think so, though. I feel it when he's gone.

The conversation with Crispin keeps running through my head. He knows things that I don't. He's got the upper hand. My eyes fall upon the journals on the shelf. They're tempting me again, even more than they were the other night.

In the entry I read, he wrote about a woman. I don't want to know about any other women. I feel inadequate enough already. But I'm at the shelf, running my fingers along the journals. Do I go back to the one I opened last time? It's the oldest. The age of it is alluring. It's hard to gauge exactly how old it is; the cracked spine, the yellow pages. Seventy years maybe.

I pull it off the shelf and open it. I flip past the first page about the woman, eager to move on. But she seems to be everywhere in this book.

"I know every day that passes brings me closer to finding her."

I shut the journal and push it back onto the shelf. Did he ever find this woman? He must not have. Because now he's with me. The love—or obsession—that fills these pages is strong; even extreme. A wave of jealousy sweeps over me. I pull a different journal. It's one of the newer ones. I open it to the first page. There's one sentence.

"I know where she is."

I rifle through the pages. It's still all about the woman. I put the journal back. She's one of his secrets. But she's not *the* secret. Crispin's face floods my mind. He could tell me what I want to know, but I have a feeling he would also tell me other things. He's dangerous. I can't get involved with him, and Michael wouldn't like him. But, Michael wouldn't know. Why would I have to tell him? He doesn't tell *me* everything.

I wish he would, though. I sit down at the table and bury my face in my hands. I want to know where he goes, but I can't make him tell me. I don't know how to deal with this. Being brought back was like being rebirthed. I have to relearn how to deal with people, how to act in situations.

I have a feeling that Crispin will soon find me. What do I do when he does? The front door clicks open. I smooth my hair and try to act like I haven't been agonizing during his absence. He looks less surprised than last time to see me awake. He's dressed in dark colors again. I suspect it's to draw less attention to himself, as opposed to a style choice.

"Where you have you been?" I ask, even though I know it's pointless.

"Just felt the urge to go for a walk."

"Did you go to Caron Park again?"

"No, no, I just walked around."

He must know of my suspicions. He must know that I don't believe him. He walks towards me, bends down, and kisses my forehead. He doesn't sit down next to me. The strange distance between us keeps growing. I feel further away from him than the last time this happened.

"Are you going to bed?" I ask.

He nods. "Yeah, I'm exhausted."

"Okay."

"You should go back to bed," he says. "It's late."

He doesn't look at me as he walks into the bedroom. I get up and turn the lights off.

CHAPTER 20

Our eyes meet. He's realized that he's defenseless. The point of my knife scrapes his throat. No gun today. It's been a crutch. I wasn't brought back to be a coward. And isn't that what I've been? If I'm going to take someone's life, I should feel it. I shouldn't keep my distance. I used to feel the life slip out of someone's bones without understanding the significance. But now I know.

He says nothing. He's on the floor, arms pinned down by my knees. He wants to live, but he can't. I drag my knife down his neck and stop at his chest, right above his heart. He whimpers. What if the situation was reversed? What if the knife was about to plunge into *my* heart? The life that I fought so hard for would be gone. How terrible that it can be taken away so easily. A weird pain shoots through the hand that holds the knife. It doesn't *hurt*, but I don't know what to call it besides pain. My hand starts to shake.

I stare, stunned. Nothing like this has happened before. Even on my first job, I was composed; steady. The man notices, too. He looks confused, then hopeful. I use both hands to drive the knife through his heart. The hope is replaced with blankness. I close his eyes and fall back. I sit a few feet away from him, watching him. That's it. He'll never breathe again, and it's because of me.

Could I have let him live? No, Mr. Winters would have sent someone else and I would be dead, too. I fumble for my smart glass and notify the cleaners. There's blood on my hands, some of it gets on the glass. I rush to the kitchen, scrub my hands, and wipe the blood off the glass. I can't bring myself to look at him again. Maybe I *am* a coward.

I walk into the elevator. The air seems so cold. My body is shivering. The wind hits my face as I step out into the street. I pull the collar of my coat up and fold my arms. I just want to get home, but the buzz of a Regulator's gun causes my feet to stop. I turn and see the unworthy being dragged off—limp, *lifeless*. No chance for a fight.

At least the man I killed today had the chance to fight. I let him fight me and I won. The faces of the two Regulators are expressionless as they drag the young woman away. What did she do to deserve this? What did she do to deserve being sent back to the cold, dark sleep? If she really had done something wrong, they would've sent me. I realize that now. But even then, the people I kill are usually victims of the twisted way this city works. Are the sins they commit worthy of punishment by death?

Everyone sins. But I've committed the greatest sin of all: I've killed. I touch my forehead with the back of my hand. It's mystifyingly cold again today, but I'm sweating. I turn back and keep walking down the street. I just need to go home. The woman they just dragged away can never go home again. I doubt she'll ever be brought back. She'll be pushed to the bottom of the list. The mark next to her name will never leave.

I clench my fists. She isn't my problem. The way this city works isn't my problem. I feel it again: the heat on the back of my neck. Crispin's here. He grabs my hand and slips my arm through his.

"I told you I'd see you again soon," he smirks. I pull my arm out of his grasp. The brashness leaves his face as he looks at me. I try to walk away, but he doesn't let me. He grabs my arm again and I have to stop. I stare at the ground, wiping the sweat off my face with hands that can't stop shaking.

He gently pulls my hands down from my face. His eyes are wide, filled with concern. Crispin doesn't know what to make of me. I don't know what to make of me either. I expect him to say something. I expect him to ask questions, maybe even make fun of me. But he says nothing. We stand silently in the street.

I don't know if I should shake him off and go home. I feel numb. Suddenly, he turns his head from side to side. His eyes narrow: scanning, searching. He pulls me down a side street. He still doesn't say anything, and neither do I. There's almost nothing here. It's small and dark, awnings spread down both sides of the road.

He leads me further into the dark and away from the crowd. Then, he stops. I'm not sure why I've let him bring me here. I'm still shaking, sweating. I feel sick. Crispin cradles the back of my head with his hand and brings me into him. I rest my head on his chest and listen to his heartbeat, and the sound of it comforts me. He tightens his hold on me and rubs my back. Pain shoots through my chest and I start to sob.

He runs his hand through my hair. Then, he speaks. From the tone of his voice, it sounds like he might be crying, too. "I know, Astrid. I know."

CHAPTER 21

The room fills with silver light from the sky for a few seconds. The bed is empty again. He leaves the house with an objective, I know. He doesn't just go out to walk. He goes *somewhere*. I go out into the living room. The lights don't turn on again. He should know by now that he shouldn't bother to switch the mode. I go to the pillar. The room illuminates.

The journals are calling to me again. But the secret that I want to know isn't in them. They're all about the woman and if I read more about her, I'll just feel worse. The love that's in those pages could never be replicated. We only get one love like that. I must not have loved *him* from the past like that, because I love Michael. I love Michael with the kind of love you can only give away once. My eyes fill with tears.

What is this feeling? Regret? I haven't felt like myself lately. Or maybe I've felt more like myself. I can't tell. Suddenly, I'm exhausted. I could stay out here and wait for him, but there's no point. I turn the lights off and walk back into the bedroom. I slip into bed and bury my head in a pillow.

But his absence is too apparent. Sleep doesn't come. I don't know what's happening with my body. *I need to sleep.* The fatigue is seeping through every part of my being, including my mind; but I can't find rest. Blurred flashbacks of being in the side street with Crispin flow through my mind. Why did I let him take me there? Why did I let him see me like that? Why did I find comfort in his presence? I thought I hated him.

The sound of the front door lock meets my ears. Michael's probably relieved that I'm not out there waiting for him. I watch him creep silently into the room. He doesn't know that I'm awake. The fatigue is starting to go away, but I'm still tired. I'm tired of him not being honest with me. I'm tired of him not telling me where he goes.

"Michael."

He stops and turns to me. I can see his eyes shining in the dark.

"I'm sorry I woke you."

"Where do you go?"

My question rings in the air. It seems to stay there—oscillating, intimidating. We stay silent for a moment, both of us scared to touch it.

"I went for a walk," he says, voice barely above a whisper.

"*Please* don't lie to me." It's too dark to tell if he looks guilty.

He stands there, not saying anything, not *doing* anything. The exhaustion I felt is being replaced by something else. I don't know what it is. But I'm on my feet now, inches away from him. He still doesn't move or speak. We're close enough to feel the breath of the other.

"Tell me," I plead.

"I can't tell you."

"Why not?" Silence again. The silence is too much with him. "Why won't you be honest with me?"

"Astrid..." His voice drifts off. I raise my arms and shove him. He steps back. "Astrid, calm down."

I'm angry. My cheeks and neck feel ablaze. And the woman. *The woman.* He'll never love me as much as he loves her. I'm inadequate. *Unworthy.* "Why won't you just tell me?"

He's trying to grab my arms. He's not trained like me. But he gets a good grip. I struggle under his hands. I don't want to hurt him. I just want him to know. I want him to know how he's making me feel.

"Astrid, stop." His grip on my arms hurts. I push my way out of his grasp. But he doesn't let me go. "Please calm down."

I scream, "Let me go!"

He steps back again. Is he repelled? His face is a mask. He's put an invisible wall between me and him, and I don't know how to knock it down. We stand there, staring at each other in silence again.

Finally, he speaks. "Go to sleep, Astrid." Then he leaves.

CHAPTER 22

"Same process as usual," says Mr. Winters. He sits back in his chair, arms folded, eyeing me. I think back to Damon Roberts. The woman in the photo looks nothing like him, aside from one thing. *The purity.* There's a pattern, or is it only in my mind? There have been so many more women being returned lately. Mr. Winters clears his throat. I've been staring at the photo for too long. I don't look at him before pushing my way out the cool, steel doors.

I'm functioning on two hours of sleep. Michael didn't get in bed with me. He slept in the living room and left me alone. I used to be alone all the time. Now, I can't bear it. I walk to the warehouse, though I don't need the car. The job today is close by. I open the trunk and rifle through the black bag. I need to make sure I feel it—the death. It's only fair to her. I pull out the roll of wire and slip it into my pocket. I haven't used it in so long.

I shut the trunk and leave the warehouse. The silver light strikes again. So bright, even in the day. It spreads across the sky for a minute, outlining more and more of the grid before it suddenly disappears.

I turn up my collar. The weather is cold today…and making me miss the consistency of seasons. Some days it's cold, some days it's warm – and

I've had enough. I wonder who's in charge of the weather. Everything in this city is under the charge of someone. *Who's really in charge of me?*

The woman today lives about three blocks away. There have only been two jobs so far that have been this close to the OR. I wonder what Crispin is up to today. I wonder if he'll find me. I don't *want* him to find me, do I? He confuses me. I run my finger across the wire in the pocket. Michael's face has been in the back of my mind all day. I showed him the ugliness of me, and he couldn't stand it.

A chill runs down my spine. I feel lost right now. I wish I understood everything better. I steal looks into the mirrored sides of the buildings I pass, just to see if anyone is following me. No one stands out in the crowd. I walk into the lobby of the woman's apartment building. A few people are scattered about, conversing. They don't look at me as I cross to the elevator. Michael's face shoots through my mind again. I wouldn't look at me either.

My smart glass gets me up to the woman's floor. The elevator doors slide open. I don't see her. Then, I hear footsteps from the next room. Confusion fills her eyes when she sees me.

"Can I help you?" Her hair is pale blond, almost white, and her eyes are blue. She looks nothing like Damon Roberts. Yet, I can't help but think of him. "Can I help you?" she asks, again.

No words come. I can't speak. The confusion clears from her face and suddenly, she stares at me like she knows me. She rushes past me, trying to leave. I can't let her do that. I grab her hair and pull her back. She fights me, but I easily dominate her. I find myself on the floor, pinning her arms down with my knees like the last time I killed. Her blue eyes stare up at me, wide with fright. She's trying to scream, but I've covered her mouth with my hand.

Both of my hands are shaking. Sweats covers my forehead. I pull the wire out of my pocket. She tries to struggle more when she sees it. I need to kill her. *But I can't.* I can't kill her. I can't do this again. The wire falls from my grasp. My ears ring. I fall back, and she's free. The ringing in my ears is almost deafening, but I hear the elevator doors slide open. Has someone come for me?

The woman is fumbling with her smart glass. My eyes start to hurt; I rub them with the back of my hand. I can't see. I can barely hear. But then, a gunshot. The ringing in my ears gets worse for a minute, then stops. My vision slowly clears. The woman is lying on the ground. A bullet's gone through her forehead. There's blood everywhere. And there's someone else.

It's Crispin. His tall frame turns around, gun in hand. Our eyes meet, and the expression on his face stuns me. I thought I hated him. But now I know I don't. He kneels in front of me and lifts my chin with his hand. "Where's your glass, Astrid?"

I hand him the smart glass from my pocket. He notifies the cleaners. Then, he pulls me up and puts his arm around my shoulders. We go down in the elevator. His touch is calming, comforting. The woman's ruined face, and the blood all about her, flash into my mind as we step out into the street. My legs start to give out, but he catches me. My voice comes out in hoarse gasps.

"She'll never be back."

He's pulling—*carrying*—me into a side street again.

"She's gone, she's gone, she's gone." The words keep coming out of my mouth. He takes my face in his hands and looks in my eyes. My rambling stops.

He sighs. "Astrid, you're okay." I shake my head. I know I'm not, and I can't remember the last time I was. "Listen to me, you're okay."

"No, I'm not. I can't do this. I can't do this anymore."

My breath keeps getting shorter and my chest hurts. He gets closer, and I welcome it. I hold onto him and steady myself.

"You don't have to do this anymore," he says.

"I have to. If I don't, Mr. Winters will kill me and—"

I feel sick. Would he kill Michael, too?

Crispin studies my face for a moment before speaking. "You're worried about Michael, aren't you?" I nod. He shakes his head. But he doesn't look angry or jealous. "Don't."

"I have to. I have to keep doing this."

"No, you don't."

"Why do you say that?"

He sighs and gently presses his forehead into mine. I tighten my hold on him.

"Because you have me now," he whispers.

CHAPTER 23

The coffee tastes even more bitter than it did yesterday. Everything seems to cut more. Michael's sitting across the table, devouring his breakfast. He pays me no mind as I study him. He hasn't paid me much mind since that night when I screamed at him, and I don't blame him. But I wish he'd look at me - or say something that *meant* something. His looks and words have been empty. Fillers for silence, patches to help us pretend like everything is fine.

He clears his throat. "How's your coffee, Astrid?"

"It's fine. How's your breakfast?"

"It's good."

He takes a bite of toast. Since when did we become so mundane?

"What do you have planned for today?" I ask.

"I have to go into the office for a couple hours," he replies. "You?"

"I don't know yet."

He nods. "Okay."

I'm not sure how we became like this so quickly. He pushes his plate away and stands up. We don't say anything to each other before he walks into the bedroom. My gaze goes to my coat by the door. I could leave. *Or I could do worse than leave.* I go to my coat and pull my smart glass out of the pocket. I could call Crispin. I could see him. Silence is the only thing that meets my ears. I don't know what Michael is doing. He might've just walked away so he wouldn't have to deal with me.

I stare at my glass for a while, yesterday's moments with Crispin replaying in my mind. If I had only known what he was really like before, would things be different? I hear footsteps from the bedroom and quickly slip my glass back into the coat pocket.

Michael emerges freshly changed. His blue eyes seem to actually see me for the first time today. He walks closer, but I know he's not coming for me. He reaches behind me and sets his hand on the door handle. I should move out of his way and let him go, but this is the closest we've been in days. It's hard to tell what lies in his eyes. He looks like he wants to say something, but he can't. Or, he won't.

"Are you going?" I ask.

"Yeah, they just called me."

I step to the side. He goes out the door. Then, I'm alone. But I don't *have* to be alone. I pull out my smart glass and ask Crispin to meet me. As soon as I send the message, I feel a pang of guilt. But Michael doesn't need to know. My glass buzzes with an instant reply. I put on my coat and head out the door. It doesn't matter. Michael wouldn't care anyways.

Crispin wants to meet for lunch. It sounds mundane, but I know it won't be. He's the furthest thing from mundane. The streets are crowded, even on a Saturday. The weekends aren't made for rest in this city. I don't know where Crispin lives, but the place he's picked is only a ten-minute walk away. *Maybe he lives close.* There's something comforting about that thought.

My thoughts don't bother me so much during my walk today. The sun is shining, and the warm glow seems to burn away the tenseness of the morning. The place Crispin has picked looks like a silver box, with the front side opening onto an outdoor dining area. As I walk up to it, I see him sitting in the shadiest spot. The shadows suit him. He waves and smiles. I try not to walk too quickly to his table. He gets up to greet me.

"Hello," I say.

Before I know what's happening, he slips a hand behind my back and kisses my cheek. The surprise on my face amuses him. He laughs as he sits back down.

"What inspired you to contact me on this fine day?" he asks. But the smile disappears as he studies me. "Ah," he sighs. "I see."

I regret having my emotions show too plainly on my face. "I wanted to see you."

The smile comes back. "I know," he winks.

His manner makes me mirror his smile. He touches the side of the table and it lights up: most of the tables at restaurants nowadays are made of smart glass.

"Alright, what do you want?" he asks. "I'll be getting the lobster."

I look down at the menu. I haven't looked at a menu in months. I hardly eat out. Michael and I just stay home...

"I'll get the same," I say.

"Perfect." Crispin swipes on the table and orders for the both of us. Then he leans forward, a curious light in his green eyes. "How are you doing, Astrid?"

"I'm doing well. How are you doing?"

He doesn't look like he believes me. "I'm doing good, now that I've seen you." Cheeky. A compartment in the wall next to our table opens, and the food slides out. "Isn't it great how fast things are nowadays? Nothing like the past, right?" There's something in his voice. It feels like he's asking more than he is.

"Yeah, it's great."

"What do you remember about the past, Astrid?"

His question freezes me for a moment. "Not much. Why?"

"I'm just curious," he shrugs. "As I've said before, you fascinate me."

"But *why* do I fascinate you?"

"Do you not think yourself worthy of inspiring such fascination?"

"I'm not sure what I'm worthy of," I reply.

"Well, you're very worthy, Astrid," he says, with a crooked smile. "I assure you."

His words unnerve me. I don't know what to say.

He calmly chips away at the lobster. "So," he says. "What exactly drove you to me today?"

Dare I tell him? He surely must not want to hear. But, I want to tell him. "There's been distance."

"Between he and you?"

I nod. Crispin folds his hands beneath his chin and studies me. "And what do you think has caused the distance?"

I hesitate. How did I end up here? Telling everything to a man I thought I hated? "You say you know his secret." I know the direction I'm heading in is dangerous, but I don't stop. Thoughts look like they're running a million miles per hour behind his green eyes.

"And did something happen in relation to this secret?" he asks.

He's dodged my question. I wonder why. "He goes somewhere at night."

"You don't know where he goes?"

"No, I don't."

"Have you asked him where he goes?"

"I tried to get him to tell me."

He looks like he doesn't need me to tell him what happened, but he continues. "And?"

"I screamed," I whisper.

"He didn't deal with that well?"

"He didn't."

Crispin leans back in his chair and mutters something under his breath that I can't hear.

"I don't know what to do. I don't know how to *fix* it."

"You shouldn't have to *fix* anything," he growls.

He seems angry. Is he angry with me? Maybe I've told him too much of what he doesn't wish to know. Maybe this was a mistake. He looks away for a moment. I've distressed him, though I didn't mean to.

I rack my head for a subject change. "Crispin, about what you said yesterday…"

"What did I say yesterday?"

"You said I didn't have to do it anymore."

The expression on his face makes me stop. He lifts one hand to quiet me and pays the bill with the other hand. "Walk with me," he says.

He pulls me up and slips my arm through his. We walk in silence for a while before he speaks.

"Do you feel like we're monitored in this world, Astrid?"

I scan the streets, the buildings, the crowd. No blatant signs of surveillance, but they—whoever *they* are that truly run this city—wouldn't let us roam without knowing.

"Yes."

He envelopes my hand with his. His grasp is warm, alive. He scans his surroundings, much like I did. There's confidence in his green eyes.

"How much do you know about paralations?"

"Sorry?"

"Are you aware of how footage can be changed in real time?"

Something stirs in the back of my mind. "I feel like I should remember something now, but…"

Crispin nods. "The wall."

"Yeah."

He gives my hand a squeeze. "There are ways that allow us to manipulate footage in real time, to make what is false seem true and vice versa. The level of deceit in the edited footage is so deep, so believable, and we called these 'paralations.' Paralations were banned in the old world when they became nearly indistinguishable from the truth, but you can't completely ban something like that. It doesn't work. People will find a way…and I found a way to bring them back for our good in here."

He points to a nearby skyscraper: tall, twisted, mirrored glass panels. "Now, a building like that has heavy surveillance," he says. "If you and I walk past, someone or *something*, somewhere, should see footage of us walking past. But what would you do if I told you we could make it seem like we hadn't walked past this building at all? That it was possible, perhaps, to make it seem like we had walked past a building somewhere else—a building we had never seen?"

I stare. His words surprise me, but his voice makes it all seem so reasonable.

"Would you believe that's possible, Astrid?"

"I believe it could be."

The corner of his mouth goes up in a half-smile. "A screen of invisibility," he says. "A screen of deception; or rather, security. You'd be free to go wherever you like, do whatever you like. And no one would be any the wiser, unless you wanted them to be."

"Wouldn't that take a lot of effort?" I ask.

"I know some very skilled people," he says.

I arch an eyebrow. "Who do you know?"

He shakes his head. "I won't tell you yet. The point is, things are easier now."

"What does that mean?"

"It means I can protect you, Astrid."

I take a moment to process his words. The calm confidence he exudes only adds to the enigma he is. "Why would you do that?" I ask.

"Because I know you aren't made for this," he says.

"And you are?"

An ironic laugh leaves his lips. "You and I aren't alike, Astrid." For some reason, I don't believe him. He and I are more alike than Michael and me. What would Michael do if he knew where I was now? Would he care? "You don't have to do this anymore," says Crispin. "I'll protect you."

"Why would you do that for me?"

He stops walking, and I follow suit. We stand there, arm-in-arm, silent. He looks at me for less than a second, and I know there are things in his mind that he won't say. I wish I knew what they were.

"Astrid," he says, voice low. He speaks my name so much, but I don't mind. I like the way it sounds when he says it. "I'm too far gone," he sighs. "But you're not. You're unspoiled."

I stifle a laugh. "We both know that's not true. We both know there is blood on my hands. We both know—"

"No." I stare at him. The expression on his face is hard to read. "You still have a chance," he says. "You still have a chance of being alright."

"I don't—"

"Trust me, Astrid." I do. Yet, I still can't make sense of his words. He sets his hands on my shoulders. "Let me do this for you."

"What would you want in return?" I ask. Nothing in this city is ever free. I know that.

As he thinks, his grasp gets tighter. Then, he lets go. "I won't ask anything from you."

"Why wouldn't you?"

"Because I care about you."

The crowd keeps milling past us. Chaos all around, but there's only quiet between us. No response comes to my mind; all I can do is stare.

"Let me do this for you, Astrid. *Please.*"

A life without killing could change me. Maybe I'd become the person Michael wants. Would he want me then?

"How would this work?" I ask. "You make it seem like I'm carrying out my jobs when I'm not? Even if you manipulate what they see, they'd know if I let someone go free because the cleaners wouldn't have a body."

Crispin shakes his head. "They wouldn't be going free." Then, I realize. "I'd be taking their blood off your hands," he says.

So, nothing will have changed—except for me. And for him. "There'd be more blood on yours," I reply.

He steps closer. "It doesn't matter anymore." He smiles, but his smile is full of pain now. "Let me save you."

CHAPTER 24

Michael's leaving again. It feels like a knife goes a little deeper into me every time this happens. I don't let him know that I'm awake. As soon as I hear the front door lock, I slip on my coat and follow him. Maybe what I'm doing is wrong. I don't know. The line between wrong and right seems to get blurrier every day.

I step out into the street. The rain is pouring heavily. I pull the collar of my coat up. Who suddenly decided we needed so much rain? I catch a glimpse of Michael in the distance. He's dressed in all black again, with no umbrella to shield him from the downpour. I tail him by a distance of about twenty yards. What would he do if he knew I was following him? Would he be angry? Would he care? Would he feel *anything*?

I thought he felt. I thought he was the most alive person in this city. But maybe I was wrong. Because he's dead with me now. Maybe it's my fault. He looks back every once in a while, but the darkness and few people shield me enough. He doesn't look like he's too worried about being followed, though.

Michael's going into a part of the city that I've never ventured into, I'm not even sure what it's called. The streets are surprisingly empty where he goes. Nervousness starts to come over me. He might see me if there's no one else around. I make my footsteps as quiet as possible and try to stick to the side of the street, lest I need to use a building for cover.

The part of the city we're in is an industrial zone. There seem only to be old warehouses, with the occasional empty, concrete space. *This* is where he goes? Why? Suddenly, he heads down an alley on the side of the street. If I follow him down there, he'll see me. I approach the alley and wait for a few moments before turning my head to look.

He's gone. The alley is empty. I've lost him. Maybe this was a bad idea. Then, I hear the click of a door opening. I rush back down the street and slip into a nearby doorway. Less than half a minute later, he walks past me carrying a black bag. I follow him again. On second glance, I realize what he's carrying is more like a box. It looks heavy-duty, almost medical. Like the containers we used in the past to transport organs.

A chill runs down my spine. *What is he doing?* We're going into a part of the city where a few people are ambling down the pavement. Still, no one looks at him as he makes his way. Does no one notice what he's carrying?

They must notice. The ones we can't see. The ones who watch us. But Crispin's explanation runs through my mind. There is a way to slip away from the ones above who see everything: change what they see. Does Michael know this? Is he invisible right now? I have a feeling that if they knew what he was doing, he wouldn't be here.

The rain has completely soaked my coat, and the chill seeps into my bones. I try to keep my teeth from chattering. Michael isn't even wearing a coat, yet he doesn't look cold. He looks determined. Soon, the route he's taking seems familiar. It's the way to his office. I wipe the rain out of my eyes.

He enters the building, and I can't follow him. I go around the side and wait. It seems impossible to find any shelter from the rain. My teeth chatter uncontrollably. I peek around the corner. The rain keeps getting into my eyes, making it hard to see. I'm so cold. I don't know how much longer I can last in this weather, but I stay. Michael emerges from the building about ten minutes later.

He still has the bag. From the way it swings, I'm guessing it's empty now. He heads back the way we came. I'm shivering now, but my curiosity is stronger than the cold. I follow him back into the industrial zone. He stops and looks behind him. A part of me wonders if he knows that I'm following him, but I've been careful. We're almost to the warehouse now. I look down at my drenched coat. If I don't go back now, he'll know that I've been out.

I watch his tall frame in the distance. I want to know what happens next, but I turn and head back to the apartment. What have I just witnessed? I'm not sure staying any longer would've helped me figure that out. Still, I wish I didn't have to go back. Perhaps I've been stupid, staying out this long. I quicken my pace. My hair and clothes are soaking wet. Water pools at my feet as the elevator in our building ascends. My heart is beating fast, but not in the way it used to when I was around Michael.

I just wish I knew what I'd seen. But I can't figure it out, and I can't make him tell me. I set my glass on the screen and let myself into the apartment. Water is still dripping down from my coat and my hair. He can't know that I followed him. I run to the pillar, turn on the lights, and take off my coat. I swipe to the laundry options and set the coat in the server to dry. I go into the bedroom, quickly change my clothes, and stash my wet outfit in the corner of the closet. Now, there's just the matter of my hair.

And the floor. I quickly mop up the puddles. The ringing from the pillar tells me my coat is dry. I pull it out and hang it up. My heart and breath are much faster than they should be now. I switch the lights off and head back into the bedroom. I have to do something about my hair, but I hear the click of the front door's lock.

I dive into the bed and pull the covers up enough to cover my hair. It's not like he'll care enough to notice anyway. I don't hear his footsteps when he walks into the room, but I know Michael's there. He brings a burst of cold air in with him.

I open my eyes. His silhouette is barely visible in the dark. He's only ten feet away, but it might as well be a mile. He changes out of his wet clothes and crawls into bed. Even now, there's distance. I could extend my arm and still not reach him. Will he ever share himself with me?

CHAPTER 25

Crispin grins at me from across the waiting room. We haven't ended up here at the same time since that day when Michael asked me to Caron Park. I walked past it today. The park is gone now. It's hard to keep myself from smiling back. He's cunning, winning. His eyes are so magnetic that I don't even realize the blonde woman has come to usher me into my appointment.

Her voice cuts into my focus. "Astrid Rayner."

I leap to my feet and follow her down the hall. She moves more gracefully today, but her demeanor is icy. I suspect the fact that my appointments usually run late doesn't do anything to thaw her manner. I don't think that'll bother her today.

Michael shoots me nothing more than a glance as I walk into the room. I take off my jacket and sit in the gray chair. He brings my stats up on the wall. I don't get nervous about him seeing how fast my heart beats anymore. He looks at the screen for a moment. *Does he realize the change in how he affects me?*

Michael turns around and stares at me. It feels like this is the most attention he's granted me in a while. My heartbeat slowly starts to climb, and I'm mad at myself for letting it. "How are you doing today, Astrid?"

"I'm doing well. You?"

"I'm happy to see you."

He sounds like he means it, but I don't know whether to believe him or not. My silence doesn't affect him as much as I want it to. He crosses the room and fills the syringe with Curat. The color is different again today: it's almost clear, barely tinted with blue. The needle pierces into my arm, and the liquid drains out of the syringe.

"Will you be home tonight?" he asks.

I try not to look too eager. "As far as I know, yes."

Michael kisses my forehead and bandages my arm. "I'll see you tonight," he says.

He walks back across the office and prepares for his next patient. Our appointment is done on time. I feel hollow as I walk out of the room. The blonde woman watches me as I pass her desk.

"Goodbye," she chirps. "Have a good day."

I turn around. This is the first time she's bid me any kind of goodbye. And though her eyes are as cold as ever, she's *smiling*. But within a second, the smile is gone and she's back to reviewing files on her desk.

"Goodbye," I echo, stunned. Perhaps she noticed how short the appointment was and said something to me out of pity. Or...I don't know. It'd cut to be pitied by the stiff blonde woman.

I don't see Crispin in the waiting room. As I exit the building, I'm tempted to wait for him, but I walk down the street. It's so easy to feel small in this city. I don't know where I'll go. I have a feeling I'll be called into the OR today. But until then, I'll let the crowd swallow me up. There's almost something comforting about being in a sea of people. At least, today it seems comforting.

But only a couple minutes pass before the comfort is gone. Dark hair, blue eyes, and the coat. The same coat worn by the person who bumped me in Lutum, the person I saw that day on the street with Crispin...

A woman is about ten yards ahead of me, frozen in the milling crowd. Her eyes are on mine, but they're empty. I stop. Her eyes are *too* empty. But she stands there like she wants something. I don't know how long neither of us moves. The sound of my heartbeat climbs in my ears.

A hand grasps my shoulder and I hear his voice. "I thought you'd wait."

I blink and the woman is swallowed by the crowd. I try not to look too relieved as I meet Crispin's smile.

"You thought about it, didn't you?" he asks. The blood rushes to my cheeks before I know what's happening. "Of course you did," he smirks. He pulls my arm through his and we walk down the street—something we seem to be doing quite a lot recently. "Where shall we go?"

Suddenly, the day seems full of so many possibilities…though I can't shake the woman's unsettling stare from my mind. I give Crispin's arm a quick squeeze. "How about you lead the way?" I reply.

A small laugh leaves his lips. "Alright, let's wander. Maybe we'll end up somewhere exciting."

"Sounds good to me."

A few seconds later, his tone turns somber. "How was your appointment today, Astrid?"

I don't know why he asks. "It was fine," I say. "Yours?"

"Oh, same as usual," he shrugs. "I was just wondering because of…you know. He's your doctor, isn't he?"

The ease that I was feeling dissipates a little. "Yeah, he is."

"And how are things working out? With him?"

"I don't know."

It's a while before he says anything. "*Idiot*," he mutters, and I have a feeling he's not referring to me.

The glass in my pocket starts to buzz, and we both know it's time. He takes my hand into his.

"I'll walk with you."

I think I understand how this will work. But, I'm still nervous, and his grasp does nothing to abate that. My thoughts and memories run a million miles per hour as we walk to the OR. The woman's face when I couldn't kill her, her face after he shot her. *What if they know? What if they find out it wasn't me? What would happen to Michael? Or would the repercussions fall solely on me?* I hope they would. I can't let anything happen to Michael.

"I'll be waiting down the street for you," says Crispin. "Close to the warehouse."

"Okay."

"Don't be nervous."

"I'll try not to be."

We're a block away from the OR now. I try to steady my breathing and my hands. He lightly touches the back of my neck. "This is where I leave you. I'll see you soon."

The feeling of security he brought is gone. I brace myself as I close the remaining distance between me and the OR. David's pale face greets me when I arrive.

"Astrid," he nods.

I nod back as I head to the elevator. The air feels colder than usual, but maybe that's just my imagination. My footsteps echo loudly as I walk down the hall. Before I knock, I hear the lock of the steel doors click open. I push my way in, and Mr. Winters fixes me with a tired gaze. There are bags under his eyes. He usually looks sleek, pristine. I've never seen him look tired.

He's sitting down in his chair, leaning over the table. "Good afternoon, Astrid," he says.

Something must be wrong. He's less cold than usual. But the anxiety I felt is starting to go away. He doesn't know or suspect. "Good afternoon," I reply.

He pulls up the profile on the table. Green text flows across the screen, then stops. A profile photo of a man fills the screen. He looks bleak, grim. Mr. Winters leans back in his chair. I set my glass on the table to copy the info. Mr. Winters sighs and rubs his forehead.

"Are you alright?"

He stares at me, surprised and narrow-eyed. "I'm fine." He looks like he wants me to leave; I oblige. I go through the profile as I make my way out of the building. I can feel David's eyes on me, but I don't acknowledge him.

Nothing about the man I'm supposed to kill seems interesting or unusual. He has a plain name: Brandon James. He lives just outside of Oriel, so I'll have to take the car. Nothing too exciting about his personality diagnosis. But the reason for the job catches my eye: his refusal to take Curat.

Another one. The memory of the transparent blue liquid from this morning jumps into the forefront of my mind. *"Look at you right now. Would you have done this before?"* That was what the woman said to me, right before I shot her. I feel like I'm starting to understand. But I'm still taking Curat, and I can't do this anymore. I can't kill. So, why are all these people refusing the substance that grants them life? Why do they choose death? I'll never understand that.

I'm almost to the warehouse when I see Crispin step into the street from behind a building. He holds out his hand for my smart glass, and I give it to him. He bites his lip and studies the profile for a minute before handing it back.

"I'll meet you there," he says, looking at the address. Have I misinterpreted the way this works? I thought I wouldn't have to go…

"The car," says Crispin.

Then I understand. The car I take is high-tech, high-security—and the warehouse is guarded by heartbeat signature. Crispin might be able to change what people see, but it'll be known if I don't take the car to the address. "I'll see you there," I whisper.

Then I head to the warehouse. My breath is shallow, my muscles tight. My ears seem to ring as I open the trunk of my car. Why am I doing this? Out of habit, I suppose. I pull the gun out of the bag. Crispin shot the last person with a gun. But they'll know if the man today is not shot with *this* gun if they do thorough inventory.

I slip the gun into my pocket and get into the car. After I input the address, the car speeds out of the warehouse. My chest keeps getting tighter the whole way. I pull my shoulders back and try to stretch myself out to ease the pain, but it doesn't work. The car reaches the address; it feels too soon. I set the timer to twenty minutes and get out. The slight ringing in my ears starts to get worse. I turn my head to scan the street for Crispin. The ringing gets louder. I can't find him.

"Astrid." I look to my left. He's suddenly appeared a few feet away. He waves me over and I follow him to a nearby alley. He holds his hand out, it's gloved now. "Gun," he says.

I give it to him. He puts it inside his coat, then gazes steadily at me. "You can wait here," he says.

"Here?"

"Do you think you were followed?"

"I don't know. I don't think so," I mutter.

"Then just stay here."

"Are you sure I shouldn't go in with you?" I ask, even though I don't want to.

Crispin hesitates for a moment before replying. "You just need to stay out of sight."

I don't think I was followed, but there's still a nagging feeling of anxiety in my chest. The streets around here aren't too crowded, but my heart jumps every time someone passes the alley. Crispin watches me for a few moments before setting a hand on my shoulder.

"I'll see you soon," he says.

Then, he leaves me alone in the alley. The ringing in my ears has stopped. But now my head is pounding. I rub my forehead and slink back into the alley, into the shadows. Nobody can see me now. Even *they* can't. Crispin and whoever he works with have taken care of that. The comfort I find in being invisible calms me.

I don't know how much time passes in the alley. It could be ten minutes, or it could be an hour. I stand in the quiet, waiting for him to come back. I still don't know why he would do this for me. I don't know why he'd be okay with taking the blood off my hands and putting it on his. I can't figure Crispin out, but I don't mind.

Michael, however, I wish I could figure out. I doubt that'll ever happen though. He'll never let me. Interesting, the way things work out sometimes. The sky flashes with silver and jolts me out of my thoughts. For the time that the light stays there, I feel anxiety shooting through my chest again.

Then, it leaves and Crispin walks back into the alley. He looks the same as he did before, nothing to show that he just took a life; I wonder how he does it. He holds out the gun and I take it back.

"Your car is waiting," he says. He sets both of his hands on my shoulders as I slip the warm gun into my coat pocket. "You alright?"

"Yeah," I say. "Are you?"

Crispin doesn't reply. He clears his throat. "Tell the cleaners."

I pull out my glass.

"I should go," he says, then starts to leave. I watch him walk away. He turns around, and the smirk crosses his face again. "I'll see you soon, Astrid."

CHAPTER 26

I push open the door to the apartment, and almost slam it into Michael. He's out of his work clothes, dressed in a crisp blue button-down and slacks. The clock shows it's barely after four p.m. Why is he back already?

"You're home early," I say.

There's a hunger—*a spark*—in his blue eyes that I haven't seen in a while.

"I wanted to spend time with you."

My breath leaves me for a moment. All I've wanted recently was for him to be like this. He reaches for my hand timidly, as if afraid to touch me.

"Do you have any plans for tonight?" he asks.

"No. No, I don't."

"I'm glad."

His grasp sends chills through me, and I'm mad at myself for it. I shouldn't still be affected by him like this. "Did you have something in mind?" I ask.

He stares at me silently for a minute before speaking, just taking me in. I can feel my heartbeat start to climb up. "You look beautiful."

I shake my head. Why is he suddenly being like this? I pull my hand out of his. I want to ask him about the sudden change, but do I break down the wall between us? Michael's the one who put it there in the first place.

His brow furrows. "What's wrong?"

I can't find the words. His eyes are wide, boring into me. I hang up my coat and walk into the bedroom.

He follows me, for the first time in a while. "Astrid."

"What?"

"Speak to me."

"Why *now*, Michael?"

He looks confused. *Does he not understand?* Maybe this was a mistake. Maybe *everything* was a mistake. My gaze shifts towards the closet. I could pack my things and leave.

"Please don't," he says, like he knows what I'm thinking.

"Why did you ask me to move in with you so quickly?" I ask.

He opens his mouth as if to say something, then closes it.

"Michael?"

Still nothing.

"You say to speak to you," I mutter. "But you stopped speaking to me a while ago."

I wait for him to say something, to say *anything*. Nothing happens.

I push my way past him and out of the bedroom. I can hear his footsteps behind me as I grab my coat, but I still leave. I pull out my glass as soon as I'm out in the street and message Crispin. I should feel guilty, but I don't. I don't bother to check if Michael's followed me into the street. He probably doesn't care enough to, and even if he did, it doesn't matter.

I've asked Crispin to meet me at the place we went for lunch other day. The weather is getting cold; the clouds are knitting together and turning gray. I see him sitting outside the silver box: he's beat me there. He's so…different. He waves at me as I approach and smiles. I smile back as I walk to him. He gets up to greet me, slips a hand behind my back, kisses my cheek.

"When I said I'd be seeing you soon, I didn't think it'd be in the same day."

"Surprise," I laugh.

"Well, it's a surprise I welcome most eagerly," he says. I settle down across from him. He's still smiling, and I'm still smiling back. But then his eyes narrow and the corners of his mouth turn down. "Tell me what's on your mind," he says.

I haven't decided where to start, but there's something about him that invites transparency. "I followed him."

"You followed Michael?"

He looks surprised. I feel a tinge of guilt, but I keep going. "The other night, he left in the middle of the night and I followed him."

"And what happened?"

His face is hard to read: the surprise has gone away and I can't tell what's in its place. "He went to a building and got a bag. A box, really."

"What was in this box?"

"I don't know. He took it to the office."

It's starting to rain; the shades close above us to keep us dry. Crispin leans back in his chair and brings a hand beneath his chin.

"You said you know his secret." I'm not handling this well. The eagerness, the pleading can't be kept out of my voice. Perhaps the expression on Crispin's face is pity.

"I did say that." His tone is cautious. It sounds like this might be a conversation he doesn't want to have. Yet, he seemed so eager before to flaunt his knowledge in my face. Why would he flaunt it if he wasn't willing to share? "Once you cross that line, Astrid," says Crispin. "You'll never be able to go back."

"But you'll tell me?"

"I don't know if you really want to know."

"Of course I want to know."

He leans forward. "Where is this coming from?"

"What do you mean, 'where is this coming from'?" I'm starting to get frustrated.

"Astrid."

We sit there in silence for a few minutes; the rain beating loudly above us and around us. I feel trapped. Nobody will tell me anything.

"Why are you here?" he asks.

"You know why I'm here."

"Why are you here asking *me* questions that you should be asking *him*?"

It's hard to find an answer. I try to find words. But I just sit there, blank-minded, looking like an idiot.

"I don't want you to come running to me just because you're frustrated with him."

"I didn't come running to you because I'm frustrated with him," I reply. I wonder if my protest is false, but I don't think so. I always want to see Crispin.

"I'm not his replacement," says Crispin.

"I know."

"I want to be something else entirely. So don't just come to me when something is wrong, don't just come to me because he's not enough for you."

"I came here because I wanted to see you."

"You came here because you wanted to ask questions about *him*."

I can't deny it. But does it *matter*?

"You'll find out everything in due time, Astrid."

Something about his voice scares me. "Why won't you just tell me?"

"You'll find out when you're supposed to find out," he says. "I'm not going to tell you."

I stare at him, confused. His enigmatic nature is intriguing, but I'm so lost. Then, I feel it. I turn my head to the left. Michael's standing about ten yards away. The rain has drenched him; his golden hair clings to his forehead. His blue eyes shift from me to Crispin, and they darken. Crispin's gaze stays on me. I wonder if I should tell him that Michael's there.

"I'm not him, Astrid."

I tear my eyes away from the golden man in the street. A feeling of dread fills my chest.

"I'm here for you," continues Crispin. "I always will be. But I want you to understand, I'm not a substitute."

"Are you trying to make me choose?"

"I'll never make you choose."

A lump appears in my throat. He'll never make me choose, but I'll have to. He gets up and I know I can't ask him to stay.

"Goodbye, Astrid."

He walks away, and I turn my head. They're both gone.

CHAPTER 27

A pain more intense than anything I've ever felt before sears through my head. All I see is darkness, even when I open my eyes. At least, I *think* I'm opening my eyes. I can't tell. The pain is all I feel. I can't move. I want to reach up and claw this pain out of my head. But my arms are bound to this chair I'm in. It feels like the gray chair at Michael's office but harder, and fitted with restraints to make sure I can't leave.

I can't escape. If the pain wasn't so heavy, I'd be panicking right now. But I don't have enough space to feel panic. My thoughts aren't coherent. I don't know where I am. I don't know what's happening. Suddenly, I see a blur of green text quickly flow past and disappear. Is there a smart glass in front of me?

Another flow of text made up of 1's and 0's passes by. My head feels like it's burning. I hear a click. I see nothing but a blank space, but everything is lighter. Somebody's turned a light on. *Who?* I hear footsteps. Someone's in the room. Have I gone blind? Have I been *made* blind? A gentle hand touches the side of my head. I brace and try to pull my arms up to grab whoever it is, but it's pointless.

The person says nothing. I feel the hair next to my temple being pulled back and parted as if to check a part of my skull. Whoever's doing this has been inside my head. I open my mouth to say something, but it hurts too much. Another gentle hand touches my lips as if to tell me to stay quiet.

Tears well up in my eyes. I'm trapped, weak, mad. The hand brushes away my tears. The touch is kind, but whoever's done this to me cannot be kind.

A needle pierces into my arm. I can usually take the Curat needles with no pain, but it's like my other senses have been heightened by my lack of vision. I let out a scream and immediately regret it: it's like a million nails have been pounded into my brain. The tears are streaming down my face now, and my nose is running. The person has taken a towel and is cleaning my face. If I wasn't so angry, I'd feel humiliated.

The pain lessens; due to whatever was just injected into my veins, I suspect. But I still can't see. Footsteps ring in my ears as the person walks away. I hear a door shutting. As the pain goes away, I'm able to feel more of what is around me. The air is frigid, like the air in a doctor's office. I try to listen, but everything is silent. Something about the space I'm in makes me feel like it's large and open; the air smells sterile, medical.

Just like Michael's office. Has he done this to me? I cast my thoughts back and try to remember how I got here, but I can't. I think I've lost another part of my past. I tug at the restraints again though I know it won't do any good. The last thing I remember is Crispin leaving and Michael being gone. But something else must've happened, because how did I end up here?

The pain is dull now. How lonely it is when you can't see what's around you, to be completely in the dark. I almost wish that the person who left would come back in. I'm used to being lonely, but I'm not used to being in the dark. The only sound in the room is my quickening breath. I try to slow it, and I try to slow the pounding in my chest.

I keep tugging at the restraints. The bands are steel and locked to the contour of my wrist. The bands around my ankles are the same and the more I struggle, the more they dig into my skin. I don't know why I keep struggling. I'm only hurting myself. But I can't stop. The steel digs in more, and I feel blood trickle down my hand. I hear the person come back into the room. He still says nothing, but I hear him frantically rushing around.

Then another needle pierces my arm. I scream again…

1's and 0's flow across my vision, pushing me awake. I open my eyes. My sight is back, but the image that meets my eyes isn't welcoming. I'm in a cold, cement room lined with steel shelves. Boxes upon boxes of vials are on the shelves. They're all varying shades of blue: light blue, aquamarine, navy. *Curat?* Different versions of Curat? I pull my arms and realize the steel bands have been lined with soft spongy material. The cuts on my wrists have been efficiently bandaged.

My hair is pulled back and I feel cool air brush against a bare part of my scalp. Something's been put inside, I'm sure of it. I study the chair I'm in, looking for a way to escape. But it's impossible. I'm thoroughly bound and trapped. My clothes have been replaced with a medical gown. I look around the room. What kind of room is this? It's not a doctor's office. At least, it's not like any doctor's office I've ever seen. There's a sense of illegitimacy about it.

I wonder how many people have passed between these cement walls, and how many lived to tell about it. I want to see what they've done to me, what they've done to my head; but there are no mirrors and no reflective surfaces. This is a dead room. A feeling of dread fills my chest. I'm more scared to find out who put me here than what they're doing to me.

I think an hour passes. The pain fades, and I realize I don't feel weak. In fact, I feel stronger than I've ever been. I scan the blue vials on the shelves. *Have I been reduced to an experiment?* The door opens. Michael walks in and I catch my breath. He's dressed in all black; the same outfit he wore the night I followed him. My mind goes blank as I stare at him. He doesn't look ashamed. There's no hint of remorse on his face. His blue eyes look at me: cold, analytical.

"How are you feeling?"

I don't know what to make of him. There's concern, but I can't see any warmth or compassion.

He steps forward and looks at the side of my head. "That'll be easily covered."

I still don't know what to make of him. I can't think.

"Your wrists have probably healed by now. We can check in a little bit." He steps back and crosses his arms. "The pain is gone, isn't it?"

The pain he speaks of is gone, yes. But it's been replaced with one that's even worse. Anger more intense than anything I've ever felt is stirring inside of me. I tug at the restraints with all my might, but I don't break free.

Michael shakes his head. "Astrid, you'll only hurt yourself."

"It won't compare to how much *you've* hurt me."

Michael's eyes widen. I can't tell what lies in them. I struggle and shake the chair again. "How is your head, Astrid?"

"What did you put in my head?"

"I didn't put anything in your head."

He's lying. I know it.

"*Tell me,*" I hiss.

He's studying me, analyzing me even more. He steps forward to touch the side of my head again. Before I realize what I'm doing, I've turned and bitten his hand. He jumps back, clutching it, but he doesn't look surprised. He crosses the room and pulls out a vial from the shelves. With a sigh, he fills a syringe and injects it into his arm.

"You'll calm down soon," he says.

I scoff.

He walks back over. "How's your vision?"

"My vision's fine."

"Good. Do you hate me, Astrid?"

I *do* hate him. I can't remember the last time I hated someone so much. "Yes."

"Good."

Good? His answer only makes me more angry. If I wasn't stuck in this chair, he'd be dead by now.

"How much do you hate me?" he asks.

"I wish you were dead."

My words don't hit him as hard as I thought they would. He doesn't look hurt. *Does he not believe me?* I meant what I said.

"Good," he nods.

I shake the chair again. I'm getting out of this room; I don't care how much I hurt myself in the process.

"Astrid, calm down."

I scream at him. He just stares. He won't touch me, not after what happened last time.

"Quite the pair of lungs you have, huh?"

I growl at him. He brings his hand beneath his chin and narrows his eyes.

"Interesting," he mutters. I notice that the mark from my bite is gone—healed. That's fast, even if one has just taken Curat. I thought I bit hard enough to pierce his skin…but his hand looks perfect.

He walks around and checks the side of my head again. "Will you hurt me if I touch you again, Astrid?"

His voice is softer now: it's sensitive, gentle. Suddenly, I feel regret. "I'm sorry," I say.

"Why are you sorry?"

"I'm sorry I hurt you." My chest feels like it's caving in. I convulse with sobs. "I'm so sorry, Michael."

"How sorry are you?"

"I'm really, really sorry."

"You don't hate me?"

"No, I don't."

"You don't wish me dead?"

"No, no, I'm so sorry I said that. I'm a terrible person." I can barely push the words out between my sobs. Tears are streaming down my face, and my nose is running again.

Michael grabs another towel and cleans my face.

"Will you forgive me?" I ask.

He sets the towel down and says nothing. His silence scares me.

"*Please*, Michael. Please forgive me."

Air passes quickly in and out of my lungs. I'm hyperventilating. He just watches.

"I'm so, so sorry. Please say you'll forgive me. Will you forgive me? I'm so sorry."

I ramble on, not quite sure of what I'm saying. He still says nothing. His silence fuels my panic. My hands and lips start to tremble.

I'm not sure how long it is before he speaks, but it feels like an eternity. "I forgive you, Astrid."

His words lift the dreadful weight off my shoulders. I stop trembling and feel light, relieved.

"*Thank you*," I say. But I can't stop thanking him. I can't stop what's coming out of my mouth. My words overlap in a blurry ramble.

Michael gets closer, his eyes shifting back and forth. "Astrid, calm down."

But I can't. The words keep coming out, except they're not words anymore. Laughter creeps into my voice.

"Astrid. *Stop*."

I can't stop. My voice explodes into high-pitched hysterical laughter.

Michael puts his hands on my shoulders. "Calm down."

I can't.

"Astrid, *please*."

My chest is so tight I can't breathe anymore. The laughter won't stop. Michael rushes across the room. I can feel the last bit of air leave my lungs. A needle pierces my arm again. Everything goes dark.

CHAPTER 28

When I wake up, I'm still bound to the chair. I feel queasy. Michael's across the room, arms folded. His blue eyes are narrow, scanning me intensely. He's still wearing the same clothes. I don't know how long I've been out. The absence of natural light in this room makes it impossible to get a good grasp of time.

"How are you feeling?" he asks.

"Sick." I still don't know what to think.

Michael slowly crosses over to me. He looks cautious, but he doesn't look frightened.

"How are you *feeling*?"

I stare at him. "I just told you."

He shakes his head, and gently sets his hand on my chest. "What's going on in here?"

I don't say anything. His touch sends bad chills through me. I feel scared and there's so much I don't know. I look away from him and glance around the room. He takes his hand back with a sigh.

"Astrid, I might have gone about this wrong."

My confusion keeps me silent. I'm trying to fathom what kind of experiment I'm undergoing. I crane my neck to try and look behind. There's a long table in front of three metal cabinets, lined with lab equipment. Then, I catch a glimpse of a laser set up in the corner, along with an operation table.

That's how he got in my head.

Was this his plan all along? Did everything happen between us so that I would end up here?

"I know you probably don't trust me right now..." Michael's voice drifts off. I make myself meet his gaze. He shifts nervously from one foot to the other. "I wish this could've happened in a different way. I mean, maybe—"

I cut him off. "What exactly have you done to me?" My nausea is abating, as is my discomfort. I feel stronger, calmer.

Confusion creeps into Michael's eyes. Did he expect me to stay afraid? "There's a lot you don't know," he says.

"So tell me."

He hesitates before clearing his throat and straightening his shoulders. "There's an implant in your head, Astrid."

"You put an implant in my head?"

"No, it was already there." He's trying to stave off the nervousness, but he's fidgeting. "It's meant to keep you from feeling."

"What?"

"The neural implant was designed and implanted to temper your emotions, in coordination with the Curat."

"What are you talking about?"

"Everyone in this city is programmed in such a way that they have the potential to be a killer."

"That's not possible."

"Astrid, look at what you do for a living."

"What?"

"You kill people. Tell me that doesn't make you question if they've changed you."

I stare at him, lost. He's waiting for me to say something.

"I don't kill anymore, Michael."

He doesn't understand. "You kill people for a living, Astrid. That's your job."

"No, I don't kill anymore," I say again.

"How is that possible?"

I don't reply. He doesn't need to know about Crispin. He doesn't need to know about anything.

Once he realizes I won't answer, his eyes shift from me to the vials on the wall. "When did you stop?"

My grasp of time is corrupted after what he's put me through, after being locked in this room. "Maybe a few days ago."

"Maybe?"

"A few days ago," I say as if I know.

He looks at me, frustrated, before gazing clinically at the vials again.

Then, I realize. "You've been switching out the formulas, haven't you?"

He turns back to me. "I've been switching the Curat in the offices with an altered version."

"When did you start giving me an altered formula?"

"A month after I brought you back."

"A month?"

"As soon as I knew you were stabilized, I started switching it out. I weaned you off the original and built you up to vastly different formulas."

"How many people did you switch it out on?"

"There are fifteen of us."

"Us?"

Michael bites his lip, as if afraid he's said too much.

"Why me?" I ask.

He deflects my question. "I should tell you about the implant," he says.

Suddenly, the chair I'm in feels overwhelmingly uncomfortable. I tug at the padded cuffs, but Michael doesn't unlock them. "What about it?" I ask.

He holds up a hand and backs towards a small table in the corner where a smart glass is resting. He picks it up and crosses back to me. "Promise me you'll stay calm," he says.

His lack of transparency annoys me, as does this chair. "Promise," I mutter.

Michael swipes his finger across the glass. I flinch as green text starts to flow in front of me again. Eventually, the flow of text stops and a set of diagnostics appears like the ones on the smart glass in his office. "Do you see your med stats?" he asks.

"Yeah." The sight in front of my eyes unsettles me. I feel sick again.

"Good," he says.

"Can you let me out of this chair?"

Michael looks up from the glass.

"Please?" I ask.

He reluctantly bends down and unlocks the bands around my ankles. Then, he stands up and starts to unlock the bands around my wrist. But he moves so slowly.

"What's wrong?" I ask.

Michael shakes his head. "Nothing, nothing."

The bands click open. I flex my wrists. Strangely, my body doesn't seem to be suffering any effects from the inactivity. I feel strong, and from how cautiously Michael looks at me, I suspect he can tell.

He clears his throat again and turns his attention back to the glass. "Walk to the door, Astrid."

I don't move.

"Please walk to the door, Astrid, if you wouldn't mind."

I head toward the steel door in the corner of the room. There's a small, silver screen next to it. A glowing hand icon appears in the center of my vision. Instinctively, I set my hand on the screen. My hand suddenly heats and the door unlocks.

"That's good, that's good," Michael mutters behind me.

I push open the door; and see nothing but darkness. As my eyes adjust, the slight glow of light from this room reveals that it's a warehouse. *The warehouse I followed Michael to?* That's no surprise. Cold air rushes through the doorway. I could run out of here and try to escape.

"I wouldn't try to leave right now, if I were you," says Michael.

I turn back around. I shouldn't leave without knowing what's in my head now. "You can read my thoughts?"

Michael holds up the glass. "Not with this," he says. "I just know you."

I stifle a scoff. "Really?"

He waves me over. "Come back."

I hesitate before walking towards him. I'm not feeling inclined to be near him, but he keeps getting closer, eyes glued to the glass. I shift back a little. "So," I say. "What exactly have you done to me?"

"The implant in your head is called Spora."

"Spora?"

"Yes. As I was saying, it was designed to temper people's emotions. To help them be non-threatening, functional members of society."

"How do unworthies come about then?"

Michael sets the glass down. "Various reasons," he says.

"Like what?"

"A little while ago, you were sent to kill a man named Maksim Smith."

My heart seems to stop at the mention of that name: the man who almost killed me. "How do you know that?" I ask.

He shakes his head, brushing off my question. "Spora keeps you cold. It enabled you to kill without the feeling of guilt or regret," he says. "It gives you tunnel vision and robs you of curiosity. When it's in your head, you might think that you feel sometimes...but it's all shallow. Imagine your emotions as a smooth, dark lake – with the richest feelings in the deepest parts. You've been told that you can stand anywhere you want in this lake and still keep your head above the water. If you swam a little further out, you'd find that the lake gets deeper and deeper...and you'd understand that what you've been told is a lie. But the Spora keeps you from wondering, from questioning, and it keeps you where you are on the shallow edge of the lake. You never know that you can feel more than you already do." Michael pauses, embarrassed like he's said too much. He clears his throat and stares back down at the glass. "All Spora implants are on the same settings and controlled by the System."

Then he brings his hand across his blue eyes, and his beautiful face crumples with pain for a moment. "No, I should tell you. They're all *supposed* to be on the same settings, but I've noticed its effect differing between brains. I haven't figured out the reason for the occasional deviant – whether it's just a glitch that happens - but the effect of Spora can be enhanced or diminished by the version of Curat as well. Maksim suffered a lack of feeling on a dangerous level. In that case, the Spora completely robbed him of his humanity. When I tried to fix him, it was too late."

I wonder who else Michael has told. The fifteen he mentioned? "What about the other unworthies? The others I killed?" I ask.

Michael's brow furrows and his eyes narrow as he looks down at the floor. "Did they really seem like they were unworthy?"

I take my time: the ones who refused the Curat, the ones who stood up to the wrong people. *Damon Roberts and his wife?* "No."

Michael nods. "The hierarchy in this city is wrong, Astrid. Whenever Spora seems to 'fail', people are put back to sleep, and they'll probably never be brought back. Or they're killed. That has to change. Someone has to change that."

"Are *you* changing that?"

"I'm trying." His voice sounds tired. He sighs and runs his hand through his hair. "I manually altered the Spora in your head so that we could view its settings from here," he says, holding up the glass again. "The implant's new default is its lowest possible power setting."

"Why not turn it off completely?" I don't want him able to tap into this thing in my head. That's far too intimate…

"Because you might need it someday," he says with a hint of a sad smile. "The Spora is an intelligence in of itself – and it's intuitive. If you end up in a place where it seems like there's no way out, the Spora will know because of the stress response in your brain…and it might be able to help."

It'll know what's going on in my head. I can't hide my reluctance, my distaste.

Disappointment lines his face for a moment. "The implant itself is extraordinary; tempering emotions was only using a modicum of its potential," he says, as if it needs to be defended.

"Why *wouldn't* they use its full potential?" I shoot back. "I assume they could completely control the population. Then we wouldn't have to deal with unworthies at all, would we?"

Michael lets out a strange laugh. "They tried that once. Something called Groupmind."

"What happened?"

"Everybody was networked together, but there was a malfunction. Half of this city's awoken population died before we fixed it. The rest experienced psychotic breaks...we ended up returning them all for their own good and repopulated with those who had been asleep," His mouth straightens into a grim line. "You should count yourself fortunate that you haven't been here this whole time." Michael's staring at the floor again. His eyes are wide, mind somewhere else. The longer I look at him, the more I understand. "I should be dead," he whispers. "Or worse."

"Why?" I ask. "You were lucky to escape with your life."

"No!" His voice comes out close to a yell. Shame creases his face. "No, I shouldn't be here. It wasn't luck. It was a guarantee that I would be fine."

"How was it a guarantee? You just said everyone was part of this Groupmind."

"Not everyone. Not me. I was part of the committee that helped implement it. We left ourselves off the network...for safety."

My heart drops. "What?"

"It sounded idealistic: a world without strife or violence, a world without pain."

I understand the desire for a world without pain. But a group consciousness? That's a world without *life*. "How could you?"

My question seems to scare Michael. "You have to understand, Astrid. You have to understand where this world was. The years before that were *terrible*. Violence ran rampant. People were taking risks because they felt immortal, risks they should *never* take. The debauchery—"

"And your reaction was to assemble everyone into some sort of hive mind?" I don't bother to keep the contempt out of my voice. He looks hurt, but I don't care.

"You don't understand what it was like, Astrid."

"You experimented on people and killed half of the population!" I can see all the muscles in Michael's body tensing. Maybe I should regret the words that just left my mouth, but I'm so angry at everything he just put me through.

He doesn't say anything for a few minutes. "I know it was stupid, Astrid," he sighs. "Believe me. But it seemed like the perfect solution at the time, and people change."

"You're saying you've changed?"

"What do you think?"

His eyes are pleading. I know what he's like. I know that the man before me isn't capable of robbing people of their individuality. He would fight with everything in him to let them keep it now...but it doesn't fix everything that happened before. "I believe you're different now," I say.

"I am."

"So what exactly are you doing? Why did you mess with this thing in my head?"

"Because I want you to help us."

"The fifteen?"

His eyes widen. "Yes, the fifteen. We all want the same thing."

"What's that?"

"To make the world right again. You won't meet everyone right away. We all have our own role to play. Many within the fifteen have never met each other or even know the full scale of the operation. It's better to know less – for protection."

Excitement starts to push out the rage left in my chest, but there's something needling into my mind. "Why me?" I ask.

He shifts uncomfortably. "What do you mean?"

"Aren't you the one spearheading this movement? I assume you recruit everyone who's part of 'us.'"

"The implant in your head functions independently of the System now," he says, brushing off my question and looking away. "The System shouldn't notice as I've put a ghost presence in to replace it. It'll still think you're connected. Now you'll be able to join the rest of us in the shadows at night."

Shadows. I think of Crispin. Has he noticed that I'm gone? But there's something else I'm worried about…

"You said 'shouldn't.'"

He still doesn't meet my gaze. My skin goes cold. "Michael, what happens if the System notices?"

"I don't know," he replies. Fear crosses his face, deep enough to be unsettling.

"You'll understand more of this as we go on," Michael says. "It can be overwhelming at first. As you adjust, the Spora might show you things such as your med stats or – " He stops, like he's run out of breath. "Since it's no longer suppressing or modifying your emotions, be careful. Feelings can help you remember."

Something that looks like a glimmer of hope flashes in his eyes, then his face goes cold. "We should go. I've been monitoring your glass. You haven't been called in."

He pulls my smart glass out of his back pocket and gives it to me. There's a message notification from Crispin on the front screen; I wonder if Michael's noticed. I can't tell anything from his face. I swipe past the notification and check the time. "How long have I been here?"

"Five hours."

CHAPTER 29

I'm alone in the apartment. Michael's gone to work. I know he couldn't stay, but I wish he had told me more. He's trying to ease me into this new world. Green 1's and 0's flow across my vision again. It keeps happening; must be a glitch while I adjust. I'm in the bathroom, staring at myself in the mirror. I've been in here for a while. There's a bald spot where he cut in to alter the implant. It's easily covered with the rest of my hair. Besides that, I look the same as yesterday. But I feel different; stronger, better, *alive.*

My med stats are in front of me, as if they've appeared on the mirror. My smart glass starts to buzz and the med stats are gone as quickly as they came. I pull the glass out of my pocket: it's the OR calling me in. I take one last look at myself in the mirror. They won't know anything has happened. I grab my coat and walk out of the apartment. The air is cold, but it doesn't bite into me today. The streets are crowded, and nobody knows that they're missing out. Nobody knows that their feelings are being taken from them.

Silver light cracks the sky. I look up but can only stand it for a second. The light seems to be getting brighter. No one else looks up at it, though it stays there long enough for me to walk three blocks. Does being cold the way they are also keep them from seeing? From noticing?

How much have I missed?

"I want you to help us," Michael said. Who are *they?* Can I really help them? I'm almost to the OR. A slight tinge of nervousness comes over me, but Mr. Winters won't know what's happened. After all, how could he?

David greets me coldly as I push my way into the lobby. His face seems even paler than usual. "Astrid," he nods.

I nod back. It might just be my imagination, but I think I can hear his heart beating all the way into the elevator. The air doesn't feel as cold in here today. The doors open on Mr. Winters' floor. My footsteps resound loudly as I walk down the hall. I knock on the steel door. There's no reply. I wait thirty seconds and knock again. The lock clicks open; I push my way in.

He looks tired again, even more so than last time. The circles under his eyes are darker. He fixes me with an exhausted gaze before speaking. "Good to see you, Astrid."

My surprise keeps me from replying right away. His friendliness is slight, but he's never exhibited anything like it before. "It's good to see you, too," I say.

Mr. Winters leans over the table and slowly swipes. He pulls up a profile and brushes his hand over his eyes.

"Are you okay?" I ask.

The hand is quickly brought back down. "I'm fine," he sighs. But he doesn't look fine. My gaze seems to make him uncomfortable today. He looks away. I turn my attention to the profile on the glass. It's a young woman, Eleanor Christian. She's exquisite. *And she has to die.* A pang of guilt hits my heart. I set my glass on the table to get in the info, then scan through her profile. There are no notes on why she's been chosen today.

"What did she do?" I ask.

Mr. Winters is still avoiding my gaze. I can see the muscles in his jaw and neck tightening. Why is he so uncomfortable? He sighs again. "She's done what everyone else has done, Astrid."

"What does that mean?"

Finally, he looks at me. "Goodbye, Astrid."

I stare at him for a moment before leaving. His behavior is strange, confusing even. He looked sick. We're never supposed to be sick in this world. I catch another glimpse of David as I walk through the lobby. *He's so pale.* I try to push them from my mind as I step out into the street. Time to focus on the task ahead of me. I never replied to Crispin's message. He was asking where I was. Will he show up today? If he does, why? *Why is he doing this for me?* He doesn't deserve my sins. Maybe I could let Eleanor go instead. Maybe she could hide. *Michael.* They could kill him to punish me. And if he's gone, what happens to *them*, the ones he leads?

Someone grabs my arm, and I can tell who it is by the grasp. I turn around.

His green eyes pierce into mine. "What happened to you?"

I'm taken aback. Can he tell? "What do you mean?" I ask.

He scans me up and down, studying every part of me. He looks like he knows, but he says nothing. I quickly hand him my glass. He looks down and scrolls through Eleanor's profile. His bites his lip like he did last time, but now his brow is furrowed. I can't tell what's going through his mind. "I'll meet you there," he says as he gives back my glass.

He leaves and I continue to the warehouse by myself. The silver light is back in the sky – and lights my path the whole way. I should've told Crispin I'd take care of it. But I go through the usual routine. I push my way into the warehouse and go to the car. I open the trunk and pull the gun out of the black bag. Then I slide into the front seat and input the address. She lives in Oriel, the place filled with people powerful enough to make a difference. Michael's voice flows through my mind again. *"I want you to help us."* Do they live in Oriel? Are *they* who I've been killing?

I have to let Eleanor go. I have to let all of them go. My foot taps incessantly as I sit in the car. I can't stop fidgeting. My heartbeat is climbing. I know what I have to do. It seems to take forever to reach the address. I set the timer to thirty minutes and jump out. I scan the nearby streets for Crispin. I walk around the side of the building; he's in the shadow of the skyscraper.

He holds out his gloved hand for the gun. I don't give it to him. "Astrid. Give me the gun."

I shake my head. "We have to let her go."

His eyes narrow. "What?"

"You can manipulate what people see, Crispin."

I can tell he understands what I'm saying, where I'm going. But he's still holding his hand out. "Astrid, give me the gun."

"You know you can let her go."

He's silent for a few seconds before bringing his hand down. "So even if *I* kill her, even if I do this for you, you're not okay with it anymore?"

"Are *you* okay with it?" I ask.

"I'm okay with keeping you safe," he says. "That's what I want."

"Then extend that courtesy to others."

His jaw clenches. He's frustrated.

"Don't you think that's right?" I ask.

"Damn it," he hisses.

"You don't think so?"

"*Yes*, Astrid. I think it's right to let her go."

"And you can manipulate what they see so no one will ever know, right?"

Crispin looks at the building. His face doesn't move, but there's a fire underneath. "Sometimes we can't do what's right."

"But you know you can do it," I say. "You change what people see, what people *know*."

"It's such a risk." His voice is tired. "If our process ever failed, if we can't trust her, if she *ever* came out of hiding."

"You know you can do it."

He stares at me, thoughts reeling behind his green eyes. "We have to give the cleaners a body," he says.

My heart seems to stop. I'd forgotten. "There has to be a way around that," I reply.

He shakes his head.

"Crispin, if you can change what people see—if you can make it seem like I'm the one killing these people—you *must* be able to find a way around this."

"I have to hand in a body when I kill for you, Astrid."

His words hit me hard, though I already knew. But I have to fight it.

"*Please,*" I breathe.

He looks away and I know he wants this, too. We stand in silence for a few minutes. The shadows shield us from the crowded streets. Finally, he speaks. "Stay here."

A chill runs down my spine. "You're going to kill her, aren't you?"

He mutters something I can't quite hear.

"What?"

"I won't kill her, Astrid," he says, louder. "Stay here." He pulls out his smart glass as he walks away. I stay in the dark and lean against the wall. I don't know what he's going to do. *But I trust him.*

Crispin returns faster than I expect. He looks a mess, but a different kind of mess than one would be after killing somebody. Hair falling into his face, hands in pockets, brow furrowed, lost in thought.

"What happened?" I ask.

"She's leaving."

"What about the cleaners?"

"Don't worry about them."

"Why not? What did you do about them?"

I can tell he's mulling things over in his mind. He looks like he wants to tell me, but can't…or shouldn't. "Everything's been taken care of," he says. "Everything will be fine, Astrid. I called in a favor."

We lock gazes for a minute. For some reason, the lack of transparency doesn't bother me with him. "You saved her?" I breathe.

"I told her she could leave."

Relief fills my chest, and I know he can tell how grateful I am. "Thank you."

The corner of his mouth goes up in a half-smile. "You can go home, Astrid."

Home means Michael, and I realize I don't want to. Right now, I'd rather stay here with him. Because I'm far happier here with him than at home with a man who can't return my love. But Crispin looks like he has to leave. There must be repercussions to deal with. How much has he risked doing this for me?

"Thank you," I say, again.

He steps forward and kisses me on the forehead. I wish the moment could last longer than it does. "I'll be seeing you soon," he winks as he walks away.

I wish he would come back.

CHAPTER 30

Michael is sitting across from me, but he hasn't spared me a single glance. We're back at the apartment having dinner. I'm not hungry. For someone who's going out of his way to help people feel again, Michael really seems not to feel much. Or maybe he just doesn't feel much for me. Did I do something to push him away?

Or is it just where we are? Maybe things would have been different in another life. It feels like we're roommates, not lovers. He doesn't want me. But he wants *something*, and that's why I'm here. Maybe everything he feels or ever felt was for the woman who fills those journals, and there's nothing left for me.

No, that can't be true. He could've lied to me, though. Was everything in the beginning simply a ploy to get me here? To get me to the point where he could use me? I'm not even sure what he wants to use me for. He wants me to help *them*. I'm supposed to find out who they are tonight.

Michael wipes his mouth and pushes his plate away. "You haven't touched your food, Astrid."

"I'm not hungry."

"You should eat before we go."

"I said I'm not hungry."

His eyes widen a little. But he doesn't push me anymore. "Alright." We sit in silence for a moment. Then, he gets up. "Are you ready to go?"

"I will be as soon as I grab my coat."

He hands my coat out to me. I try to take it, but he doesn't let go. "This might all be a little unsettling for you."

He looks concerned. I gently remove his hand from my coat. "I'll be fine," I reply, but I can't keep my voice from quivering.

He grabs my arm. "You're very brave, Astrid."

"Don't call me brave for dealing with something that was forced upon me."

I can feel him tense up. He clears his throat as he turns around and opens the door. "After you."

We ride down silently in the elevator. He tries to grab my arm as we move through the lobby, but I dash ahead outside.

"Astrid! Wait."

I stop. *"What?"*

Michael opens his mouth as if to say something, then closes it. He looks like he's at war within himself. "No, no," he mumbles. "This isn't the time."

"The time for what?" I ask.

He starts walking again. "We have to go."

I follow. Even though I'm frustrated with him, I know I'd still follow him anywhere, and that makes me mad. I pull my collar up, then push my hands into my pockets. The night is too cold.

Michael slows his pace and lets me catch up to him. "How was your day, Astrid?"

His question catches me off-guard. I thought small talk between us was long gone. "It was fine. How was yours?"

He ignores my question. "Did you see anyone?"

A memory flashes through my mind of Michael in the rain, watching me and Crispin. I could tell him the truth. I *should* tell him the truth. Because telling the truth would be right. But I shrug. "Just the usual."

"You were called into the OR?"

"I was, yes."

"But you said you don't kill anymore."

"I don't."

He stops walking again. "How does that work?"

I keep going. Recently, I've felt things so clearly. I've known things; things that I should do, and things that I shouldn't. But I still don't know if I should tell him. He hurries to catch up and puts a hand on my shoulder. I turn around. "I can't tell you."

Because it doesn't matter if I want to tell him. It's not only my secret. It's Crispin's as well. I start walking again. He matches my pace, brushing his arm against my shoulder.

"Does *he* do it for you?"

My heart feels like it's about to lurch through my chest for a moment. "Why do you ask that?"

"Because that man would do anything for you." He sounds bitter, like he holds a grudge.

"What makes you think he would do anything for me?"

Michael scoffs. "Because I saw the way he looked at you."

"Appearances can deceive," I say.

"Who is he to you, Astrid?" he asks. I can feel his gaze piercing into the side of my head.

"A friend."

"Of course," he replies, unconvinced.

"Who is he to *you?*" I retort.

He's silent for a while before replying. I realize we're on the way to the warehouse. Michael just stares straight ahead, brow furrowed. The quiet starts to unnerve me then finally, he speaks. "He's someone who could take you away."

"And would that be so bad?"

"That would be unbearable."

He shoots me a glance, and it only lasts a second. My heartbeat is climbing, and I hate myself for it. Maybe he actually cares. Or is this just part of an extended ploy? Of course Michael wouldn't want Crispin to take me from him. He needs something from me, *but what?*

We fall silent again. The streets are empty. Our footsteps seem to echo in my ears. Finally, we reach the street where the warehouse is. Michael grabs my wrist. "What are you doing?" I ask.

"Are you nervous, Astrid?"

"A little, but I'll be fine."

"If you get *too* nervous, you can tell me." He won't let go of my wrist.

"I'll be fine," I say.

"If you get too overwhelmed in there, just tell me. It's normal for there to be episodes after the Spora is altered."

Episodes?

I tear my wrist away. *"I'll be fine."* His gaze locks onto mine. I feel confused. *Everything* about him confuses me. "Why wouldn't you be able to bear it if I was taken away?" I ask.

His blue eyes shift back and forth. "Don't you know?"

I wish I did. A shuffling sound meets my ears, and Michael turns away to look. I see someone dart into the warehouse.

"We should go in," he says. But he doesn't look like he wants to. "Come on, Astrid." He leads me to the door and holds it open for me. I step in. The interior is completely illuminated tonight; all the light makes it look a world away from the dark place I was kept in. There are only four people: one woman and three men. They all eye me suspiciously as I walk towards them, except for one.

"Is this really her?" asks one of the men. He has dark skin, dark hair, and charming eyes.

Michael nods. "Yes."

The man breaks into a smile and holds out his hand. "I'm Luke."

I shake his hand. "I'm Astrid."

"Nice to meet you, Astrid. We've all been waiting for you." Yet, from the faces of the others, I doubt his words. He beckons to the other three. "This is Ruth," he says with a wave toward the woman.

She has bright red hair and a mouth that droops at the corners. Reluctantly, she holds out her hand. I take it. "Nice to meet you, Ruth." She doesn't say anything.

Luke nods to the other two men: one sandy-haired and lanky, the other darker and shorter. "Astrid, meet Thomas and Noah." They say nothing. I don't think they want me here.

"Good to meet you both," I say.

Michael clears his throat and steps forward. "Alex won't be joining us tonight."

Alex. Why does that name sound so familiar?

"Why isn't he coming?!" snaps Ruth.

Michael steals a glance at me. "He's taking care of something."

"Taking care of what?" snivels Ruth.

Thomas puts a hand on her shoulder. *"Ruth."*

Her chin goes down and her shoulders slump forward. "Sorry. It's not my place."

Luke smiles at me. "We're happy to have you here, Astrid." But again, I think he only speaks for himself. He turns to Michael. "Did you tell her what we're doing tonight?"

"No, I didn't," Michael replies. "But I suspect she has an idea."

I don't, but I take a look around the room. Five black bags are stacked in the corner of the room, like the one Michael carried when I followed him.

"Are you switching out the Curat?" I ask.

"She's bright, isn't she?" scoffs Ruth. There's so much contempt in her tone, and I don't know why. Thomas puts his hand out again to quiet her, but she dodges it. "Is she coming with us?"

"She is," replies Michael.

"Who are you pairing her up with?"

Michael crosses his arms. "She's coming with me."

Ruth smirks. *"Of course* she is."

"The Spora has only just been altered," says Michael. "She needs to be with me in case anything happens."

Ruth raises an eyebrow. "You could send her with Luke."

I can see the muscles tense in Michael's jaw. "She's coming with me," he states, voice low.

He and Ruth lock gazes for a minute. The others look as if things like this happen often.

"Alright," she mutters.

"It's best if Michael's the one she goes with," Luke says, nodding.

Ruth shakes her head as she walks over to the bags. She mutters something under her breath I can't quite hear as she slings one over her shoulder. She heads back and stands in front of Michael, head held high. "Are we gonna do this or what?"

Michael shifts uncomfortably. He runs a hand through his hair. "Luke, could you pass out the bags?"

"Yes, of course." Luke grabs the bags and hands them around. I pull open the top of mine. It's thick and sturdy. Michael heads into the room where I was kept, and the others follow. I trail behind. A chill runs down my spine as I step through the door. It looks as cold and unwelcoming as it did when I was last here. The chills run to my fingertips. I don't like it. The chair is in the middle of the room: bands open, waiting for whoever Michael chooses next.

A warm voice cuts into my thoughts. "Are you okay?" It's Luke.

"Yeah, I'm fine."

He smiles and suddenly, I feel a little better. "Okay," he says.

Michael's watching me; he looks away as I catch him. "Thomas," he says. Thomas steps forward, and Michael carefully fills his bag with the modified Curat. He fills the others' bags as well, then it's my turn. He doesn't look at me. "Alright," he says. "I think we're all good."

"I'll see you later, Astrid," waves Luke.

The three file out of the room. Then, it's just me and Michael. "You don't have to do this," he says.

"Why else would I be here?"

All I get in reply is silence.

"I'm used to more demanding things than this, Michael."

He still won't look at me. He puts his hands in his pockets.

"Where's your bag?" I ask.

"Well, you're coming with me."

"It's not like one of these bags holds enough to replace an entire office's supply of Curat."

"It's not supposed to," he says. "We replace a limited amount and use the modified version on the few we choose."

"And how do you choose?"

"We choose those who can help us."

Damon Roberts and his wife flash through my head. "Like hackers?"

Michael looks stunned. He waits for a few moments before replying. "Yes. We replace the Curat first and monitor them. If we notice them questioning their surroundings or experiencing dissonance, then that's when we modify the Spora." He lifts a hand like he's about to touch me, then pulls it back. I wonder if I can ask more. Would he tell me more? Michael clears his throat and looks away again. "We should go."

I follow him out of the room and out of the warehouse. He's uncomfortable tonight. Maybe he was never comfortable around me.

"So are the others like you?" I ask, as we walk the route to his office. "Doctors, too?"

"They're doctors," he says. "I suppose you could say they're like me."

"You think you're different?"

"I've been awake the whole time, and I used to be a Renewer. There aren't many like me."

"You think you're special?"

He shakes his head. "I think I'm different."

"I can't even imagine what that must've been like. Being awake all those years."

He reacts like I want him to. "There was a lot of trial and error with the early versions of Curat. Sometimes, it was like my mind wasn't mine."

At last, some details. "And now?"

"I've regained as much of it as I can."

"How much is that?"

He's silent. No surprise. The streets aren't busy. Only a few people filter past as we make our way to his office, and they pay us no mind. I wonder how many times Michael has walked this path before to do what we're about to do.

"When did you first think of switching out Curat?"

All he gives me is more silence.

I can't keep the frustration off my face or out of my voice. "Of course," I hiss.

"Don't think I don't want to tell you, Astrid."

"What else am I supposed to think?"

He brushes his forehead with the back of his hand. "You can think what you want."

"I know. Because you don't care."

"Don't you get it?!" he snaps. "It's *because* I care."

"But you don't trust me," I reply.

"I trust you," he breathes.

"Then why don't you tell me? Why don't you *share?*"

He holds his hands out, like he's begging for mercy. "Protection."

"What are you protecting me from?"

"There are things you don't know. Things you *shouldn't* know. Don't mistake my lack of transparency for lack of trust."

"How else am I supposed to interpret it?" It feels like I've reached the end of my rope with him. But I still love him, and that cuts into me more than anything else.

"Interpret it however you want," he says. "But know that I trust you."

I clench my fists. "Yeah, whatever."

"I *love* you, Astrid."

Before I can even think, I strike him across his face. "Keep things from me. I can deal with that. But don't *lie* to me! Don't give me hope when there is none." Then, I see the red mark across his cheek. *Did I do that?* "I'm so sorry." I hold my hands up, but I don't know what to do. I'm paralyzed. His eyes narrow.

"It's fine," he says.

He walks ahead without me. It takes a little while before I can bring myself to move. When I do, I stay a little way behind him. I feel so much shame. I want to beg him to forgive me, but somehow, I don't think he wants that.

"Catch up, Astrid." I quicken my pace to catch up but keep a few feet between our shoulders. Silver light glows around us. I can tell the light is spreading across the sky, brighter than last time. The time between the lightning strikes – or whatever they can be called – is getting shorter. Michael looks up and I'm amazed his eyes can stand it. It's hard enough for mine to look at his upturned face. But he looks at the sky like it might shatter and fall in on him…

Michael freezes in his steps, and so do I. Is this light more than what we're told?

Then I see her. The dark-haired woman with the coat. She's straight ahead, silver gleaming off her hair and fair skin, hollow blue eyes searing into mine again. She wants something, I know. *But what?*

The light leaves and the woman begins to leave, too. I follow her for a few paces but she turns down a side street and by the time I look around the corner, she's nowhere to be seen.

"I didn't mean to make you upset before," Michael calls out behind me. "I'm sorry."

I want to ask him about the light in the sky, about the disappearing woman, but I'm hyperventilating. I feel sick but I don't know why. Michael rushes to my side.

"Astrid, are you alright?"

"I'm fine," I lie between gasps. "You say the implant kept me from feeling. But sometimes I think I feel as much as I did before."

"I *did* start giving you the modified version of Curat quite early."

"And yet, you didn't believe that I felt."

"I made a mistake."

"You pushed me away."

"Don't let me push you away again." He says, voice hoarse.

My breathing starts to normalize but now there's a pounding in my head. "It won't be up to me."

He takes a deep breath. "You're right." We're almost to his office. A part of me hopes to make it the rest of the way in silence. But that doesn't happen. "Just don't leave again," he says.

"When did I leave?" He says nothing. I'm getting too used to his lack of response. Still, a piece of rage stirs in me. "When did I leave, Michael? I've *stayed*. I'm here right now. *You* left."

"I made a mistake, Astrid, but don't act like this is completely my fault."

"What did *I* do?"

We've reached the office. He glances at the door, and I can't tell if he thinks it offers escape or interruption. "You let *him* back in," he whispers.

I know who he's talking about, but it doesn't make sense. "I let him *back* in?"

Michael's cheeks flush. He looks like he thinks he said the wrong thing. He crosses to the door. "Let's go." He sets his hand on the door and opens it with no trouble.

"I assume you've got someone manipulating this and making sure no one ever finds out you or the others are replacing this Curat," I say, as we enter the dark lobby.

"Yep."

"The programmers?"

"Yep."

"So those are the rest of the fifteen?"

Michael hesitates before replying. "The rest of them are mostly engineers."

His words were so carefully chosen that I know he's hiding something, but I also know it'd be pointless to push right now. We make our way down the hall, to his office. There *must* be more connecting him and Crispin than just me. They both use the same approach to slip into the shadows.

Once we're in the office, he holds his hand out for the bag. I give it to him, and he switches out a shelf of Curat for the alternate vials.

"Why did you bring me here?" I ask.

"Because you're going to help us."

"You keep saying that, but I don't know what you mean. Everyone there tonight was a doctor. I'm not a - "

"This is only the first step," Michael cuts in, zipping up the bag.

"You can't go around replacing all the individual vials of Curat by hand," I say. "You're not going to have me doing this myself. So, really, *why* did you bring me here?"

It's dark, but I can see his cheeks flush again as we leave the office. "I've kept a lot from you," he says.

"I know. And you still do."

I'm about to open the front door when he slams his hand on it. I turn around. His face is inches away from mine. "I'm *trying*, Astrid. I brought you here because I want to share with you. I really do."

I can't remember the last time we were this close. "You want to share what?"

He's getting closer. "Everything."

I can't let myself give in. I *won't*. But the longer we're like this, the more I feel my restraints failing. He kisses me. I close my eyes.

CHAPTER 31

I stare up at the white ceiling. There's something comforting about the blankness of it. I'm not sure what time it is, but the sun isn't up yet. I look over to the side. Michael isn't awake yet. He looks peaceful. I haven't ever seen him look this peaceful. I bury my face in my hands. Maybe I've made a mistake with him. The hold he has over me is so strong and I hate it because he might be more grief than it's worth. I'm too confused. *I'm too mad.*

I get out of bed and cross to the bathroom. The lights illuminate as I walk in. I lean over and splash water on my face. I reach for a towel, but the sight in the mirror makes me stop. Why do I look different? I get closer to my reflection. There's something about my face that is new, but familiar. *Purity.* Like Damon Roberts. But how can that be? I'm not like him. He was kind. I've done far too many bad things to ever be like him. Yet, here I am, and my face is smoother, eyes unclouded. *Why?* My med stats show up for a moment, everything is normal. Actually, everything is better than normal. I'm healthier, stronger. I dry myself with the towel and walk back into the bedroom.

Michael's blue eyes peek at me over the covers. "Hey," he says.

"Hey."

He looks like he's expecting a kiss. I sit down next to him and oblige.

"I'm happy," he smiles.

"What are you happy about?"

"I'm just happy that you're here."

I believe him. But it feels like it's too late. I don't know what last night was, and I don't know if we'll ever become what we could've been. Because I don't know if I should want that. He runs a hand through my hair and pulls me into him. The sound of his heartbeat is one of the best sounds in the world. Michael *is* my weakness. Is it okay to be weak? I tear myself away.

"What's the matter?" he asks.

"Nothing."

"Do you have to go? Were you called in?"

I could lie and say yes. I feel like I need to get away and think. But I shake my head. "No, but I think I might go for a walk."

He starts to get up. "I'll go with you."

"No!"

As soon as my reply's out of my mouth, I bite my lip. Michael arches an eyebrow. "You don't want me to go with you?"

"I just need some time by myself."

His eyes narrow. "Are you going to see *him*?"

"No. I just need to go for a walk to process some things."

A few seconds pass before he replies. "Okay. I trust you."

I kiss him on the forehead and get up. I can feel his gaze on me as I put on my clothes. I turn around and he looks away, cheeks flushed.

"I'm glad you're all mine," he whispers.

But I can't agree with him, because I don't belong to anyone. I fake a smile as I leave the room. The cold air brushes against me as I step out into the street. All I've wanted was him. All I've wanted was for him to want me. I should be happy. Everything should be fine. But I can't shake the feeling that something about this isn't *right*. It's something I've felt strongly since the day Michael altered the implant: whether something is right or not.

I bump a countless number of shoulders as I make my way down the street. I want to go somewhere nobody goes, maybe a park. I'd like to go to Caron. I feel a pang in my chest at the thought of how it's gone now. I didn't really care before. Now I care about things like that. I guess the Spora really did stunt everything.

Suddenly, a friendly voice interrupts my thoughts. "Hello, Astrid. Good to see you." It's Luke. He grins at me. His friendliness is infectious.

"Hi, Luke. How are you doing?"

"I'm doing well. Couldn't let you pass by without saying hi. Where are you off to?"

"I'm not sure."

He studies me for a moment, then nods understandingly. "Just one of those days, huh?"

"Yeah, just one of those days."

"I get you," he smiles.

"I'm glad. I don't think many people do."

Luke lets out a laugh. "It's easy to feel that way."

"Do you feel that way?"

"Oh yeah, all the time."

His mouth suddenly sets into a straight line. "By the way, best not to mention to Michael that you saw me."

"Why not?"

He lowers his voice to just above a whisper. "He'll get all strange about the two of us being seen together in public. You know, he'll get paranoid about somebody watching, connections being made."

"Do you think his concerns are valid?"

He shrugs. "Probably."

"Why'd you come say hi to me then?" I ask.

"You looked like you needed a friend."

I can't help but smile back as I look at him. The others don't like me, I know. But I like Luke. "So what's your story?" I ask.

"I was brought back eighteen years ago. Been a doctor the whole time. Michael recruited me about a year ago."

"Only a year ago?"

"Everything's pretty recent. The others you met have been recruited over the past six months." *Ever since he woke me up.* "Anyway, that's the short version," says Luke. "It's not as interesting as yours."

I stop walking. "*My* story?"

He stops walking, too. "Well, yeah."

"What is my story?"

His brow furrows. Then, realization floods his eyes. "You don't know," he says.

My heart is racing. I can feel my neck getting warm. "Michael didn't tell you?"

"No, he didn't."

"Alex didn't tell you?"

"I don't know who Alex is," I mutter, trying to keep the frustration out of my voice. I wish he would just *tell* me.

Luke looks he doesn't quite believe me. "But he's *Alex.*"

"That name means nothing to me."

People have been filtering past us on each side. But something out of the corner of my eye catches my attention, and I turn my head.

Two Regulators are marching towards us, guns in hand. I look back at Luke. He's noticed, too. There's fear in his eyes, and I'm sure there's fear in mine. Are they coming for me? Or are they coming for him? I can tell he doesn't know either. A notification pops up showing that my heartbeat is climbing to a dangerous level.

Do we run? But it's too late. A sharp buzzing meets my ears, and I see Luke's body crumple into the arms of a Regulator. Before I realize what I've done, I've slammed my fist into the face of the other Regulator.

"No!" I scream.

I try to reach for Luke, but the other Regulator is pulling back on my collar. I reach back and elbow him in the gut.

"Get her, too," growls the man who's holding Luke.

But then I hear the buzzing sound again, and then a thud. The other Regulator is lying on the ground, lifeless. Someone pulls on my arm and leads me away.

It's Crispin. I don't know where he came from. "Go home, Astrid." I stare at him, uncomprehending of what's just happened. He grabs my shoulders. "Go home, Astrid. I'll take care of this." I still don't move. He shakes me. "*Go*, Astrid!"

I turn and run. My heels feel as if they've been set alight. Tears start streaming down my face. And they don't stop for a long time.

CHAPTER 32

Michael stares at me: wide-eyed. "He was returned?" I nod, wiping the tears off my face with my sleeve. "But *how*?" he asks.

"I don't know. Suddenly, the Regulators were there, and we didn't know who they were coming for."

He covers his mouth with his hand and walks across the room. His shoulders hunch forward and his head drops. We stand there, enveloped in silence for a few minutes. Finally, Michael speaks. "*Why?*"

My face is still covered with tears, despite my best efforts to brush them away. "I don't know."

He sinks down to the floor. "He was a model citizen," he says, voice hoarse.

"Do they know? Do they know about what you're doing?"

Michael shakes his head. "If they knew what was going on, they would've come for *me*, or..."

"Or who?"

His blue eyes look at me for a second before snapping away. "Alex."

Again, the person whose name I've heard mentioned so much, yet know so little about. "Who is Alex?"

Michael opens his mouth as if to say something, then closes it.

"Luke mentioned him before he was taken," I say.

"What did he say about Alex?!"

From Michael's reaction, I can't tell if he loves this person or hates him. "He was surprised that I didn't know my story. He thought that you or Alex would've told me by now." I would've expected such a vague explanation to confuse Michael, but he looks like he understands perfectly.

"Yeah," is all he says.

"Who is Alex?" I ask again.

Michael doesn't answer, but I won't accept the silence this time. "I need you to tell – "

"You will meet him when he is ready."

I've never seen him look so stern. There's a shadow in his eyes. He turns away and looks down at his hands.

"As much as I want it to be, it isn't my place to tell you about Alex."

Blood rushes to my cheeks and neck. I want to push him to give me an answer but from his voice, I can tell that I'm treading on thin ice – and if I go further, I might fall into a part of him that I don't want to see. This is a mess. *I'm* a mess.

The memory of Luke falling into the Regulator's arms sears my mind again. Chills run through my body. I rub my arms to abate the sudden cold I feel. "Do you have any idea why they took Luke?"

"I'm trying to figure it out," he sighs. "He honestly was a model citizen. Did his job, didn't cause any drama, didn't disrupt the balance."

"Except he disrupted the balance by working with you."

"But they don't know!" His darkness stuns me again for a moment. His cheeks flush. "Sorry, I'm just confused."

I push my hands into my pockets. "So am I."

He runs a hand through his hair. "He couldn't have done anything to warrant that."

"But he must have," I reply. "He must have if they don't know what you're up to."

Michael gets up. "Him somehow being human surplus is the only reason I can think of."

"But he's a doctor. Doctors don't end up as human surplus because we *need* them."

"Unless we don't need them anymore."

"How would that even be possible?" My heart falls as I realize it wouldn't be a surprise. Everything could become automated. Even killing people could be done by a machine. And then where would we be? We could all be classified as unworthy, so who could be allowed to stay?

"That's the problem with this world," says Michael. "The lack of humanity. It's all about what one *offers*. Humans are judged by the same standards and requirements as machines. It's a wonder anyone is awake right now."

I shudder. How did the world become so cold? "But then what's the point?" I ask. "The people who decide who lives and who dies are human. They can't rid the world of humans, because then they'd be gone, too."

"Astrid, there's something I haven't told you - " Michael pauses. The invisible top of the hierarchy; does he know who they are?

A pounding on the door interrupts us before I can question him more. I shoot a panicked look at Michael, and he shoots one back. Have they come for us? He motions to me to be quiet, then points towards the bedroom. I start walking. The door clicks open. Every muscle in my body tenses as I turn back. But the sight surprises me. It's Crispin.

What surprises me even more is Michael's face. It isn't just that he looks like he knows Crispin, but that he knows him well. "What are you doing here?" he asks.

Crispin doesn't look at him. His green eyes are glued to me. "You didn't tell him?"

My neck feels warm as I shake my head. What is going on? "No, I didn't."

"Tell me what?!" snaps Michael.

I turn back to him. "He found me right as Luke was being taken away. He kept me from making things worse and told me to go home."

Michael's lips curl into a sneer. "He just *found* you, did he?"

Crispin steps forward. "Michael—"

"You found out through the System, didn't you?" asks Michael. "That's how you got there just in time to save her. Well, that's no surprise."

Crispin's eyes narrow. "I went there for Luke!"

"Don't act like you don't always know where she is. And if you went there for Luke, why didn't you save him?!"

"Because I found out too late," protests Crispin. "By the time I got there, they'd already gotten to him."

"*Why* were you too late?"

Crispin ignores his question. "Every single one of us is a model citizen, there is no reason that any of us would ever be considered an unworthy."

Michael turns his back and starts pacing. "You should've been there. You should've prevented it."

"That could've ruined us," mutters Crispin. "We can only do so much."

"Luke is gone!" cries Michael. "He's *gone*."

A pained look crosses Crispin's face. "I tried to get him back. I really did. But I couldn't."

"Why?" asks Michael, voice low.

Crispin stares at him. I can tell there must be so many thoughts running through his mind. "He'd already been marked as Returned in the System. Too many knew. Just be glad they didn't take Astrid with them," he replies. "I made some adjustments. Her involvement in the incident has been wiped."

"And the Regulators?" asks Michael.

"They've been taken care of," says Crispin.

My heart seems to stop for a moment. "Did you kill them?" I ask.

Crispin shakes his head. "No, I didn't."

"Then how did you take care of them?"

"Pressure points," he mutters. It takes me a moment to figure out what he means.

"Blackmail?"

"Of a sort. It's easy to manipulate footage to make it seem as if *they're* the ones who misacted."

"But they were only doing their job."

Crispin's green eyes pierce into mine, and I know he understands. "Almost nothing is right in this world, Astrid."

Michael lets out a bitter laugh. "I'm sure you've figured out by now that he'd mess with the lives of the innocent to protect you."

"We're all far from innocent," says Crispin.

Michael looks over at me, as if he expects me to take his side and protest. I don't, though. I just want to know why Crispin is here. "Why didn't you tell me you were a part of this?"

Crispin hesitates and exchanges glances with Michael before replying. "I wanted you to feel safe with me," he says.

"And you thought I wouldn't if you told me?"

He takes my hands in his. "I know what it's like to get that implant altered, Astrid. I know it's hell."

"So?"

"I wanted you to have someone removed from all of that. Someone who you trusted that would make you feel safe."

"I still trust you." I think the ease with which I admit that surprises or scares him. Then, it clicks. "You just said you know what it's like to have the implant altered." His grasp on me tightens. Confusion floods my head. "Yet still, you…" my voice drifts off.

"Yet still, he kills," says Michael, no small amount of contempt in his voice.

Crispin says nothing, but he doesn't let go of me and strangely, I don't want him to.

"How?" I ask.

His mouth straightens into a grim line. "It's complicated."

"He would do anything for you," scoffs Michael.

"But why?" I ask. The longer I stare at Crispin, the more I feel like there's something I should know. There's something I should *remember*. I feel like Crispin knows what I'm thinking. He shifts uncomfortably, as if afraid of being found out. But what is there to find? "What is your part in this?"

He and Michael silently exchange looks again. "Might as well tell her," says Michael.

"Tell me what?"

Crispin drops my hands and steps towards him. His brow furrows with concern. "Are you sure?" he asks. It sounds like his words hold more than the question implies.

Michael watches him for a minute before shaking his head. "You're in charge." He steps around Crispin and crosses to me.

"I thought *you* were behind everything," I say.

"No. *He* is. He's the one who started all of this."

"What?" I ask. Crispin looks helpless, racking his brain for ways to explain. Suddenly, green text flows across my vision. I try to stop it, but it keeps going. My head starts to hurt. The damn implant. I wish I could reach in and claw it out.

Crispin grabs my arm. "Astrid, are you okay?" My legs give out, and my vision starts to blur. "No, no, no," he rambles, catching me as I fall. I feel disgustingly weak. "It was too soon to tell her this much, Michael," he says. "She hasn't adjusted."

I can make out Michael's figure leaning down, then feel his hands on my neck and cheek. "She's been fine until now. Even when I took her to the meeting, even when Luke was taken, even..."

My eyes drift closed. My consciousness begins to slip into black.

"Well, this is different, isn't it?" asks Crispin.

"Why?"

"Because it's me," Crispin says. "And the more she feels, the more she might start to *remember*."

CHAPTER 33

A harsh pain fires through my brain. It takes such an effort to open my eyes. The first thing I see is Michael's face. He looks concerned, worried out of his mind. "What happened?" I ask.

"The Spora caused you to have an episode." His hand is on mine. I wish it wasn't. "I'm really sorry, Astrid."

"For what?"

"I told him to tell you."

"I should've known anyway."

Michael shakes his head. "Your health is important," he says.

"And I'm *fine*."

I've been laid down on the couch. I look around for Crispin. But of course he's not here.

"He's not here," mutters Michael.

"I can see that."

Michael takes his hand from mine and leans back. "He's got a hold of you again."

"Again?"

I know there's a story from the past. I know Crispin is a part of it, but I don't want to hear about it from Michael. I get up. My limbs are slightly numb. I steady my breathing and stand still. Michael watches me.

"How are you feeling?"

"I'm feeling fine."

"Are you sure?"

"Yes."

He raises his eyebrows. "Okay."

"Where did he go?" I ask.

"He left," grumbles Michael. "He had some things to take care of."

"Did you make him leave?"

He stares, wide-eyed. "You think I would do that?" he asks.

He looks hurt, a small part of me regrets asking him. I turn my head to look out the window. It's dark outside. "How long was I out?"

"About eight hours," he says.

"Eight hours?!"

I still haven't moved. Taking a step feels like it might be too much right now. Michael continues to watch me for a minute before speaking. "Come with me," he says.

"Go with you where?"

"The bedroom."

I scoff. "Seriously?"

"Just come with me." He walks into the other room. I still don't move. He comes back out. *"Astrid."*

"Fine." My legs feel slightly shaky as I make my way into the bedroom. Michael's brought a heavy-duty silver box out; Lord knows from where. Secrets run rife in here, apparently.

"What's that?" I ask.

He opens the box to reveal two vials and a syringe. "Do you ever wonder why everyone has to go in every week to get their Curat injection? Why not just create a formula that wouldn't require such frequent injections? Surely someone would've come up with that by now."

"I have wondered that," I admit.

He pierces the top of the vial with the syringe needle and fills it. For some reason, I can't help but observe his process intently. The liquid is a completely different color—a light purple.

"It's a show of power," says Michael. "Of dominance."

"What is?"

"The fact that if you don't go in for your weekly Curat injections, you revert to your true state. It's a way of controlling everyone, subjugation."

"So it's intentional?" I ask. "The accelerated aging without the Curat?"

Michael nods as he empties the contents of the syringe into my arm. "Of course we created an advanced formula. We spent so long working on it."

"But they don't want the public to have access to the advanced formula?"

Michael disposes of the needle. He doesn't need to bandage my arm, the area where the needle penetrated has already healed over. "When the general population was a part of the Groupmind, there were talks of switching over to the advanced formula. People would never need to worry about aging, deteriorating. One injection and they'd be immortal."

"And what happened?"

Michael clears his throat. "Well, the Groupmind failed. Suddenly, we needed to implement a different way of keeping control. A different method of subjugation."

The tone of his voice stuns me. He sounds so nonchalant.

"We?" I ask.

Suddenly, it's as if his muscles freeze. "I told you I changed, Astrid. The rudimentary state of the Curat is a test. Everyone is required to come in every week. Everyone is required to take this injection that helps stunt their emotions, keeps them cold and efficient. It's the perfect way to weed out those who are different."

"But how can there be people who are different?" I ask. "The control is so thorough."

Michael sits on the edge of the bed and runs his hand through his hair. "The Curat is supplementary. It keeps you young, yes. It also stunts emotion and feeling, *but* the Spora is really what controls you. The Curat should technically only numb you a little, but the Spora is what robs you of most of the feeling. Before it goes into your head, Spora is no larger than a grain of sand. But it expands upon implantation into a mesh that covers most of your brain. Then it sends signals that affect the limbic system, the part of your brain that deals most significantly with feeling and curiosity."

"So can you negate the effect that Curat has on emotions by hijacking the Spora?"

The corner of Michael's mouth goes up. "Without the Spora stunting emotions, the Curat's effect on feeling is much less significant."

"So, like I asked before, how are there people who are different?"

Michael shifts uncomfortably. "There are those who fight it. We don't know how. Once they figure out they've been influenced in a way, they think it's the Curat. That's why they stop coming in." His brow furrows. "*He* fought it."

"Crispin?"

A glint of confusion shines in his eyes before he nods. "Yeah, Crispin. He fought harder than anyone else before."

I'm not even surprised. He *would.*

"You fought it to a point," says Michael.

"I did?"

"You didn't let it rob you completely of feeling."

"But I killed people."

"Still though, Astrid." He looks like he doesn't know what to make of me.

"What?"

Guilt crosses his face. "I misjudged you in the beginning." He might've. But I also know he was right. It didn't matter if I somehow tried to fight. I didn't feel as much as I should've.

"I probably didn't fight enough. It got the best of me."

Michael gently grabs my arm. Every time he touches me, I feel regret. *Why?* "However little you might think it matters, you fought it without knowing. That's extraordinary, Astrid." His hand moves up my arm, and my muscles tense. I can't deal with his touch right now.

I turn away. Michael looks disappointed. He sighs before leaning back.

I can tell he'd rather be talking about something else. He'd rather be *doing* something else. I try to push the thought out of my mind.

"When are we leaving for the meeting?" I ask.

"But you're not feeling well."

"I'm feeling fine."

"You're not needed. You should stay and rest."

"I'm not needed?! I was *there*. I saw Luke taken away."

"And I'll explain it to the group," he sighs.

Michael sounds as if he's trying to calm a petulant child. But Luke's face races through my mind, the sound of the gun, his limp body. *"I'm going."*

He lets out a little scoff. "Alright. Fine. We'll leave in an hour."

We sit in silence for a while. It seems like he's slowly getting farther and farther away from me. He's staring at the floor. I feel guilty. Because I'm doing what he did to me. I'm pushing him away. I've put up a wall and I'm keeping him out. But as I turn my head to look at him, the guilt goes away. I'm really just a tool for him. He brought me back, he changed me. Why? So I could help him. And I will help him. I'll help in any way I can. But I don't know if I can do more than that.

I run my finger across the skin where he injected me. "What exactly did you give me?"

Michael's mouth goes into a half-smile. "Now I only have one of those left."

"One of what?"

"It's the advanced formula," he says. "You'll never need another Curat injection. I'm not able to replicate it; I've run so many tests but there's something else in it I can't identify, they got rid of the formula when they found out and I…my mind has some memory lapses when it comes to that time."

It feels like my heart stops. But a notification flows across my vision showing the opposite: my pulse is high and climbing.

Michael leans forward. "What are you thinking?" he asks.

Maybe I've been wrong about him.

CHAPTER 34

Confusion and distrust are spread across everyone's faces.

Ruth's arms are crossed and her eyes are narrow. Maybe not so much distrust from her as distaste. She looks like she can't wait to spit me out. "You just let him go?" she asks.

Guilt fills my chest. "It didn't go smoothly, Ruth."

"It didn't go smoothly? He was *returned*."

She walks toward me. Michael tries to shield me, but I don't need him.

"I hit the Regulator in the face. I screamed. I wanted to bring him back. But it was too late," I try to keep my voice from breaking.

She stops. Her hair is wild, cheeks flushed. "I don't care what anyone else believes," she hisses. "I don't see the point of you."

The guilt in my chest becomes heavier. I don't see the point of me either. I don't know why I'm here.

"That's enough," growls Michael.

Ruth scoffs as she backs away. Thomas speaks up. "You're being too hard on her, Ruth."

"She was brought back for us!" snaps Ruth. "Do you really think a revolutionary would've just let him go? No. Look at her. She's a fucking shell of what she used to be."

Thomas' eyes widen. "*Ruth,*" he whispers.

Suddenly, the blood rushes to my head. *A revolutionary.* "What did you say?"

Ruth looks back at me; I think her disdain is more than it was a minute ago. I can tell she wants to unleash *something*, a tirade of abuse maybe. I don't know, but Michael stops her before she can.

"Luke is the subject that matters here. Save your thoughts on Astrid for yourself. Can anyone think of any reason why the Regulators took him?"

This time, it's Noah who speaks up. "Did they find out he was disrupting the balance?"

"No," Michael replies.

"Are you sure?" asks Noah.

"They don't know about us, okay?" Silence falls for a few seconds before Michael breaks it. "We're all safe. No one knows about us. People are returned either because they disrupt the balance or because they're human surplus."

"Are you suggesting he was sent back because he's human surplus?" asks Thomas. Michael nods. "But he's a doctor. Doctors are never returned, they're retrained and moved at the worst."

"You know he wasn't sent back for disrupting the balance," Michael replies. "So what does that mean?"

"You don't know what you're talking about," says Thomas.

"*Think about it.*" Michael's eyes are narrow. There's something almost menacing about him in the moment. I feel a tinge of fear, and I wonder if the others do, too.

The words are out of my mouth before I realize. "They're eliminating the need for doctors."

"But how?" asks Thomas. "Or why?"

"There are many possibilities," replies Michael. "They could be automating the dispensing of Curat, they could be planning on returning a great number of people, shutting down entire parts of this city, who knows."

"You do." Ruth's words cut through the air. "You know."

The hairs on the back of my neck stand up. Michael fixes Ruth with a gaze I can't read.

"You wouldn't have said those reasons if you didn't," she goes on. "Am I right?"

"There have been whispers about automating the dispensing of Curat for years," says Michael. "There have been whispers about the other things, too."

"But whispers are whispers," Ruth replies. "And *you* don't give whispers credit unless you know something."

I can tell by the beating of my heart and the look on everyone's faces that we all want her to go on, but Michael clears his throat as he crosses his arms. She's gone too far for him. "The point is we have to consider these possibilities seriously."

The group falls silent. How terrible would that be? If everyone here was suddenly gone, like Luke. Michael shoots me a glance, gauging my reaction. I still know I would do anything to protect him. He directs his attention back to the group. "We have to act fast."

Ruth straightens her back. She's been quiet for the past few minutes. She's never quiet. "Act fast and do what exactly?" She keeps going before Michael can reply. "What's *your* end goal?" She walks quickly towards Michael, almost like she's going to hit him. But she stops, inches away from his face. "Because sure, we're going to topple the System, win our freedom, everyone gets their feelings back…that works for the rest of us but I don't buy it with you, Michael. *You're* working toward something else. What is it?"

Michael doesn't flinch, and neither does Ruth. He says nothing. He stays silent. Defeat creeps into Ruth's eyes. So, it's not just me he freezes out. *Why won't he say anything?*

Michael steps around her and walks over to the stack of bags. "We should get these out," he says.

Ruth seems glued to the ground, but Thomas and Noah follow. They begin to fill the bags. I can't look away from Ruth. Her cheeks and neck are aflame. Suddenly, she turns her head and fixes her eyes—bright with rage—on me.

"*What?*" she asks.

"Nothing. Want me to get your bag for you?"

To my surprise, she doesn't shoot back some scathing reply. The rage is replaced by calculation as her eyes travel over Michael…then the others.

"No," she replies, quiet. "I don't." Then she walks away from me. Michael hands her a bag already filled with Curat. She grabs it without slowing her pace and storms out of the warehouse into a flash of silver light. That's the second time the grid has sparked this hour.

"Well, then," sighs Michael. "Let's get a move on."

The cold wind bites into my face as soon as we're outside. I pull the collar of my coat up. Thomas and Noah say nothing as they leave in the opposite direction. Are they frustrated with Michael, too? The streets are almost empty, and I welcome the open space.

He doesn't speak for a bit. I stare at him, wishing that I could *see* something that would help me understand more. But the Spora only tells me things about myself.

It takes a few minutes more for us to reach his office. He opens the door. "After you," he says.

"Thanks."

It feels even colder inside than it does outside, but Michael doesn't seem to notice. I follow him through the waiting room and down the hallway into his office. He begins to switch out the vials.

"Something that's terrible," he says. "Is that we have to consider all of the people Luke had started to convert as lost causes."

"I'm sorry."

"So much work, for nothing." I reach my hand out to help him, but he shakes his head. "It's alright. I got it."

I say nothing as he finishes replacing the Curat. It seems like he appreciates the silence, or perhaps just the lack of questions. But now, Ruth's words are stuck in my mind. She had a right to ask. What is *his* end-goal? I know he has one. We head back into the waiting room. I'd almost forgotten what happened the last time we were here. He hasn't. I feel his eyes burn into me as I push open the front door. The quiet envelopes us again as we head back to the warehouse, but it's too much, and I have questions.

"Ruth's right, isn't she? You're working toward something else."

He lets out a bitter laugh. "So, you're asking too."

"Well, of course I'm asking," I say. "After everything you've done to me, I have every right to ask." Rain starts to fall. Every drop that falls on me feels ice cold, almost like snow.

"I can't tell you, Astrid."

"Why not?"

He rubs his forehead. "There are things you will find out. There are things you *have* to find out. But not yet."

"Why do you have to hide so much, Michael?"

"Astrid – "

"What did she mean when she called me 'a revolutionary'?"

For a moment, he looks like the wind's been knocked out of his lungs. "Astrid, please, not yet."

There's desperation in his voice, and it makes me want to accept his plea. *Could I be okay with not knowing?*

We're almost back to the warehouse. A tall figure cuts across our path, and my heart skips a beat. It's Crispin.

"What are you doing here?" snaps Michael.

Crispin brushes off his question and walks up to me. "Astrid, are you okay?"

"She's fine," Michael says.

Crispin shoots him a cold glance. "I'm asking *her*."

He turns back to me. "What are you doing out? You were ill. You should be resting." His hair is a mess, and the rain has soaked through his clothes. I wonder where he's been.

"I'm fine," I say. "But it's cold, you should get out of this rain."

Crispin shakes his head. "Let me take you home, Astrid. You need to rest."

"*She's fine*," hisses Michael.

Crispin looks at him, eyes narrow, as if trying to decipher his words. "Did you—" he stops.

They stand there, just staring. "Get over it," growls Michael. "She doesn't need you to look after her."

Crispin's brow furrows before he turns back to me. "Astrid, you know you can always talk to me. Whatever you need, I'll be there." He looks even more worried than he did before. I wonder why.

Michael squeezes my hand. "Come on. We're going home."

I go along with him, even though I want to stay with Crispin. Because there's no point in staying right now. Crispin watches us walk away. His cheeks flush in anger, and I know the anger isn't because of me. It's because of the man next to me, the one who's pulling me away. I turn my head to look at him: golden hair plastered to his forehead, blue eyes that remain unflinching despite the rain. Should I turn around? Should I be walking away from *him*, instead?

CHAPTER 35

"And how are you doing today?" Michael asks as he pierces my arm with the needle.

How strange to be having small talk in the place we snuck into last night. What's even stranger is that I don't need the liquid he injects into my veins anymore. "I'm doing well. How are you?"

Michael disposes of the needle and shoots me a quick smile. "Doing great, thanks."

He could be lying. I don't think he's truly been happy since he's been with me. But how would I know? And appearances must be kept up. There are rules to adhere to. That's why I'm here.

"You're free to go," he says.

"Thanks," I reply. then I leave. No delays. No long appointments like we used to have. The blonde woman smiles at me as I leave the room. "Have a great day!" Her voice has started to sound eerily robotic every time she says goodbye to me. Nothing changes. Not her manner, her inflections or anything. She looks away before I can reply. I wonder if she averts her eyes out of pity, or maybe she just doesn't care. Probably the latter. I'm not wearing a coat today. The weather is almost unbearably hot. Such a change from last night. The flushed cheeks and wet brows of the people who pass me confirm that it's not just me. *What is going on with the weather?* The silver light has flashed across the sky so many times today that I've lost count.

My thoughts are diverted by the sound of a Regulator's gun. A young woman falls limp, and they take her away. It seems like more and more are being returned every day…or maybe I just notice it more now. I wipe the sweat off my forehead with the back of my hand. Only a couple more blocks left before I'm home. I hope to glimpse Crispin as I pass the mirrored building, but I don't. Did I make a mistake last night? Should I have stayed with him? I *wanted* to stay with him, so why didn't I?

Because there would have been no point. I could've walked the other way and left Michael. But what then? Nothing. I don't think I'm supposed to leave him. I don't know. The heat might be getting to me. I wipe the sweat off my brow with both hands. My building comes into sight, and I'm so relieved. I rush inside, the air in here feels freezing by contrast. The elevator seems to take too long to ascend. When it finally reaches my floor, I step out, open the front door and stop.

"I can tell you're *very* happy to see me." Crispin's sitting at the table, arms crossed, mouth curved into a smirk.

A smile spreads across my face, I can't help it. "Really? How can you tell?"

"Your face is glowing." Blood rushes to my cheeks. I must look revolting. I walk to the kitchen to grab a towel. "Hey, hey," says Crispin. "Calm down. You look great."

I wipe myself off and look at him. There's amusement in his green eyes. "It's too hot outside today," I say. "I can't remember any days being this hot since I came back."

The amusement quickly leaves. His mouth straightens in a grim line. "Yeah, I can't either. And I've been here longer than you have." He sits silently in deep thought, and I'm loath to interrupt him…but I have to tell him something.

"I'm sorry."

He snaps out of his thoughts and fixes me with a confused stare. "About what?"

"About walking away from you."

Something like shock crosses his face, and he looks lost. This heat has slowed us all down. "Last night," I clarify.

"Right," he replies, hoarse.

"You were being kind, and I wasn't kind in return."

"You don't have to apologize at all," he says, and wipes a thin layer of sweat from his forehead. "Any chance I could get some water?"

I cross over to the pillar and get two glasses of water. "Thanks," he says, as I settle across from him.

"Of course." I've never seen him panic, but something close to it is in his eyes right now. Did I say something wrong?

He frantically downs some water before he speaks. "How are you feeling?"

"I'm feeling infinitely better," I reply.

"Good. That's wonderful. I'm glad…" Crispin finishes his water and runs a hand through his hair. "Astrid, I want to apologize."

"For what?"

"I shouldn't have let Michael tell you about me, about how I've started this resistance."

"You're sorry I know now?"

"No! I'm sorry that I hurt you." His eyes are wide, tone filled with guilt.

"But you didn't hurt me. That was the Spora."

"I let Michael tell you, though. And that was what triggered it. I should've told him to keep silent."

I reach my hand out, and he takes it. "That's not on you. That's on Michael."

"I swore to always protect you. If anything happens to you, it's on me."

My heart stops for a moment. "When did you swear that?"

He shakes his head, like he's said too much. "A long time ago." His grasp on my hand tightens. "I'll be better from now on."

"But you don't need to be any better," I say. "You're being too hard on yourself. I'm fine, really, and I'm not your responsibility." He doesn't say anything. He just sits there, holding my hand. A question that's been on my mind since yesterday tumbles out. "You're from the past, aren't you?"

A hint of a smile appears on his face. "We knew each other very well."

The rest of the questions come out. "How did we know each other? What happened?" I bite my lip. I sound too eager.

"What makes you think something happened?" he asks.

"Because of where we are."

He leans forward. His hand moves up my arm to my shoulder. "With remembrance comes pain, Astrid."

The hurt in his expression scares me. Did I do something to him? Maybe I don't really want to know. "What about Michael?" I ask.

"You knew him, too."

"Knew him well?"

Crispin hesitates before replying. "Very well. Something I should tell you, Astrid, is that Michael was different back then." He takes my silence as a sign that he should go on, and he's right. I should know, even though I'm too scared to ask. "The best way to put it is that he was more human back then. I know it seems like I judge him harshly, and I do. But don't think too badly of him. In his way, he *does* care about you."

I stare in disbelief. "You're defending him now?"

He breaks into a smile. "That wasn't easy. It's not like I wanted to, but I felt like I should."

"Why?"

"Because things need to be fair if you're going to decide."

His words snag in my mind. "A decision?"

A buzzing sound conveniently interrupts us. He pulls his smart glass out of his pocket and shoots me a sad glance. "I have to go." I follow him to the door. I want to pull him back. I want to make him stay. He gently touches my neck and presses his lips into my forehead. "We'll be meeting again soon, Astrid."

And I can't wait until we do.

CHAPTER 36

I can feel Michael watching me in the mirror. "What?" I ask.

He turns around and gives me the once-over. He's dressed in the same dark clothes that he usually wears to the meetings, as am I. "You look nice," he says.

I stifle a laugh. "Me? Are you kidding?"

His blue eyes widen. "You always look good."

I smile. He steps forward and slips a hand behind my back. I still want him, but I shouldn't. Because what we were is gone. Maybe it was never real, maybe it was all in my mind. Whatever it was, I know it's broken now. I shake my head. He freezes.

"What's the matter?" he asks.

I gently push him away and step back. "I think we both know we shouldn't."

His eyes narrow. "What do you mean?"

"What is this, Michael? Was *this* ever anything?" He comes towards me and I put a hand on his chest to stop him.

Alarm crosses his face. "What are you talking about?"

"You want me to help you. For all I know, everything you've done has just been to keep me close."

His eyes are wide. He looks frightened, and a pang of guilt hits my heart. "Of course I wanted to keep you close," he says. "I *love* you."

And I believe him, but it's too late. "I love you, too." I don't know what else to say. It's hard to look at him.

He doesn't do anything. His expression doesn't change. He just stands still.

"We should probably go."

I turn around, but he grabs my arm. "Please don't leave," he gasps, voice hoarse. "Please don't leave me." Fear fills his eyes. Is he really that scared of losing me?

I remove his hand from my arm. "I won't leave," I say. "But whatever we had, whatever *this* was, is done."

"Then what are we?"

What are we? A moment ago, this was so simple in my mind. What else would we be but friends? But we stand there, staring...and the longer I look at him, the more confused I get, the more I wonder if this was right. "I'm sorry," I whisper.

He shakes his head as he steps around me and heads out of the room. "Save your apologies, Astrid. They won't do any good."

Neither of us says anything on our walk to the warehouse. I don't know what I'm doing. I should know that I did the right thing, but I don't. Regret is creeping through every part of my being. His was the first face I saw when I was brought back. I trusted him. I loved him so quickly. I moved in with him so eagerly. I was lonely. If I had other people—if I had *anyone*—it would've been different, and then maybe we wouldn't be as cold as we are. But I guess that's what happens when you go too quickly, you burn out.

The warehouse comes into view, and I welcome the sight of it. I breathe a sigh of relief. A break from the silence: other faces, other people to talk to. That's what I need. Michael speeds to the door. It almost closes behind him before I catch up. I walk into the warehouse and the blood rushes to my cheeks.

Thomas and Noah look up as we stride in. I know from their reaction to Michael that they can tell something's happened.

Thomas runs a hand through his dark hair. "You alright?"

Michael's eyes seem to shoot daggers at him. "It doesn't matter."

Thomas looks at me suspiciously, as if he's figured out that I'm the source of Michael's anger.

"Where's Ruth?" asks Michael.

"It's early," says Noah. "I'm sure she'll be here soon."

Michael crosses his arms. "She better."

"Is Alex coming?" asks Thomas.

The quiet that follows makes it seem like he's just asked the wrong thing. All of us, except Michael, look around uncomfortably. When Michael finally answers, his voice is barely audible.

"He's not."

Both Thomas and Noah stare at me now. *Is Alex not coming because of me?* It feels like that from the way they look at me. But why would Alex – whoever he is - not want to see me?

"Is Alex a doctor like the rest of you?" I ask, but it's like I asked a question to the wind. Michael ignores me, and Thomas and Noah just continue to stare.

"Ruth's late," snaps Michael, jaw clenched. The other men finally avert their gazes, now muddled by discomfort.

"I'm sure she'll be here soon," I say.

He looks at me for a second, and I wish he hadn't. Because what's in his eyes makes me shudder. I'm not sure what it is—coldness, hurt. *Hate?* Could he have crossed that line so quickly? We all stand there in stillness. No one wants to say anything, or maybe no one dares. The door opens and the sound of rushed footsteps ring out. I turn my head. She looks like she's been pulling at her hair. Her eyes are wide with fright. Her chest heaves with quick, shallow breaths. She looks like she's been running.

"Sorry I'm late," gasps Ruth.

I want to ask if she's alright, but Michael speaks first. "Where have you been?"

Ruth tries to steady her breathing, but she doesn't succeed. "I think I was being followed."

"By who?" asks Michael.

"I don't know."

Michael's fists are clenched, his cheeks red.

"Michael—" starts Thomas. But he's cut off.

"Did you lose them?" asks Michael.

"I…I think so," quivers Ruth.

"So help me, if you've been taking risks—"

"I haven't," says Ruth, shaking her head nervously. "I haven't."

Thomas crosses in front of me and grabs Michael's shoulder. "Michael, back off."

Michael shoves Thomas away, then regret crosses his face. But he doesn't apologize, and it doesn't look like anyone expects him to. He walks to the bags in the corner of the room and hands them out. I don't follow them into the other room when they go to fill the bags with Curat. I want distance between me and Michael, however short it lasts. Without him right there, it's like I can breathe for the first time since I pushed him away.

Ruth is the first to leave the room. She doesn't look at me as she walks past. Her steps are close, nervous. The door clangs shut behind her. Were there really men following her? Considering the terror on her face when she arrived, I should believe her. There's something about her that keeps me from being completely convinced, though. But then why was she so scared? And what would it mean if men were really following her? Luke's face flashes through my mind again, his eyes rolling back into his head. A chill runs down my spine. Could that happen to Ruth? Could that happen to all of us?

Thomas exits next, and Noah follows close behind. They both glance quickly at me as they leave the warehouse. Then, Michael comes out. He still looks just as angry.

"Michael—"

"You don't need to come with me," he says. He doesn't look at me as he heads out. "I should've just told you to stay home."

The door clangs behind him. I look around the warehouse, not knowing whether to stay or go home…or go somewhere else. Maybe Crispin's free. Would he want to see me or is it too soon?

The door creaks open. For a moment, I think Michael's come back. But then, I see the pile of red hair.

"Ruth?"

"I want to talk to you," she rushes over, bag swinging wildly.

She seems calmer than when she left, but I've never seen her like this. She's only ever looked at me like she hated me. But now, the only thing in her eyes is urgency.

"What's wrong?" I ask, because it's obvious from her face that *something* is.

She skids to a stop close enough for me to feel her breath. "Don't trust him."

"I'm sorry?" It's like every inch of my skin has gone cold.

"Michael," she breathes. "Don't trust him. He's not what you think he is."

Now it's like my skin is turning into ice. "What do you mean?"

"There's someone else in your life. Choose him instead."

Crispin. "What do you know, Ruth?" I get closer to her and she backs away.

"I know we haven't been…friends," she replies. "But I had to say something. I'm sorry I've been so cold to you, but I've been jealous."

"Jealous?" I echo.

"You've got two people who care deeply for you here, and I have no one," sniffs Ruth. "My wife isn't awake, and it's too risky now to get into the System to try and bring her back."

My head is spinning. "I'm so sorry."

She runs the back of her hand across her eyes. "I'll get to her someday. I'll figure it out. But that isn't the only reason I was so cold to you. I was — "

I wait as she wipes her eyes again and takes a deep breath.

"I was angry," she says.

I want to get closer to Ruth, as if closing the distance will reveal everything I didn't know she was keeping from me.

"Why?" I ask.

A look of apology crumples her face as she backs toward the exit. "Because I didn't choose you," she says, just loud enough for me to hear.

Then the door shuts and everyone is gone. I'm alone again.

CHAPTER 37

Sweat streams down my face. It's unbearably hot again today. I wipe my brow with the back of my hand. Maybe I shouldn't have walked, but I always walk and I needed space to think. What Ruth said last night keeps spinning in my head.

He's not what you think he is.

There's too much that she – that everyone – is not telling me and my patience is wearing thin. There are questions burning in my mind and I will only leave them unanswered for so long…

The glass in my pocket buzzes. I pull it out. I already responded and said I was coming in. Whatever the job is, it must be urgent if they bother to tell me again. They never message me twice. I try to motivate myself to quicken my pace, but my feet still seem to drag. Maybe because it's too hot. Maybe because the OR is the last place in this city I'd ever want to go to. But it is what it is.

Equally sweat-streaked people bump into my shoulder countless times as I push through the last block to the OR. The crowd is making the heat worse. *Why is it so hot?* Finally, I reach the OR. A burst of cold air hits me in the face as I walk in. I stand still for a moment, just basking in the coolness. David watches me: somber, pale, stringy-haired, haggard. He looks worse than last time. Surely heat couldn't do *that* to him.

"Hello, David."

"Astrid," he croaks.

"Are you alright?"

He seems to turn an even paler shade. He coughs as he looks away. "I'm alright." I've never seen such an obvious case of misspoken words. But I walk past. Mr. Winters is waiting.

The elevator doors open on his floor, and I frown in disappointment. The air is humid, almost as bad as it is outside. I head down the hall and knock on the steel doors. They click open right away. Mr. Winters is sitting in his chair, a blanket laid across his lap. He doesn't look as bad as David does. *He looks worse.* He lifts a tired hand and starts to pull up a profile on the table. But he's slow, and it's taking far too long.

"Are you alright?" I ask.

He says nothing. I rack my brain. What do I do? Do I take him to a doctor? *Should I do nothing and hope he dies?* I don't know how he—or David—could've ended up like this. No one is ever sick in this city. But there seems to be a lot about this city that I don't know. Finally, he manages to bring up the profile. My heart stops. Cold face, red hair, grim mouth. It's Ruth.

Mr. Winters is sitting back in his chair, his hands covering his face. It's a good thing he didn't see my reaction. So, they're taking another one of us. Except this time, it's worse. Because they don't want to give her the chance of coming back.

"My wife isn't awake, and it's too risky now to get into the System..."

Pain runs down my neck and shoots to my fingertips. I flinch. There's no reason listed for Ruth's return. Mr. Winters brings his hands down and shoots me a mournful look. He wants me to leave. I set my smart glass on the table to get the information, then I oblige.

The air is too thick; it feels like I'm swimming through it as I head to the elevator. When I reach the first floor, David is slumped over his desk. I rush over to check his pulse. I feel relief as a steady beat meets my fingers, but he doesn't wake up. I leave the OR. Any energy I have seems to leave as soon as I step into the scorching street. Everyone's pace seems to have slowed since I went in.

I pull Ruth's profile up on my glass. *Luke*—and now her. They're taking us out, one by one. Or is it something else entirely? Michael insisted they didn't know about us. Would only a fool be so sure? *They.* The top of the hierarchy I know so little about. Yet, I feel Michael knows it well. He might've even been a part of it…what if he still is?

Someone bumps my shoulder. I turn around in time to catch a glimpse of the woman in the dark coat. It couldn't be anyone else.

"Hey!" I call out. How can she bear wearing a coat in this heat?

She shoots a hollow glance over her shoulder before disappearing into the crowd. I elbow my way through, but she's nowhere to be seen. Again.

Crispin grabs my shoulder. I always know what his grasp feels like. "Hey," he says. He seems just as miserable as I do in this heat, and he doesn't even know yet. "What's the matter?" he asks. I want to tell him about the woman, but there's something more important right now.

I hand my glass over, and he looks at the profile. His face freezes. "What? Why?"

"There's no reason listed," I say.

"Do you think they know?"

"Michael said they didn't."

"If he said they didn't, then they don't."

That takes me by surprise. Because I trust him, and if he trusts Michael… "Why are you so sure?" I ask.

"Whatever else Michael has proven himself to be, I know he's wise and trustworthy."

What does he know that I don't? But the clock is ticking, and something has to be done about Ruth. "Should I meet you there?"

He doesn't reply, lost in thought.

"Crispin."

His head snaps up and he hands my phone back. "Yeah, sorry. I'll see you there."

Ruth lives just outside of Oriel. Not close enough to walk, especially in this weather. I go to the warehouse. I seem to spend a lot of time in warehouses nowadays. *Appearances must be kept up.* I open the trunk of the car, grab a holster band and secure it around my hips, under my shirt. Then I rifle through the bag of weapons, pull the gun out and load it.

I get into the car and input the address. It speeds out of the warehouse. My thoughts are running too fast. Even the cool air blasting inside the car does nothing to calm me. *Why was Ruth picked?* Can we even let her go? My thoughts lead nowhere. I figure out nothing. I've put the gun on the seat next to me. I don't want to touch it, but the car stops and I have to.

I set the timer to thirty minutes, tuck the gun behind my waist, and get out. As soon as the car rounds the corner, I see Crispin. He looks determined. From the way he walks, I can tell his thoughts have gotten him somewhere.

"Stay here," he commands. He heads into the building, and I wait. I'm not sure how long I stay there. It seems like an eternity, but it's probably only a few minutes. Sweat pours down my face again. The sun is glaring a little too harshly, and the silver light that suddenly lines the sky suddenly makes it unbearably bright. I can't stay out here, and I *have* to know.

I go into the building. There's no one in the lobby. I set my glass on the screen, and it gets me into the elevator and up to Ruth's floor. The doors slide open.

"I'm sorry, really. I'm so sorry."

"Tell me what you've done, Ruth."

They both turn their heads as I step into the room. Crispin looks less surprised than I expected. Ruth looks perplexed. She turns back to Crispin. "You brought her?"

"She was the one who was supposed to take care of you," Crispin replies.

"Take care of me?"

"I'm supposed to kill you," I say.

Ruth's face blanches. Her mouth hangs open. "I didn't know it would be that bad."

Crispin steps towards her. "Tell me," he says.

Ruth's hand covers her mouth. I can see tears fill the corners of her eyes. This was not how I expected it to go…

"I was trying to do a good thing," she whispers. "I thought…I thought if I altered the Curat—"

"Altered it how?!" snaps Crispin.

"I thought if I made them *sick,* that it would…it would be good. It would help us. We would get rid of a big part of the problem with this city."

"Made who sick?" asks Crispin.

Ruth shoots me a frightened glance, and I know who she means. "Mr. Winters and David," I say.

She nods. "I'm their doctor."

Crispin's eyes narrow. "Who else?" he asks.

"I have a list," quakes Ruth.

"Give it to me."

She pulls out her smart glass and swipes to a list. "Here you go," she says, handing it to Crispin.

"Are you serious? You stored it on *here?*"

"I'm sorry!"

"This is probably how you were found out, Ruth!"

"I'm really sorry," gasps Ruth. She looks like she might start sobbing at any moment.

Crispin scans the list. "Why is Luke's name on here?"

"Uh—"

"Luke's name is at the top of a column," he says. "Did you convince him to give out your version of Curat, too?"

Ruth doesn't speak. But the guilt on her face says enough – and the blood flows to mine. *Luke was her fault.* I walk towards her, but she backs away. "You were mad at me for letting Luke go. But what happened was because of *you.*"

Her chest begins to heave with sobs. "I know, I know, I know it's my fault."

"Was everything you said yesterday some sort of ploy?" I can barely get the words out. "Were you trying to throw me off? Were you trying make this some sort of friendship so you'd have an ally when everything crashed around you?"

"No, no, no," she gasps. "My God, no. Astrid, I swear…"

She crumples to the floor. Crispin and I let her cry. I wish I felt pity for her, but I can't. Neither of us goes to comfort her. Finally, Crispin speaks. "You took a huge risk, Ruth. You could've ruined everything." All she does is louden her sobs. Crispin pulls her up. "You know what you have to do. You have three minutes to pack a bag."

He pushes her and she runs into the other room.

"Now you know it wasn't your fault," he says. But I don't feel relief, because it doesn't matter. It won't bring Luke back. Crispin takes me in his arms, I'm not sure why. But I don't push him away.

Ruth rushes back into the room, bag in hand. Then, a deafening shot rings through the air. I reach for my gun but there's nothing there. Ruth lays on the ground, blood pooling around her head. Every muscle in my body seems to freeze. I think Crispin's saying something, but I can't hear. I can't stop staring at Ruth.

Crispin puts a hand on the side of my head and makes me look at him. "We had no other choice. Where's your glass?" I can't speak. He searches my pockets and pulls it out. "Astrid, I'm notifying the cleaners. We need to go."

CHAPTER 38

I've been staring at the blank, white ceiling for a while. I feel taken advantage of. I brought the gun. Would he have killed her anyway? Or did she die because I was there and presented him with the opportunity? I don't know if he did the right thing. Killing will never be right, but she might as well have killed Luke.

No. Luke was only returned – and he made his own choice to help Ruth. Crispin put a bullet in Ruth's head. *So much blood.*

I don't know why exactly she came back to talk to me last night. I don't even know if I can trust anything she said.

"My wife isn't awake, and it's too risky now to get into the System…"

She looked so distraught when she told me. How could that be a lie? If it's true, now she'll never see her wife again.

I cover my eyes with my hands and try to think harder, try to figure things out better. But better thoughts don't come, and clarity seems impossible. I hear the front door's lock clicking open. Then: "Astrid."

I bring my hands down from my face. Michael's blue eyes are looking down at me, filled with concern and confusion. "Astrid, are you alright?" I nod, but I know he can tell that I'm lying. "Can I help you up?" he asks.

"No, thanks. I'm good."

I expect him to walk away, especially with the way I've been treating him. But he gets down on the floor next to me. "Something's happened," he says. "Tell me what it is."

I really don't want to tell him. It was hard enough to admit it to myself. I fill my lungs and try to keep my voice steady. "Ruth's dead."

He doesn't move. He doesn't even speak for a long time. We just lay there, still. I thought I left pain behind in the past; I thought everyone had. But could the pain in this world be worse? I can't even remember.

But everything hurts so damn much right now.

When Michael breaks the silence, his voice quivers. "How did it happen? Did you do it?"

"No!" I cry, as if I could blame him for thinking that.

"Who did it?"

Tears begin to fall out of the corners of my eyes. "I was supposed to, but I couldn't. She was changing the Curat. She was making people sick. She even recruited Luke, and that's why he was taken."

"Tell me who did it, Astrid. Please."

I can't voice my reply above a whisper; and for some reason, I can't bring myself to say his name. "It was *him*." Michael knows who I'm talking about. It feels like it takes too long for him to say anything. And I need him to say *something*. "It was wrong, wasn't it?" I ask.

"Of course it was wrong," he mutters. "*Killing* is wrong."

I turn my head to look at him. "What should he have done instead?"

Michael's mouth presses into a straight line. He wipes his eyes with the back of his hand. "I don't know."

"I didn't know he was going to do it," I say. As if my lack of knowledge erases my part in it. But I know it doesn't.

"Who did she make sick?" asks Michael.

"Mr. Winters and David from the OR, and some others. There was a list. But we've been letting all of my targets go…"

"If he let her go, they would've been onto you. Because if Winters was personally affected, he'd want to see the body himself."

I turn over onto my stomach to get a better look at him. "You know Mr. Winters?"

"I know almost everyone in this city, Astrid." Pain covers Michael's face. He stares at the ceiling, like I did for the past few hours. "He did it to protect you," says Michael. "He did it to protect all of us."

"Would you have done it?" I ask.

"No, I wouldn't have. He can pull triggers that I can't. That's why he's been able to do all of this."

"All of what exactly?"

Michael hesitates before replying. "He built the surveillance protection from the ground up. The fact that we're able to move out in the open and stay under the radar; I would never have thought it possible. Then, the plan of who to bring back, even the idea of modifying the Curat. That was all him."

"How?" I ask.

"Unlike everyone else, he didn't want to be brought back. He didn't want to be here, Astrid. He was one of those who wanted to die in the past. When people are renewed and the Spora is implanted, most of the time memories and urges go away. But the implant didn't work on him like it did on others. He fought it so hard."

I ask the next thing on my mind, but I think I already know the answer. "What did you do?"

"I altered the Spora in his head. I gave him his mind back."

"He was the first?"

Michael nods. "He was."

"Why did you do it?"

"Because I was tired of who I was," says Michael. "And I thought he seemed like who I wanted to be. He had fight in him, and I hadn't seen fight like that in so long." His hand slips into mine, like he's asking for comfort. I give it a gentle squeeze. "But even with the full command of his emotions—his *thoughts*—he still did things that I couldn't believe."

So much blood. I rub my forehead, trying to push the thought from my mind. The question is out of my mouth before I realize: "Why?"

"He's driven by a greater purpose. He wants to save this city, and if he has to kill a few people to do so, then he'll do it." He takes a deep breath in. "Hell, he even might save the world while he's at it." *The world.*

Michael shoots me a glance. "You didn't think about it, did you?" I shake my head. "What lies beyond this city is a whole other beast, Astrid."

I'm scared to ask what he means because I never wondered about the world beyond this city. I never wondered about anything. Now, Michael squeezes my hand. "Don't blame yourself, Astrid. You didn't have your mind."

Chills run under my skin. How terrifying that something as small as the Spora could rip so much apart from so many people. I would ask him about the world out there right now, but this grief makes me feel like I'm falling in on myself. I can barely make sense of the thoughts in my head. Michael starts to get up.

"You're leaving?" I ask.

"I have to go meet Thomas and Noah and tell them what happened." His blue eyes lock onto mine. "You don't have to come," he says. He doesn't want to be alone.

"I'll go with you." I hold out my hand, and he pulls me up.

CHAPTER 39

The meeting was hell. Explaining that Luke being returned was bad enough, but explaining that Ruth *died?* Michael was the one who told the story, but he left Crispin and I out. No one knows that I was there and saw her lying in that pool of blood. I know Michael has his reasons and it's probably for the best, but I can't help but feel like we've lied...

I lean against the window, hoping that the cold surface will soothe me. But the sudden silver light makes me step back. I manage a glimpse before it becomes too much. Not only is it getting brighter, but it stretches further and further across the sky each time. The weather is unusually chilly today. The clouds are gray, and the icy rain falls on a shivering population. No one knows how to deal with weather like this because no one's had to. Are the weather controls glitching or is there something else going on?

I hear Michael come out of the bedroom and turn my head. He scans me, and his eyes take me in hungrily. He stands tall, but I know loss has crushed him. I want to reach out and draw him in—and maybe I should, but I don't.

"Hey," he says.

"Hey. You alright?"

The corner of his mouth goes up in a sad half-smile. "No, but there's nothing to be done about it right now."

I walk over to him. "You know I'm here for you."

"You mean because we're roommates?"

"No, because I'm your friend, and I care for you," I whisper.

He studies me for a minute. Then, he puts a hand on my shoulder. "Thanks, Astrid." He brushes his lips against my forehead. I watch him go out the front door. I want to follow him. I want to take his hand and comfort him. But I just pushed him away two days ago. Am I simply wanting what I don't have? The buzzing in my pocket interrupts my thoughts. I pull my glass out. It's the OR. A sinking feeling appears in the pit of my stomach. When will this end?

I head into the bedroom and put on a hat, scarf, and warm socks. Then I cross back out and grab my coat. I wonder if I should catch a cab instead of walking, or even the rail. But, I find myself out in the street, pushing my way through the crowd. Despite my heavy clothes, every muscle in my body seems to be freezing. My breath is a white cloud, lingering in the air even after I've passed. It feels like it should be snowing. All the faces around me have rosy cheeks, red noses, teary eyes. I wonder if any of them are worried about this weather and what it could mean.

But none of them wonder or realize. None of them care and none of them feel. *I felt.* Because Michael started giving me the modified Curat early, right? But Crispin felt. I scan the rosy faces. Are there more like me? Are there more like *him?* My teeth chatter and I pull my coat in tight. Only a few more blocks until the OR. The sound of a Regulator's gun buzzes in my ears. I shut my eyes and don't turn my head. I can't look anymore. I can't hear that gun without seeing Luke's face. I quicken my pace, push my freezing muscles. I want to get out of this street.

I reach the OR and walk into the lobby. David still looks ill, but his brown eyes gaze at me intensely. I know he's trying to figure out something, though I don't know what.

"Astrid."

My feet start moving again. "David," I nod.

I feel strange. My hands are numb, and my chest is tight because of the way he looked at me. Suddenly, I'm nervous. I close and open my hands, trying to regain the feeling. He still watches me as the elevator doors close. When the doors open on Mr. Winters' floor, the same balmy air as last time envelopes me. But I welcome it this time. I unbutton my coat as I head down the hall. I knock on the steel doors, and they unlock right away. Mr. Winters' pale face greets me.

"Astrid," he wheezes.

"Mr. Winters."

He stares at me for an uncomfortable minute before speaking. "I just wanted to thank you."

My heart stops. "Thank me? Why?"

He fixes me with empty green eyes. "For being such a good employee, of course." But his voice is empty, too.

A chill runs down my spine. What is he playing at? "I do my best," I say, even though it's a lie.

Mr. Winters' eyes are still on me. Does he know I'm lying? A few moments of silence pass before he speaks again. "I can tell." His attention turns to the table. There's something going on. His strange demeanor sends a sudden layer of nervous sweat to my forehead and palms. He slowly pulls up a profile. I lean over the table to study the text and photo. The man is of an unassuming appearance: mouse-brown hair, light brown eyes, pale skin. He's also of an unassuming name: Ryan Jensen.

The reason for killing him makes me catch my breath. "How many did he kill?" I ask.

"Four."

"Four!" I cry. "Why did nobody catch him?"

Mr. Winters studies me, and I feel myself falter under his gaze. "It doesn't matter," he sighs. "What matters is that we're doing something about it now."

The way he speaks makes me feel like I'm taking up too much of his time, as it usually goes. I set my glass on the table to get the info, then I leave. *Four women are dead because of this man.* I cover my face as the elevator descends. How was he not caught? Would the Spora not stop him? Words stir in my head, Michael saying that the implant can create people like Maksim Smith. A shudder rumbles through my body. David is leaned over the desk, resting, and watches me as I leave. The cold air outside hits me like a brick in the face. I button my coat again and pull my collar up.

I keep my head down as I walk the street. Ryan lives closer than most targets do, only about four blocks from here. I stop at the warehouse to pick up the gun. The air is warmer inside. I resist the temptation to bask in here and push myself back out on the cold street. Then I feel it: the grasp on my shoulder.

"Astrid!" Crispin always know where I am. He always knows what I'm doing. *So much blood.* I can't look at him without also seeing Ruth's head shot out by the bullet.

"Crispin."

I hand him my glass, same as usual. Do we let him go, same as usual? *He didn't let Ruth go.* I shake my head. "I think this one needs to be killed."

He shoots me a narrow-eyed glance before studying the profile on the glass. Then, he grabs my arm and slips it through his. "Let's walk."

The closeness bothers me today, even though it usually doesn't. He scans the crowd, but I know he's just using them as a backdrop for his thoughts.

"What is it?" I ask.

"I scared you the other day, didn't I?" His question knocks me speechless for a moment. "You don't have to lie to me, Astrid. I know I scared you."

"You killed her."

"She was trying to kill David and Mr. Winters. That would've drawn attention to you. You would've been found out." I stay quiet. It's like I can't find words today. He stops and faces me. I have to look at him, but I don't want to. "I would do it again," he says. "I would do it again to save you—to save *us*. What do you think of that?"

I don't know what to think, and it scares me.

Crispin's eyes burn into mine. "It's different when you know the person, isn't it?"

He's right. It is. We start walking again. "So," he says. "About this man."

"What about him?" I ask.

"Well, you don't want to let him go?"

My cheeks start to turn red from rage. "What kind of question is that? He killed *four* women!"

"But you would've let Ruth go."

"Because she was *Ruth*."

"And yet, she was trying to kill David, Mr. Winters, and many more." His words hit me harder than they should. "Do you see, Astrid? Your rules of deciding who to spare and who to kill; have you thought them over?"

I feel inadequate. *Rules of deciding who to spare and who to kill.* I haven't thought them over. I shouldn't have to make any personal rules like that. "What are you going to do?" I ask. "Are you going to let him go?"

Crispin shakes his head. "No. Because he'll kill again."

"Are you saying that it's right this time?" We're nearing Ryan Jensen's building. It's tall: massive spirals of steel and glass.

"Killing is never right," he says. "But sometimes it's for the greater good." And suddenly, I understand what Michael was saying. I see how Crispin could save this city. He leads me into the shadows around the side of the building and holds his hand out for the gun. I give it to him. He slips it into his coat pocket and squeezes my shoulder. "I'll be out soon."

I watch him leave, then slink further back into the shadows. I want to run away and hide. Be alone. Sort out my thoughts. Maybe I've misjudged everyone and everything. It feels like barely five minutes pass before Crispin comes back out. He hands the gun back to me, and I slip it back into my coat pocket.

"Tell the cleaners."

I pull out my glass and swipe to notify the cleaners. I can feel his green eyes piercing into me as I do. My cheeks start to get warm.

"What?" I ask.

His mouth curves up into a small smile. It always amazes me how quickly he can smile after he sins. "Astrid, I want to see you more."

"We see each other practically every day."

Crispin clears his throat. "Anytime we're together, it's during times like this," he says. "Times where I'm covering for you or scrambling to make sure you're alright…or when you come to me with problems." My chest tightens with guilt. I only ever see him when he's *doing* something for me. There's eagerness in his gaze. I don't blame him for wanting more.

"I'm sorry."

He lets out a soft laugh. He's just killed someone and already he's able to laugh. "Astrid, you don't have to apologize."

"It's not fair to you," I say. "I shouldn't be relying on you to do so much for me."

"I *want* to be doing all of this for you."

"Why?"

My question rings out in the air and is left unanswered. I don't ask again; I'm not sure I could handle knowing anyway.

Crispin sighs and puts his hands on my shoulders. "Just let me see you more. Please."

It's hard to look at him. Because his face and voice are pleading, and I want to give in. But everything in me is screaming that I shouldn't. Because of the blood, the killing, *everything he does for me.* I owe him. I force myself to meet his gaze. "Okay." His grin beams at me. Then, a buzzing sound meets our ears and the grin disappears. He pulls out his smart glass. Suddenly, he looks so tired. "You alright?" I ask.

He puts the glass back in his pocket. "I'm better when you're around." He runs his hand through his hair. I can tell he doesn't want to leave, but he leans forward and kisses my forehead. "I'll see you soon, Astrid." He walks away and leaves me dreading the next time I see him.

Because I think he might have a little more of my heart than he should.

CHAPTER 40

It's dark, and Michael isn't home yet. I get up from the table and cross to the window. I brush my fingers across the glass, then quickly pull my hand back. It's even colder than it was earlier in the day. People are rushing through the street, eager to escape the frigid air. I pull my smart glass out and message him. I hope he's alright. Although, why wouldn't he be?

I slip the glass back into my pocket. It sits there, its presence feeling heavier than it should be. He doesn't reply. I thought I wanted to be alone to sort out my thoughts. I've gotten nowhere, and the quiet is too much. I fall back on the couch and cover my face. Then, the glass buzzes. I yank it out and stare at the screen. It's not who I want.

It's Crispin. Our conversation from earlier in the day has been churning in my head these past few hours. He said he wanted more, and I agreed to give it to him. But now he's calling on the agreement *so soon*. The air inside of this apartment feels stifling. I go back to the window. It's cold, I know, but I need to clear my head.

I put on a hat, scarf, gloves, and bundle myself up in the thickest coat I can find. Still, I don't know if it's enough to help me handle this weather. The stores here aren't equipped with clothes for extreme cold. But then, who would've thought? Who knows why this is happening? I slip my glass into my pocket and exit the apartment. The elevator feels slow today, like the weather's slowly freezing it, too. The air bites into my face when I step out into the street. I pull my scarf and coat collar up.

Red-cheeked faces rush past me. I doubt anyone's out here because they want to be. *Except me.* My feet carry me down side streets and past rows of skyscrapers. I don't know where I'm going. My eyes water from the wind. I wipe the tears away with the back of my hand. The smart glass in my pocket keeps buzzing. I pull it out. It's still not Michael.

Notifications keep flying across my vision about the extreme weather. The Spora is telling me to go home. But I don't. My surroundings start to look more and more familiar and I realize I've somehow ended up on the path to the warehouse. The meeting isn't for another four hours, and I doubt they even want me there. I'm unnecessary. Whatever they've said about needing me is bullshit. I think. I rub my face with my gloved hands. My eyes are starting to water more and more.

Luke's warm smile floods my mind, followed by Ruth's earnest face that night in the warehouse. The more I replay that night, the more I believe she truly wanted to warn me.

"He's not what you think he is..."

When I bring my hands down, I see him. He's about twenty yards in front of me. I'd recognize Michael's walk anywhere. He's clad in the same dark clothes he always wears to the meetings. I stop for a moment. Do I rush to catch up with him? He never replied when I asked him where he was. My feet start to move again, but I stay behind him. Why am I following him? I should either catch up to him or leave.

I trail him, staying about fifteen yards behind. I don't need to get closer, because I know where he's going. Every time he rounds a corner out of sight, I know where he'll be next. He's going to the warehouse. The glass in my pocket has stopped buzzing. Crispin must have given up. I would be relieved, but my chest is too tense. *What is Michael doing?*

It's easy to stay in the dark. A lot of the lamps on the street to the warehouse have gone out. There's barely enough light to make out Michael's frame. A dark figure crosses the street and walks over to Michael. I stop in my tracks. That's another walk I'd recognize anywhere. I move towards the side of the pavement that's farthest from the street, out of the light from the streetlamps. They've gone down the alley right next to the warehouse.

I try to keep my footsteps as quiet as possible. It feels like I'm being pulled toward them. *Why?* Why do I so desperately want to know what they're saying? I pause at the corner before the alley. Their tones are hushed, but I can still make out the words. I peek around the edge of the wall. They're standing a few feet away from each other.

Crispin lets out a sigh. "Why did you want to see me?"

"I needed to discuss something with you," Michael says, arms folded across his chest.

"Could you hurry up?"

"Are you *actually* pressed for time?"

Crispin pulls his smart glass out and checks it. "I guess not," he says, disappointed. I feel a slight pang of guilt.

Michael's brow furrows and his mouth straightens. "Why did you just check your glass? Who are you waiting for?"

"No one."

"Alex," says Michael. "Don't lie to me."

Alex? My heart beats so fast it feels like it'll pound straight through my chest.

"Who do *you* think I'm waiting for?" Crispin retorts.

"What did you say to Astrid?" asks Michael. Crispin stays quiet. Michael steps forward. *"Tell me, Alex."*

A pain sears through my head. My knees buckle for a moment, and I sink to the ground. Why is he calling him "Alex"? He's *not* Alex. He's Crispin. But the pain in my head is getting worse. I pull myself up. I can't hear anymore, there's no point in staying. I have to get home. I stumble down the street. My ears are ringing. My eyes are stinging from the cold and the pain is getting worse.

I run my hands across the buildings to keep me upright. It seems to take forever to walk the path home. I'm only a block away from the apartment now. I can barely see, barely breathe. The silver light comes and makes everything even harder. But I force myself to stay up, force myself to get home. I push my way into the lobby. I think someone asks me if I'm okay, but I hurry into the elevator. Sweat covers my forehead. I try to lift my hand to wipe my face, but it's trembling too much. Finally, the doors open. I step out and lean against the wall.

Everything seems blurry. I make it through the front door and fall to the floor. Everything is fading into each other.

Alex?

I'm starting to remember.

CHAPTER 41

A hand touches my arm, and my eyes open. The familiar white ceiling above greets me. Then, a familiar voice.

"How did you sleep?" asks Michael.

I turn over to look at him. His eyes are wide, innocent. He doesn't know. I try to remember how I got from the floor to the bed, but I can't. "I slept well," I say, though I honestly have no idea. "What about you?"

"I slept well, too. Thanks for asking."

The sun's barely up. He leaves his hand on my arm. We sit there, not saying anything. We used to fill these early hours with something else. Did I make a mistake? An image flashes through my head. *Someone surrounded by fire.* I can't see who it is. It's like they're wrapped in shadows despite the flames around them.

My body is paralyzed for a moment. I saw this in my past. Somewhere in the back of my mind, I know who it is...

"What are you thinking about?" he asks.

I can't tell him, and it's not because I don't want to. It's because I don't know. I cover my eyes, try to clear my head. It doesn't work.

"You alright?"

I turn over, let him fill my vision. Despite where we are, I still think his face is perfect. I can't find a flaw, no matter how hard I try.

"Yeah," I smile. "I'm alright." He smiles back. It's beautiful. "How about you?" I ask.

He looks surprised. "Me? I'm fine."

Snippets of his conversation with Crispin in the alley flow through my mind. *Alex.* The pain sears through my head again, but not as bad as last night. I try not to wince. Michael's brow furrows.

"Are you sure you're alright?"

"Yeah, I'm fine. Why wouldn't I be?"

He studies me for a minute before his brow relaxes. "I have to go."

"I know." I wish he didn't have to. Because even with the pain, I'm enjoying right now. He gives my arm a squeeze, then gets out of bed and starts to get ready. I turn away. I want to pull him back. *Someone surrounded by flames.* Over and over. I try to remember when it happened, who it is. But I can't and the pain gets worse every time that image flashes into my head. Why can't I see them? How is their face obscured by shadows in the middle of all that bright light?

I feel a warm kiss on the side of my head. "I'll see you later, Astrid."

I turn around to kiss him back, but he's already gone. The front door lock clicks, and I'm alone. My smart glass buzzes. I know who it is; it's as if he *knew* Michael had just left. *Does* he know? I scan the room I'm in. Could Crispin—*Alex*—be watching? Pain shoots through my head again. I wince as I pick up the glass.

He's asking to meet again. My heart drops into my stomach. I don't want to, but I can't piece together the memories flying through my head. I message him back and say okay. A knock resounds through the apartment. I jump to my feet. *Is he here?* I glance down at what I'm wearing. I need to cover up more. Another loud knock rings out. And another.

"Fine, fine," I mutter.

I cross into the living room and open the front door. The smirk he wears fades as his jaw drops. "Wow."

"Why are you here?"

He brings his eyes back up. The smirk manages to creep back. "Aren't you happy to see me?" I keep quiet. When he speaks again, there's a glint of insecurity in his tone. "Can I come in?"

I hesitate, then step aside to let him through. I might as well. He strides in and flashes me a grin. I grab a blanket off the sofa and drape it over my shoulders.

"Don't cover up just for *me*," he winks.

"Why are you here?" I ask.

The audacity and brashness leave his face. "You didn't answer any of my messages from last night." He sounds sad. I feel a pang of guilt. "Why didn't you?" he asks.

I rack my brain for answers that aren't a lie. "I had to think a bit. Clear my head."

The corners of his mouth turn down. "Are you alright?" *Someone surrounded by fire.* The pain shoots again. I clutch at my head. He rushes forward and grabs my shoulders. "Astrid, what happened?"

I bring my hand down. "What do I call you?" I ask.

"What?"

"What's your *name*?"

He stares, and I know he understands. "Did you follow him last night?" he asks. I nod. There's sorrow in his eyes, and something that looks like regret. "Put some clothes on," he says, voice low.

I scoff. "What? Am I distracting you too much?"

"I need to show you something."

"So show me."

"Not here."

Silence envelopes us for a moment.

"Fine," I mumble, and go into the bedroom.

I pull open the wardrobe and throw on some clothes. A black ribbon hanging on the side grabs my attention. It sits there, gleaming in the light. I never noticed it before. I pull it down and use it to tie my hair back. *Why is he here?* Yet, I can't help but feel a small sense of relief that he is because he'll tell me. He'll explain everything I don't know; and I want to know, don't I? I walk back out into the living room. He's gazing at the bookshelf.

"Anything there catch your eye?" He spins around, and his jaw drops again. "What?" I ask.

The color has suddenly gone from his cheeks. He looks as if he's just seen a ghost. He takes a minute to compose himself. "We should go," he says.

He offers me his hand, but I don't take it. I head over to the door and he lags behind. The way he's acting today is strange and confusing. I look back at him. "Keep up."

He hurries into the elevator. The doors open and we cross through the lobby. I can feel his eyes on me. A gentle breeze hits me as we step out into the street. The weather is pleasant today, unlike the extreme bouts of cold and heat we've been having. It's a nice change not having to wade through a sea of sweat-streaked or half-frozen faces.

"Where are we going?" I ask.

Every time I look at Crispin his eyes are wide, stunned. What's the matter with him? He clears his throat. "Just follow me." It feels like we walk for miles. Perhaps it's because neither of us says anything. The tension between us is too palpable. I can see the muscles in his neck straining. Eventually, the surroundings start to look familiar. We're taking the path to Oriel.

Finally, Crispin breaks the quiet. "Why did you tie your hair back today?"

"Because I felt like it."

"I see." His tone is odd, choked.

"Why do you ask?"

"Just wondering," he shrugs.

"Why are we going to Oriel?" I ask.

"We're not going to Oriel."

"Then where are we going?"

He stops in front a building: tall, grand, silver spires and glass. "Here," he says.

I follow him into the lobby. Some dark-haired girl waves at him on her way out. He waves back, then shoots me a cautious glance. But I don't care. He swipes his glass on the screen and we both step into the elevator. I can hear his shallow breaths. He's nervous.

The elevator doors open and my heart skips a beat. "This is your place?"

"Yeah."

It's not what I would've expected, although I'm not sure what I expected. The place is clean, covered in warm tones. The furniture is lived-in, comfortable. The walls are lined with paintings. "Did you do all of this?" I ask.

His cheeks flush. "Yes."

I walk around, taking in all of the art. He stands in the middle of the room, fidgeting. The subjects of the paintings contrast greatly, but there seems to be a recurring theme. *Pain.* Even his painting of a park seems so full of hurt. I'm not sure why. Is it the shadows? The darkness? Maybe it's just me. I stop at a painting of a fountain. "How long have you been painting?" I ask.

"Ever since they brought me back," he says, and his voice shakes a little. Chills keep flying under my skin. The scenes in these paintings seem so familiar. He goes on. "Even with the Spora on its original setting, I was painting. It was like there was something in me that had to get out. I think, when I showed them to Michael, that's when he realized I was fighting it."

I step away from the wall and stare at him. "You showed these to Michael?"

He nods. "When I was first brought back, I was angry. My head wasn't adjusting to the Spora properly. He told me to train more—run, fight, anything—to take my tension away. For some reason, painting worked. I told him about it, and he asked to see." I turn back to the paintings. No wonder the pain is so apparent. They're beautiful, but so dark. "There's one I really wanted you to see," says Crispin.

"Which one?"

He hesitates before backing towards another room. "This way." I follow him, my heartbeat running faster with each step. We enter a bedroom. It's also furnished with warm, comfortable colors...but the sight of the far wall makes me forget to breathe. On it hangs a painting. *A painting of me.* Except, I look different. There's resilience in the eyes, head held high, shoulders back. And my hair is tied back with a black ribbon. I glimpse myself in a nearby mirror. No wonder he looked like he saw a ghost. My knees go weak. I back onto the bed. He sits down next to me. His eyes are piercing into the side of my head, but I can't take mine off the painting.

"What does this mean?" I ask, voice hoarse.

"That's you, Astrid."

"I can see that."

"It's you a long time ago." I tear my focus away from the painting and look at him. "It was the way I remembered you, when I came back."

A tear falls out of the corner of my eye, burning my cheek on the way down. I don't know why I'm crying. My head starts to hurt again. "How could you remember me?"

"Because you were my world."

Someone surrounded by fire. Is he the someone? "I don't understand. I don't remember."

"So I'll tell you," he whispers. He holds his hand out for mine. I still don't want to touch him. But he reaches and takes my hand in his anyways. "You and I were—" he stops.

"We were what?"

He takes a deep breath in. "You were my wife, Astrid." *No.* His words feel like a slap in the face. He goes on. "We were in love." I don't want to hear this. I want him to shut up.

"Stop!" I cry. He stares, and I see that I've hurt him. "I'm sorry. I just—" He takes his hand back. I turn back to the painting. We sit, quiet. My chest hurts. It feels like my heart is breaking. *Because I wanted it to be Michael.* Why did I think it could've been Michael? I'm so stupid. Another hot tear rolls down my cheek. "What do I call you?" I ask.

"Call me whatever you want," he mutters.

"What's your *name*?"

Silence fills the room for the next minute before he speaks. "Alex," he says.

"Why did you tell me your name was Crispin?"

"It belonged to someone close to me, and I didn't want to tell you my real name, because a part of me was scared of you remembering."

I shift my gaze back to him. Suddenly, it's like he can't look at me. "Someone close to you?" I ask. "Tell me."

He leans over and buries his head in his hands. "I never wanted to be brought back. I wanted a normal lifespan. When I died, I wanted it to be just that—complete death." He breathes a deep sigh as if to calm himself, then continues. "But when I came back, I believed I was supposed to wake up…because I couldn't remember what I'd decided. For all I knew, I *had* chosen life. Either way, they didn't let me die." He looks up at me. "Crispin was my brother. He chose life. I've looked for him, but I can't find him anywhere. I've hacked into the System to try and find him, but nothing. Fate? God? Call it whatever you want. I've ended up here living and he's nowhere to be found."

Crispin—*Alex*—reaches over and gives my arm a gentle squeeze. "Is this too much for you?" he asks.

"No," I reply. But my head is pounding.

"I'm just thankful Michael ended up being my Renewer," he says. "He kept tabs on me, tried to help me. He *did* help me." His voice starts to break, but I'm not sure if it's out of gratefulness or bitterness. "I owe everything to him."

The painting keeps pulling my focus away from him. "You remembered everything?" I ask.

"I remembered *you*. You were the only thing that filled my head for months after I woke up."

A question snags in my mind that I'm afraid to ask. But it's bothering me almost as much as the pain in my head. "You didn't remember our children?" Pain contorts his face. A chill runs down my spine. Why did I need to ask?

"We never got there, Astrid."

"You just said you were my husband."

He covers his face with his hand. My question hangs in the air, unanswered for minutes.

Impatience sweeps over me. My hands start to shake. I need him to tell me, or just say *something*.

"I remember children," I say. "They were mine."

"They were yours. Not ours."

I stare at him, stunned. His expression doesn't give anything away. "If they weren't ours..."

His mouth curves into a bitter smile. He shakes his head. "Who do you think?"

"I don't know."

"Michael."

A lump appears in my throat. More tears burn my cheeks. I can't tell if I'm relieved, or shocked, or something else.

Alex watches me, his face growing colder by the second. "That's how he we knew each other. He stole you from me."

CHAPTER 42

I press my forehead against the window. It's cold again. The people in the street below me are bundled up, rushing inside or back to their homes. The sunset is broken by what seems like the thousandth flash of silver light today. Michael should be home soon. What do I say when I see him? *Why* would I say anything? Is there any point in telling him I know now? What would happen? I close my eyes. I don't know. The glass keeps getting colder. But I feel too hot and it's refreshing. I press my palms against the window as well. I stand there for a while, letting the cool seep in through my skin to calm me. Then, I hear the front door click open.

"What are you doing?"

I turn around. Michael's staring at me with an amused grin on his face. I can't help but smile back, even if my chest is tight with anxiety. "I was just watching the people in the street."

Michael walks over and looks out the window. "And what were your thoughts as you watched the people in the street?" he asks.

"Everyone looks cold."

He lets out a small laugh. "That they are," he says.

The tip of his nose is tinged red from the cold. I rub his arms. The smile stays on his face. "Do you need a blanket?" I ask. "Tea? Anything?"

He shakes his head. "I actually need to go out soon."

My heart drops. "But you just got back."

His mouth straightens. "I have to meet someone," he says.

"Who are you meeting?"

Michael opens his mouth as if to say something, then closes it. We stand there in silence for a few seconds. "I'm meeting *him*."

"Alex?"

His eyes widen. And I wonder if I've said the wrong thing.

"Do you—"

"I know who Alex is."

I feel his muscles freeze. Confusion lines his brow. "How?"

"He told me," I say, then bite my lip. Should I tell him I followed him the night before? A strange light fills Michael's blue eyes. He lifts his hand and gently touches my brow.

"Do you remember?" he asks.

Regret sweeps over me. "I don't."

His face falls. "Oh," he breathes.

"I wish I did."

He shoots me a sad smile. "Are you feeling alright?"

"My head was hurting earlier," I reply. "But now it's fine. I'm just…I don't know, confused."

He gets closer, gaze locked onto mine. "Your head doesn't hurt anymore?"

"No, it doesn't." I can tell thoughts are running a thousand miles per second in his head. "What is it?" I ask.

"Usually if there's pain, it means you're remembering. Are you sure you don't remember anything?"

Someone surrounded by fire. Do I tell him? I draw air deep into my lungs. "There's one image that's been flashing through my head"

"Of what?"

Chills run down my arms. "There's a fire," I whisper. "And someone standing in the middle of it."

The color leaves Michael's face. His lips fall open. The hair on the back of my neck stands up.

"What is it?" I ask.

No answer. He looks out the window and I know he's using it as a canvas for his thoughts. I run my hands up his arms to his shoulders. "Is there something I should know?"

His head snaps back around. "No, there isn't," he mutters. "Not yet." He reaches out and pulls me close. I rest my head on his chest. His heart rings out, comforting me with every beat. "Can you see who it is?" he asks.

"I can't."

I can feel all the muscles in his body tense up even more. He tightens his hold on me. "Are you sure?"

I focus, try to make everything clearer. It doesn't work. "It's like they're wrapped in shadows in the middle of all that bright light," I say. Michael's heart begins to beat faster. I look up. "What is it?"

He stays silent for a few moments before speaking. "You're remembering."

I pull him as close as I can. "I just wish I remembered you."

"You do remember me."

"What?"

Michael's cheeks are flushed, his eyes glazed over with sadness. *Is the someone him?* But it wouldn't make sense. No one could survive what I see in my head.

"How about you tell me?" I push. "How about you tell me the important things?"

He laughs quietly. "I wouldn't know where to start, Astrid. There's you and me. And I don't know if you're ready for that."

I study his face, trying to piece together his thoughts. But I get nowhere. "Why wouldn't I be?" I ask.

"You and I…things go beyond us. We were always caught up in things that were bigger than just us." He leans back and takes my face in his hands. "So, you see, if I told you about us, I'd have to tell you about everything." The pain on his face scares me. My heart drops into my stomach. We stand there, gazes locked. I want him to kiss me. I want us to go back. But he lets go of me and starts to walk away. "I have to go," he says. "Alex is waiting."

"When will you be back?" I can't keep the hunger out of my voice.

He turns around. "I don't know yet. Hopefully, I won't be away too long."

I shoot him a smile. He smiles back. Then, he grabs his coat and leaves. I stand still. Just wishing he would come back. *The journals.* I look at the bookshelf, lined with so many. So many about the woman. I walk over and run my fingers across the bindings. But I don't pull them down. I don't go through their pages again because I know now. The woman is me.

CHAPTER 43

A buzzing sound knocks me out of my sleep. I roll over, reaching for my smart glass. My fingers find it and I bring the screen into view. I'm being called into the OR. I cast a look around the room. Michael's sound asleep. The sun isn't even up. I can't remember the last time I was called in this early. I get out of bed and put my hand to the window. It's still freezing. I run to the bathroom to wash my face. Then, I slip my warmest clothes on. I give Michael a quick kiss on the forehead before heading out.

People brush past me as I step out into the street. Their cheeks are rosy, breath like ice in the air. They're in a rush to get inside, and I don't blame them. I wish I could've stayed in the warm bed with Michael. I pull my scarf up over the bottom half of my face and brace myself against the wind. Despite the cold, I feel good. I feel *happy*, and I'm not sure why, but I feel peace. I'm being called into the OR to do a horrible thing. But the anxiety that usually comes over me is nowhere to be found. Michael's smile flashes into my head.

Everything will be fine. This will all be over soon. As the OR comes into sight, I realize I've walked faster than usual. Maybe it was the cold nudging me along. But the faster I deal with this, the faster I get to go home. People keep bumping my shoulders in their hurry. I'm not even annoyed today. I push open the door and stride into the OR's lobby. David's light brown eyes watch me. His flaxen hair is slicked back today.

He looks carefully groomed, pristine, far healthier than last time but still pale.

"Astrid," he nods.

"Good morning, David."

I think my cheery demeanor surprises him. His mouth falls open. He arches an eyebrow. I walk into the elevator and press the button for Mr. Winters' floor. The air in the OR is freezing as well, but even that isn't dampening my spirit. The doors slide open. I briskly head down the hall and knock on the big steel doors. Half a minute passes and they still don't open. I knock again. The lock clicks. I push my way into the office.

Mr. Winters is sitting in his chair, his brows pressed down over green eyes that are more intense than usual. His suit is thick and a knitted blanket is laid across his lap.

"Good morning," I say.

He doesn't immediately reach for the smart glass like he usually does. He just sits there, scanning me. The unease that was so absent starts to creep in. Mr. Winters' expression continues to darken the longer he looks at me. I open my mouth, but I can't think of anything to say.

"How are you doing, Astrid?" His question stuns me. There's something grating about his voice today.

"I'm doing well. And you?"

"I'm doing well," he says. "Thank you." He folds his hands and studies me. My chest tightens more and more with every second that passes. Finally, he reaches over to the table and starts to bring up a profile. I sigh in relief, but it turns out to be too soon. Green text flows across the screen before being replaced with a face. David stares up at me from the table.

Mr. Winters' gaze pierces into me. Chills run through my body. Every one of my muscles tightens. "What's the meaning of this?" I ask.

Mr. Winters slides open a drawer built into the lower half of the table. He pulls out a gun and sets it on the table. "You're going to take this gun into the lobby and shoot David."

I lean over the table, searching for reasons listed. There's nothing. "Why?" I ask.

Mr. Winters' eyes narrow. He presses his lips together and leans forward. "Why are you asking questions?"

Then, it clicks in my head. This is a test. *But why?* I rack my brain and realize there are so many possible reasons. Which one is it? What does he know? It feels like I'm falling, even though my feet are on the ground.

"The gun," says Mr. Winters.

I start to go numb. The gun's in my hand and I don't even feel it. Mr. Winters' gaze is glued to me. He must see what this is doing to me. *What do I do?* I turn around and leave his office. If I don't do this, they'll know. Michael, Alex—and everything they're working for—are all at risk. Everything rests in my numb hands.

My footsteps ring in my ears as I enter the elevator. When I exit, it's like I'm floating. David's at his desk, per usual. He looks at me, brow furrowing a little with confusion at the weapon in my hand. I stop directly across from him.

"Astrid," he says.

His face goes even paler than usual when he realizes I'm not leaving. Why doesn't he run? If I don't do this quickly—if I show hesitation—they'll know that I'm not like how I used to be. If they find that out, everything will be ruined. I raise the gun. David's eyes go wide.

"What are you doing?"

I don't say anything. I just pull the trigger. A high-pitched ring fills my ears. He slumps back, neck craned unnaturally, blood spilling out everywhere. Then, I set the gun down on his desk. Mr. Winters isn't in the room, but I know he's watching. I don't call the cleaners because I know he'll take care of it. I start walking towards the lobby door, careful not to walk too fast or too slow. They can't know that anything is wrong.

The wind bites into my face as I push my way out into the street. The sun is just starting to come up. Sweat covers my forehead. I'm shaking, but it's not from the cold. *I just killed David.* What would've happened if I didn't? They would take me in for interrogation, burrow into my mind with their tools and dig around. They would find out everything. They would find out about Michael, Alex, the meetings, the altered Curat.

Everything they had worked for would be for naught, and everything that could've been would become impossible. I *had* to kill David, right?

"Killing is never right. But sometimes it's for the greater good." That was what Alex said. He would understand. But Michael wouldn't understand, would he? Maybe he shouldn't have to, because it isn't *right*. What I've just committed is the greatest sin. Is there anything worse than taking a life? I rub my face. I realize I've been walking without paying attention to where I'm going. I check my surroundings. It looks like I'm on the way home. Hot tears run down my cheeks.

I'm such a fool. I thought I would never have to do this again. I tricked myself into believing that I had changed; that all of my past sins were because of the Spora and Curat. But it's me. I have no excuses, nothing keeping me from my true self. I just killed David. I wipe my tears with my sleeve as I enter the first floor of my building. The lobby is empty. I don't think anyone that lives here has a job that requires them to be up this early except me. What a horrible occupation this is, and what a horrible human I am.

The elevator seems to take forever to ascend. My scarf is stifling me. I take it off and unbutton my coat. Finally, I'm out on my floor. I can't reach the front door fast enough. I'm still shaking. My chest wracks with sobs as soon as I'm inside the apartment. I slide down against the wall and bury my head. Michael's rushed footsteps resound as he hurries out of the bedroom. But I don't look up.

"What's wrong?"

I can't manage a reply. He kneels in front of me, reaches out, and gently lifts my head to look at him. His gaze locks onto mine. He looks like he understands what's happened. But there's no hate or judgment. Michael pulls my head to his chest, and he just lets me cry. "I can't do this anymore," I say, voice coming out hoarse.

He tightens his hold on me. We sit there in silence for a while before he speaks.

"This will end soon, Astrid. I promise."

CHAPTER 44

There's me, Michael, and Alex. I don't know how I feel about this. It's awkward. They're both lost in their thoughts sometimes, shooting glares back and forth at other times. I pull my coat tightly around me and sit on the floor. We're at the warehouse. It's almost time for the meeting. We're just waiting on Thomas and Noah. Michael covers his eyes with his hand. I'm not sure what he's going to say tonight, but I know it will be important.

Alex's focus has shifted to me. It's so strange. Now that I know his real name, it makes sense. He could never have been anything but Alex. I called him by the other name for so long, it still slips out. But he's Alex, and I used to know him so well.

There's a storm brewing under his calm surface. We've barely said anything to each other tonight, which is probably good. There might be too much to say. Anytime I talk to Michael, I can feel Alex's green eyes burn into my cheek. So, I've just stayed quiet. The only sounds in the warehouse are our breaths.

The sight of David's slumped body haunts my mind. The sight of the blood flowing down to the floor. I buried myself in bed today. I shed tears for hours and still, I have tears left. I wipe my eyes with the back of my sleeve. Alex is still looking at me. I lift my chin, meet his gaze again. But I wish he'd switch his attention back to Michael.

"Leave her alone," mutters Michael.

Alex's head snaps around. "I'm not doing anything," he says.

"Stop it." Michael shoots him another glare.

Alex scoffs and crosses his arms. The door clicks open. I get up and brush myself off. Thomas strides in, followed closely by Noah. Their jaws drop when they see Alex.

"Where have you been?" gasps Thomas. From Noah's stunned face, he's thinking the same thing.

Alex puts up his hand, as if to calm them. "I've been busy."

Noah throws me a glance. "Was it because of *her*? You stopped coming after she started." Nobody says anything. Noah finds his answer in the silence. "Well," he says, dry. "Glad to see that's sorted."

Michael steps forward. There's no color in his cheeks. It's like the thoughts that have been running through his head all day have drained him of energy. "I've come up with a plan," he says. Silence again, except for my heartbeat ringing in my ears. Michael clears his throat. "I know I've explained the relationship between Curat and Spora before. But you should all know as much as possible."

He runs his hand through his hair. "Most of the general population can't survive without Curat: it's what's keeping them young. If everyone around here ended up with a body that was their actual age, we'd end up losing over seventy percent of the population. Normal Curat helps to repress feelings, keep people cold. Its effect on emotions is only significant because of it working in tandem with the Spora in everyone's brains. The Spora is on a lower power setting, though, because…well, because of what happened before."

The Groupmind. I shudder before I can help myself. Michael notices. He looks even more tired. "The thing about the Curat is its effect on emotions will be minimal if we're able to modify the Spora," he says. "We can essentially give everyone most of their minds back if we manage to get into the implant."

I feel a bit lost, and I can tell Thomas and Noah are as well. But it seems like Alex understands, and he looks angry. "We can't do that."

"Can't do what?" asks Thomas.

Alex's mouth curls up in disgust. "Do you want to tell them, Michael? Or should I?"

Michael looks even paler now. "I'll do it," he says. He takes a deep breath and braces himself. "There's a way to link the Spora into a network within the System, but only the Spora that hasn't already been manually altered. So all of you would be left out of it," he says. "But if we link the rest of the Spora, we can hack into that network and modify them all at the same time. Give everyone their minds back at once. This city would be saved." A chill runs down my spine.

Thomas steps forward. "Why haven't we done this already?"

Michael and Alex exchange glances. The golden-haired man shifts uncomfortably. "Because the last time all the Spora were linked it didn't end well."

"The Groupmind," I whisper, words out of my mouth before I realize. Silence comes over the room again. This time it's eerie. Alex's gaze is burning my cheek again. I don't look at him, because I know he wants me to give him a sign that I'm feeling the same way that he is, that linking everyone would be a mistake.

The deaths and psychotic breaks.

Noah finally breaks the quiet. "What Groupmind?"

What other choice do we have?

"A long time ago, the world was a really terrible place," says Michael. "We'd rid ourselves of the Infirmum and figured immortality out. But with the immortality came skewed morality. With the way the world was going, it wasn't going to be around very long."

"So you decided to put everyone into a Groupmind?" gasps Noah.

Shame crosses Michael's face. "It was an escape from the horribleness. We controlled people's settings, in a way. There was peace."

"There was a malfunction," scoffs Alex. "More than fifty percent of the population that was awake, died. The rest went insane." His cheeks are flushed with anger, and his rage spreads to Thomas and Noah.

"Then we can't do that," says Noah. "It's too dangerous."

Michael begins to look ill. I have to speak up. "We don't have any other choice." Alex's expression makes me feel like I've just crushed his heart. But I believe in what I'm saying.

"There is always another choice," says Alex.

I keep my breath steady, gaze at him levelly. "Death and insanity…or numbness, Alex. Which would you choose?"

"There is always another choice," he repeats, face flushed.

"Which would you choose?"

He stands there, lips parted but silent. He knows what he would choose – he just doesn't want to say it. I look around at the others. "What would the rest of you choose?"

Nobody says anything. I steal a look at Michael. The color is back in his face. I straighten my back. "Michael's just told us our best option. Our *only* option if we want to put an end to this. Isn't that what you all want?"

Everyone's standing still, eyes wide, frozen. I raise my voice. "Well, isn't it?"

Thomas speaks. "I want that."

Noah looks around…his brow is furrowed in conflict. He opens his mouth and I still hope that he's going to agree with the rest of us, though I know from his eyes that he won't.

"I can't go along with this." He's barely able to push the quiet words out. "I have to go. I need to think."

"Noah – " Michael follows him across the warehouse, but Noah breaks into a run and the warehouse door clangs shut behind him. The golden-haired man stares at the door for a few minutes before walking back to our silent group.

"Well," he says, hoarse. "Everyone's entitled to their own opinion. None of you have to go along with this."

I stay quiet; Michael should know of my loyalty. Thomas shifts his weight from foot to foot. His attention bounces around the room, like he's reformulating his opinion, then his gaze stops on Alex…

Alex doesn't speak. His chest is rising and falling rapidly. His jaw is clenched. The way he looks at me makes me realize he feels betrayed. But this isn't about him. This is about the city, and I know this is what he wants. Now we all stare at Alex, waiting for his reply. Then -

"Tell me the details." Reluctance glimmers in his eyes as they lock onto mine. "How are we going to save this city?"

"You're going to help?" asks Michael.

"I'm certainly not going to let you execute this plan alone," says Alex. "Especially as Astrid is so determined."

Michael opens his mouth as if to speak, then closes it. It takes a while before he manages any words. "You're a good man."

"A good man wouldn't become involved in a plan that puts the whole population of this city at risk," Alex replies, voice flat. "If I was a good man, I would have run out before Noah."

"They're dead anyway," says Michael. "Do you remember what that was like, Alex? They're not like you. They're not capable of fighting the way you did. At least, this way, we're giving them a *chance* at life. Better to risk everything for the possibility of life than remain without it."

Alex studies his face for a moment, thoughts reeling behind his eyes. "For the greater good."

Michael nods. "For the greater good. There are too many implants to modify one-at-a-time without being discovered. And we're running out of time."

Alex shoves his hands in his pockets and lifts his head high. "So, what's the plan?"

"There's a control room we made for the Spora network when we formed the Groupmind," says Michael. "It was sealed off after the attempt failed. But I know where it is. If we get in there, I'll be able to link the implants again."

Alex shakes his head. "How do you know the control room will still work?"

"Because I'm the one who sealed it off."

"You left it connected to the System in case you had to use it again in the future?" asks Alex, not bothering to keep the disgust out of his voice.

Michael shakes his head. "It's powered down. It'll reconnect once I turn it on."

"How long will it be until someone realizes it's back on?" I ask.

"If we're lucky, a minute," says Michael. "Seconds is the most likely bet."

Alex shakes his head. "I can get someone to hack in and cloak it."

The corners of Michael's mouth turn down. "That won't work."

"Why not?" I ask.

"Because it will literally pull all of the Spora in this city—present company and a few others excepted—back into a network within the System. You can't hide linking millions of people together like that."

"You better work fast then," scoffs Alex.

Michael presses the back of his hand to his forehead, as if trying to cool himself. "I wish I could say I was the only one who was going to be put at risk, but I need someone to go in with me. I might need help."

"I'll do it," I say. There's no way I'll let him go anywhere without me. Michael and Alex look at me with the same unreadable expression.

"It's not safe," says Michael.

"I know. That's why I'm going in with you."

Alex's eyes are piercing into me. He's shaking his head frantically, like he wants me to change my mind.

"I'm going in with you," I repeat.

"No," begs Alex. "Don't do it."

But I won't change my mind. I force myself to meet his gaze. "I'm going with Michael."

"Well then, I'm going, too. Wherever you go, I go," says Alex. He turns to Michael, face contorted into a bitter smile. "Looks like you get both of us."

Michael stares at me. "Are you sure?"

"Of course I'm sure."

"Nice to see you're worried about *my* safety, Michael," laughs Alex. But his laugh is empty, and the sound of it sends chills under my skin.

Michael narrows his eyes at him. "I have a feeling you'll be fine." He turns to Thomas. "We'll need you to keep eyes on the area around the street entrance to the control room. Just make sure that if someone tries to trap us…we can get out in the end."

I stare at Michael, confused. Thomas stares, too. "Trap you? Who would want to do that?" He asks.

Michael stares back for a few seconds before shrugging. "The area is filled with crazies."

"Where's the control room?" asks Thomas.

Michael looks around at all of us before speaking. Then, he takes a deep breath. "It's in the middle of Lutum."

CHAPTER 45

The glass has frosted over. I've gone to the pillar to turn up the heat countless times, but it's still cold. I wrap the blanket I've draped over my shoulders as tightly around me as I can. I can't tear my eyes away from the window. I can barely see outside, and it fascinates me. What are the people in the streets doing? They could barely deal with the weather when it was half as cold as this. What are they doing now?

Lutum. There are people who seem to live in the streets there; and some of the apartment buildings are devoid of any heating capabilities. How will the residents survive? Curat keeps you young, strong—but not strong enough to deal with temperatures like this. A pang of worry hits my chest. Someone needs to do something. Who is controlling the weather? *Who* is doing this?

Michael strides in. He hasn't gone to great lengths to bundle himself; he only wears a sweater and slacks. But he doesn't look cold at all. "Hey," he says.

"Hey."

He kisses the side of my head. Then, his brow furrows with concern. "You look cold. I'm so sorry."

"Why are you apologizing?" I ask. "It's not your fault."

His mouth curves into a small smile, then he looks at the window. "You can't see *anything*."

"It's beautiful in a way," I say.

He lets out an ironic laugh. "I can only imagine what it's like outside."

"Do you *have* to go?" The outside that the window conceals is suddenly frightening. I don't want him to go out into the cold. I want him to stay safe in here…with me.

"Yeah, I have to. But not yet," he winks.

I smile, because there's no better sight or feeling than him. He steps behind me and starts rubbing my arms. Immediately, I feel warmer. I reach behind me and bring him in as close as possible.

"What were you thinking about?" he asks.

"When?"

"When I came into the room just now. You were lost in thought, I could tell."

"I was just trying to imagine what it was like outside."

"And?" he asks.

"The people in Lutum. What's happening to them right now?" Michael stops rubbing my arms. "Their buildings have poor—or no—heat. Will they die?"

Michael stays quiet for a little, mulling over the question. "They might," he says.

My heart sinks. I'm suddenly too cold again. "What can we do?" I ask.

"It's the *weather,* Astrid. There's not much we can do." But his voice is hollow.

"Michael, we know everything in this city is controlled by *somebody.*"

"I wish it wasn't."

I turn around and look at him. His calm expression's been replaced with one of shame. *Why?*

"It's not your fault," I whisper. "Why are you looking like it's your fault?"

He forces the shame off his face with a painful smile. "What else has been on your mind?" he asks.

He's eager to change the subject. Do I let him? I want to push him to tell me whatever is behind his shame. But something that was circling in my head when I woke up comes back into my mind. "I've been thinking about David."

Michael tightens his grasp on me. "What about him?"

Chills run down my back. "Why have me kill him? He didn't do anything. If they suspected me of something, why not just take me in and interrogate me?"

"Are you sure he didn't do anything?"

"He was *David*. He'd never do anything to warrant that. Whoever runs this city, whatever they'd tell him to do—he'd do it. I *know* he would never do anything."

"I don't think it was a test, Astrid."

"But David didn't *do* anything."

"I think he'd completed his purpose."

I stare at him, stunned. His cheeks are flushed, and a glimmer of anger has crept into his blue eyes. "What purpose?" I ask.

Michael sighs. "Life is strange when you can't be killed."

"Everyone can die. What are you talking about?"

A quiet alarm rings from his pocket. He pulls his smart glass out. "I have to go," he says.

I reach for him, but he's already pulled away.

"Wait. Michael…"

He gives me a hug. "I'll see you later, Astrid. We'll talk more then."

The door closes behind him. The lock clicks. I stand, hand still outstretched, feet glued to the ground. I keep turning his words over and over in my mind, and they don't make sense. Because everyone can die. *Can't they?*

CHAPTER 46

This is the coldest day yet. I can hardly feel my face; the wind has numbed it. My eyes tear up and my breath freezes in the air before me. I wrap my scarf around the bottom half of my face, then quickly shove my hands back into the shelter of my pockets. The air is filled with snow, but I can't even tell where it's coming from. I know snow usually came from the sky before. But the white particles that fill the air are swirling in all directions: seemingly coming from the sky, the ground, everywhere at the same time.

Mr. Winters was back to his stilted self today. It's like he never asked me to kill David. He went through the normal process without shooting me any suspicious looks, with no mention of the fair-haired man I killed. The sight of David's slumped body fills my mind again. He hasn't been replaced. The lobby was eerily empty. They haven't put in anyone else to greet the people who work at the OR. Surely greeting people who work at the OR wasn't his only purpose…

The sound of a Regulator's gun rings in the air. I turn my head. They're dragging away a young man. I can't see his face. Everyone rushes to clear a path for them, like they're scared. Hasn't everyone always feared the Regulators, though? There's always been the looming threat of being returned. I shift my focus back to the street.

Another Regulator's gun rings out. This time, they're taking somebody on the opposite side of the street. It's a woman, her red curls peeking out from underneath a woolen hat. *Ruth.* Her bloodied red hair, her face shot out by Alex. *Luke and his kind smile.* They pass through my mind. It's like I can't look at anything without being reminded of someone who's been killed. I turn back and continue down the street.

I think I've turned the corner to the warehouse where the transportation options are. But it's hard to see, and I'm distracted. I feel like a mess today. I wipe the tears from my eyes with the back of my gloved hand. Someone grabs my hand before I can put it back into my pocket.

"Astrid. Are you alright?" Alex tightens his hold on my hand and scans me.

"Yeah, I'm fine," I say. "You?"

"I'm fine. Glass?"

I pull out my glass and let him see the job info. It's a woman today, another one who's refused to take Curat.

"There are others like you," I say. "Others who try to fight."

Alex narrows his eyes as he goes through the profile. "She won't get far without the Curat though," he replies. He sighs as he gives the glass back. "Is there any point in killing her when she'll be dead soon anyway?"

"It could cause disruptions," I say. "The mere sight of someone making a stand like that; who knows what it would do?"

Alex shakes his head. "That's not the way to make a stand."

"At least she's doing *something.*"

Suddenly, it's as if every muscle in Alex's body freezes. He looks past me, a strange light in his green eyes. I turn to see what he's looking at. A small stream of people is steadily crossing in front of us. But there are two figures directly across from us who are standing still. They're both beautiful. But then again, everyone in this city is beautiful. One is a woman, the other a man.

It's the woman from Lutum with the coat. The man is similarly colored, except his eyes are darker…

I know him from somewhere, but where?

I grab Alex's arm. "Who are they?"

He says nothing, but he slips his arm through mine and starts leading me down the street. I pull back.

"Alex, it's too cold to walk all the way."

"Just humor me for a little," he says. But his voice has gone hoarse, and the color has left his cheeks.

"Who are they?" I ask again.

Neither of us has looked back. I can feel that they're following us, though. Alex feels it, too. He wouldn't be acting like this if he didn't. "They're the worst kind," he says. I start to turn my head. Alex's fingers dig into my arm. "Don't look back, Astrid."

I study his face. He's not scared. He's angry. *Why?* "Are you going to tell me what's going on?" I ask. I don't even know where we're going. The snow covers the streets and the buildings, it blurs my vision. Everything looks the same. "Look, the target lives just outside of Lutum and it's way too far to walk in this weather. We have to go, otherwise—"

Alex stops. "We'll get rid of them."

I stop, too. "How?"

"I want you to go down this side street and around the building."

I feel like I should be scared. My heart would be racing if my mind wasn't filled with how *cold* it is. I head down the side street, sandwiched between two skyscrapers. The snow is blowing into my face, hurting my eyes.

I raise an arm to shield myself. But for some reason, it doesn't help at all. It's like whatever's in the air has a life of its own, swirling all over the place. I swear there's some flying off the ground and going back into the sky. I turn the corner of the building and find myself on a street far emptier than the one from which I came. I know someone's behind me. I wonder which one of them it is. *What happens if I look back?* I want to. It's like I'm being pulled, drawn to turn around. I walk half the length of the building, then stop. I need to look. I glance over my shoulder.

The man is a few yards away from the edge of the building. He doesn't stop, even though he sees me looking at him. Then Alex rounds the corner, running. He wraps his arm around the neck of the man, as if to strangle him. Without even thinking, I rush back towards them. The woman comes around the corner now. Her eyes narrow when she sees Alex. I run faster, heart pounding in my ears. The woman goes for Alex;

she elbows him in the face and the man slips out of the stranglehold as if nothing's happened. I run as fast as I can, but I can't get there fast enough.

Alex fights them both off as best as he can. He's skilled, trained like me. But they're quick, more skilled, almost superhuman…

The man grabs Alex from the back, and the woman kicks him in the stomach. She kicks him again, and again, and again. I push myself off the ground and ram my fist into the side of the man's head as hard as I can. I hear something snap and he lets go enough for Alex to get away from him.

The man's eyes narrow, his head is tilted forward, he's walking toward me with quiet ferocity. There's something more subdued about him. He was savage with Alex. Now he looks calculated, menacing—but there's something else that puts me off about him, something I can't figure out.

His eyes are a strange mixture of black and deep blue. I know I've seen him before…

The elevator. He was in there, studying me, as I went to tell Michael I would move in.

Out of the corner of my eye, I see Alex fighting the woman. I can't tell if she wants to kill him. Tears pour out of my eyes, brought on by the stress and cold. The man keeps walking toward me, calm. I keep backing up. Chills are running through my body, pushed into shudders by the freezing weather and fear of the man in front of me. *He's not doing anything.* He just keeps walking. *Who is he?*

The woman kicks Alex in the chest. He's fighting hard, but his movements are slowing down. He needs help. I run forward, trying to go around the man so I can kick myself off the building to bring down the woman. But the man is fast. He grabs the collar of my coat and slams me to the ground. I lay there for a few moments, staring at the white sky, trying to get my breath back. My head is pounding. The man could kill me right now, but he doesn't. He just watches…like he's curious.

Finally, air comes back into my lungs. I jump up. He won't let me go around him, and I can hear Alex's muffled groans with every blow that hits. I try to hit the man in the face, chest, knees; he blocks everything. Then, I see it: a glint of silver under his coat, strapped to his thigh. *He has a knife.* I modify my movements into distractions. He doesn't even notice when I take the knife from him. But he notices when I stab him in the side.

Alarm crosses his face. Blood oozes out, dying the snow. I kick him in the back and he falls to his knees. The woman is too preoccupied with hurting Alex to pay attention to the man, or maybe she doesn't care. They're still throwing blows at each other. Alex has a bloody nose. The woman looks pristine. Her ice-blue eyes shift to me when she sees me running. I block her for a little bit; but then she kicks me in the stomach and I drive the knife into her thigh, slicing it as I fall back. Blood spatters onto my arm, some hits me in the face. I must've struck a vein.

Surprisingly, she says nothing. There's no yelp, no cry of pain. But alarm crosses her face as well. Her focus shifts to the man kneeling in the snow for a second, and Alex rams his fist into the side of her face. Then, he leans back against the side of the building, chest heaving, trying to wipe the blood from his nose.

The woman stumbles towards her companion. My hand is still clutched tightly around the handle of the knife, but I won't use it. They're both bloodied and defeated. I don't know who they are, but I won't kill either of them. Although with the way blood is pouring out of the girl's thigh, maybe I already have. She grabs the man and they leave. What did they want? *Who are they?*

I watch them until they stumble around the side of the building and slip the knife into my coat pocket. Then, I turn back to Alex. He's slid down to the ground, eyes looking up to the sky. A few people are crossing us in the street. No one stops.

"Alex—"

"I'll be fine."

I kneel in front of him. "Strange method of getting rid of them."

"It's the only way that works."

The woman's blood is streaming down my face. I wipe it off with my sleeve, and there's something weird about it. The blood-stained snow where the man fell catches my eye. I've been covered in blood before, *seen* so much blood before. This isn't it. The snow has shifted colors—going from a pure, bright red to deep purple. The longer I stare at it, the more numb I feel.

"Alex, who are they?"

He lets out a bitter laugh before bringing his head forward. His green eyes pierce into mine. "I hope you never find out."

"Why?"

He opens his mouth to say something, then changes his mind.

"If you know who they are, then please tell me something," I beg.

Alex still looks angry. Whoever they are...he *must* know them. "I'll tell you one thing," he says.

The sky suddenly floods with silver light. Its reflection off the ice and snow nearly blinds me. I close my eyes. It's like the light is searing through my eyelids. Then, the glow stops. When I open my eyes, Alex is staring at me - and the anger has been replaced with pity.

It takes a minute for him to say anything, but when he does my heart stops. "They're *his* kind."

CHAPTER 47

I swipe through all the options on the pillar and request my second glass of brandy. Almost instantly, the pillar parts to reveal a full crystal glass. I down it, then request another. This time, I grab the glass and walk to the window. It's much colder in here than it should be. The heat function isn't broken, but it's not working like it used to. A little warmth starts to flow through my veins from the brandy. I sip it and try to calm myself. I can't get the sight of the stained snow out of my mind, and I can't stop hearing Alex's words. *"They're his kind."*

That was all he said. His nose stopped bleeding, he brushed himself off, and we went to the edge of Lutum to take care of the woman. I asked no more questions because I was scared. I'm a coward. I gulp down the brandy and walk back to the pillar. The frost on the window blurs the view too much anyway.

I put the glass back and request another, then sit down on the sofa. The alcohol is barely affecting me. It might be because of the long-lasting Curat that Michael gave me. I set the glass down and bury my face in my hands. The man and woman from earlier today weren't human. They were something else. Shudders wrack my body.

My heart is pounding, spurred faster and faster by what I'm scared to think about, the possibility I'm afraid to admit. Alex knew who the man and woman were. He knew *what* they were. And he said they were *"his"* kind. There's only one person he could be talking about. I empty the brandy from my glass.

Why am I here? I'm not sure I would've chosen life if I had known it would be like this. I push the glass away from me. Restlessness sweeps over me. I get up and start to pace. "They're *his* kind," keeps ringing in my mind, over and over. I clutch at my head. *Stop, stop.* But it doesn't stop and I start to feel sick. I stay still for a moment, cover my face with my hands, try to steady my breathing. It helps a little. When I bring my hands down, I see them. *The journals.*

I decided a while ago that I was done with that. They're Michael's journals, his private thoughts. It'd be wrong if I went through them, but I can't look away. Before I realize what I'm doing, I'm at the bookshelf, running my hands across the bindings. I pull one down. I can't tell how old it is, and I don't care. I just need to see.

"Better a life of loneliness than a life with anyone except her."

I know he's talking about me, and I don't know how to feel now that I do. There's less jealousy, but it's not totally gone. I'm jealous of my past self: she had everything taken from her and still, her life was better. I rifle through the pages.

"I swore to myself that I would bring her back, and I won't stop until I do."

"I've put a plan into place: but it won't be easy."

What plan? I turn the page, but it's the last one and nothing's written on the back. I push the journal back onto the shelf. It's almost impossible to tell which one comes next. They're not ordered chronologically; there are journals with cracked bindings placed here and there. I choose the one on the far-right side of the shelf. I flip through the pages, pausing now and again.

"Would she still love me if she knew what I have become?"

I freeze. There's an idea in the back of my mind—an idea that's been growing since I saw the snow, and it feels like the words that I just read have validated it. I don't know what to do with the journal in my hands. Do I keep reading? Do I put it back? I stand there, book open, the same page staring back at me. The journal should be put back. I shut it with a snap and lift it to put it back on the shelf, but there's something in its place that wasn't there before.

A small black notebook is lying on its side, blocking the back part of the journal's place on the shelf. I reach in and pull it out. It must've been laid on top of the journal when I pulled it; I didn't see it before. It's well-worn leather, and half the size of any of the other books on the shelf. I return the journal and turn my attention to the black notebook. I run my finger along the cover: it's been bent, scratched. I can tell from looking at the side that the pages have been roughly handled; they're ripped around the edges, and I think some pages have been torn out entirely.

Every fiber in my being is telling me not to open it, but I do. I stare at the page, unsure of what I'm looking at. A minute passes before I make any sense of what's written. There are two columns: one is a list of dates, the other is:

"Eyes—Complete
Skin—Experimented on Partial (Hands)
Heart—Upgrade
Bone—Transition Started"

It keeps going on. I flip through the pages, trying to find a place where it ends. But the whole book is filled. I don't think I'm breathing. I *can't* breathe. *Procedures.* It's a list of procedures. Done on Michael? Or did he do this to others? My heartbeat is ringing in my ears.

"Brain—Experimental Enhancement Begun"

I sink down to the floor, rifling through the pages. My body begins to go numb. I don't know, and I can't understand…or maybe I don't want to. The front door clicks open. I can't tear my eyes away from the notebook. I hear Michael walk in, but he says nothing. Silence fills the room for minutes before I can bring myself to look up.

His eyes are wide and filled with shame. His cheeks are red. He stares at me: mouth half-open, lost. I stand up and walk over to him. He still doesn't say anything. I hold out the notebook, but he doesn't take it. I grab his hand and push it into his grasp. We stand there, gazes locked. It's like we're both afraid to break the silence. But the longer I look at him, the more I need to know.

"Tell me what this means," I whisper. "*Please.*"

CHAPTER 48

My hands are folded in my lap. I don't know how long I've been sitting at this table, waiting. Waiting for him to say something. Waiting for him to explain and clear the fear that's in my heart. But I have a feeling that when he finally does speak, it won't do anything except confirm what I fear most.

Michael sits across from me, notebook closed in front of him. His cheeks are flushed. His chest rises and falls so quickly. I can hear his shaky breathing from here. He looks up at me, blue eyes wide. "I wish I could ask you to promise that once I'm done explaining, nothing will change. But that's too much to ask."

I lean forward and try to get him look at me. Still, he won't look up again. "Just tell me."

"I don't know if it's something you can live with, and I don't want to lose you."

"You stand to lose everything if you don't tell me," I say. "Because my mind is coming up with the worst things imaginable. So *please,* tell me."

Michael shakes his head. "I doubt the worst thing you can imagine comes close to this."

"Try me."

He sets the notebook down and leans forward. He can't stop fidgeting. His hands are moving, his foot is tapping. Then, he goes still. "Astrid, do you remember what the world was like just before you were put under? Has anything else come back to you?"

I shake my head. "All I get is the image of someone surrounded by fire…"

"I see," Michael sighs. He pushes the notebook away from him, as if he doesn't want to look at it. "We began the practice of putting people under in the cryotubes because it was our best option. Claims of the Curat formula and what it could do were greatly exaggerated at the time, and you knew this because I was working on it…and I told you everything," he says. "You still decided to go under, even though there was a chance you'd never be brought back."

A pang of guilt hits my chest. "I chose to leave you?"

"You believed in me," Michael shakes his head. "You believed I would perfect the formula to save you and me." He reaches for my hand, but changes his mind and pulls back before I can touch him. "You believed I'd find a way to give us a new future, a new life. Not one that was filled with pain. We went through so much, Astrid. We lost *everything*. In the end, all we had was each other. That was why you chose to go under, and that was why I let you."

Everything he's saying strikes me as true, but I can't remember. I have nothing to give proof to his words.

"We were both old back then," says Michael. "Not like how we are now: young, strong. We were old and as much as we didn't want to admit it, our bodies were failing." He goes quiet again. I catch my breath. He looks just as scared as I am of what he's about to say. "It was me and a team of twenty working on the Curat. We spent *years* tirelessly researching, testing, reformulating…we were given a group of test subjects…" He buries his face in his hands.

"How many test subjects?" I ask.

"Fifty," he says.

"What happened to them?"

Slowly, he lifts his face and I see his scars. He's looking past me at something unseen. "We lost all of them within the first ten years." He takes a deep breath in, trying to regain his composure. "By that time, we'd progressed enough to have a good idea of which direction we needed to go in with the formulation. We started testing on ourselves because we *had* to. I held off on that for as long as I could. But we were all old. Our bodies were failing. Our *minds* were failing."

My heart beats faster and faster as I wait for the bomb to drop.

"We realized that if we were failing in that section of innovation, we had to make up for it in another. Otherwise humanity would never survive. So, we turned to upgrading ourselves."

"Upgrading?"

Michael nods. "It started with bionic body parts." He flips the notebook open to the first page and turns it around so I can see. "There was a team of about ten brilliant tech innovators. They knew we weren't progressing as fast as we needed to with the Curat formula. They'd secretly been working on bionic body parts – limbs, organs, everything. We were desperate. We went to them to try and partner, to develop *anything* that could prolong our lives. But when we went to them, they already had everything we needed."

He points to the top of the page. "It started with the eyes," he says. "We went on to replace other organs. Then we began experimenting with artificial skin that would never age and that would protect us better…" His voice drifts off when he looks up at me. I don't know why. It's like I'm not able to move, not able to think. "Astrid." His blue eyes are piercing into me. The blue eyes I love so much, and they aren't actually his. They aren't actually real? "Astrid, I'm sorry."

He reaches his hand out to me and I take it, hardly knowing what I'm doing. "Why are you apologizing?"

"Because I failed," he says.

We sit there, hand in hand. I run my finger across his skin. It feels like my skin. It feels *real*. I would never have been able to tell it wasn't. My brain slowly starts to come alive again. My thoughts reel, and one spins to the front. There's a question I want to ask, a curiosity that weighs heavily within. "Michael," I say. "The entry at the bottom of the page. Did you experiment on your brain?"

He takes a sharp breath in. I feel his muscles tense up underneath my hand. "This one you might not be able to get past," he replies, voice low.

"Just tell me the truth." I have to know, even if it ruins everything. I tighten my grasp on him. I *won't* let it ruin everything.

"We'd had so many struggles with the formulation," says Michael. "We wondered if we needed an intelligence beyond ours." He tightens his hold on me, too. "It started out as sectional enhancements. We'd developed advanced replacements for certain parts of the brain that could be seamlessly integrated."

"Artificially intelligent implants?" I ask.

"Essentially. Once we started enhancing, we made so much more progress. Our formulation evolved at a ridiculously fast pace. We made leaps and bounds. The Curat formula that I gave you? The one you'll never have to take again? We came up with that within a year of the cognitive enhancements."

He gets quiet again. His hold on me is shifting past the boundary of tight and into desperation. "There are some—well, *most* decided to convert entirely."

Now, I understand why he looks so uneasy. My heart is racing. When I speak, my voice comes out hoarse. "What about you?" I ask.

"Would it matter, Astrid? If you couldn't tell already?" He's staring at the table, ears and cheeks flushed. I don't remember ever feeling this confused.

"How much of your mind is still yours?" I ask.

His head snaps up. "All of it!" he cries, voice just short of a yell. Then, regret crosses his face. He looks so *hurt*. Guilt sweeps over me.

"I'm sorry," he mumbles. "I didn't mean to. Look, Astrid, all of me is real. *Please* believe that. Please believe that everything I feel for you— everything I have *ever* felt for you—is real."

My breath wavers. How can I believe him if almost everything he ever was has been replaced? But I believe him. *And I still love him.* Am I being stupid?

"What are you thinking, Astrid?"

"I'm thinking that I believe you." He looks so relieved. The corner of his mouth quirks up into a half smile. I wish I could smile back at him, but I feel like I'm falling. Something in the back of my mind tells me that I should've known, that I should've been able to tell.

Still, there are things I need to ask. "Two people followed me and Alex today, a man and a woman. We confronted them," I say, Michael's expression darkens as I go on. "I lifted the man's knife when he was coming after me and ended up cutting him and the woman. They bled…but it wasn't *blood*. Some of it fell on the snow, and it turned purple after they left. Are they like you?"

The entirety of Michael's face and neck have flushed crimson. "Yes," he mutters, voice filled with anger. "They are."

"Why did they follow us?"

He wears the same expression Alex did when I pressed him for information. But he answers. "There were other people in your life – in *our* lives before. And when you left, there were others still with me, but I became so lonely…"

Michael looks out the window as if he's filtering through memories. "I did something terrible, Astrid. I tried to bring back those I shouldn't have – and when I did, they weren't even themselves."

Confusion muddles my thoughts again. "What do you mean?"

"I created something else entirely."

Then, it clicks. "They were never human in the first place."

Michael looks strangely relieved. "At first they were merely copies of real people, but the capabilities I gave them were so great…they turned into things I didn't recognize." He pauses, lips parted, hesitating. "Did you go after them first?"

"Alex did. I had to help."

"They're wired to be non-confrontational. They avoid direct violence if possible. But if Alex went after them first, that makes sense. They react as humans would: fight or flight." He shifts uncomfortably. "And some of them are extremely protective of each other…"

"How much does Alex know about them?"

Michael draws a quick breath in like a hiss. "I told him everything."

And yet, Alex didn't tell me. *"I hope you never find out."* Perhaps it was an act of kindness. "Why did you tell *him* everything?"

"When Alex's Spora was altered, he began to notice so much. And it was weighing on me, Astrid. They'd killed all of the people who had been working on the Curat before…and I don't know what happened to the engineers who'd worked with me to create their bodies. Alex was a familiar face. When he voiced his suspicions, everything came pouring out."

"Why not tell me earlier?"

He looks at me like I should know. "Because I was afraid what you would think of me."

I still don't know what to think of him. My thoughts about him are spinning into nowhere. But I have other questions.

"If they avoid violence, why did the man have a knife?"

"I don't know. I'm not in the inner circle anymore. I don't know how they've evolved," Michael leans forward. "But I'm still me. I'm still human. Please believe that."

I run my gaze over him. He *looks* human. I've seen enough of this world to know that humanity is a strange thing. I wasn't even human for a while, was I? I doubt many of the humans in this city actually deserve the name. If you can't *feel*, then where's your humanity? The way Michael's looking at me, he feels the most of anyone I've come across in this city. He's not like the man and woman from earlier today. They were cold, calculated. He's different.

"I believe you."

He breathes a sigh of relief. "Thank you."

We sit there for a minute before either of us speaks again. Something he said has been spinning in my head, over and over. "Why would they send a warning?" I ask. "Why make me kill David?"

The color leaves Michael's face. He shoots a glance at the window: it's frosted over, like it has been the past few days. "I suspect they've concluded that *something's* going to happen," he says. "They want to keep me in line."

He looks back at me. "And it's not like we hide. Anyone can see that you and I—" He stops. I wonder why he doesn't finish what he's saying.

"So, it was a warning for you?" I ask.

"If they wanted to affect me, the best way is you."

I lean back in my chair, thoughts running a million miles per hour. "They must know I can feel. If I'd been asked to kill David six months ago, I could've done it easily: no questioning, no hesitation. But why not go after you directly?"

"Because they think of me as one of them," says Michael. "I told you they're wired to be non-confrontational. Direct violence goes against what they stand for, unless it's viewed as self-defense. But I don't know if this happened because they know you can feel. It might've happened because they know how *I* feel. And when you have to do things like that, it kills me. We might be safe…for now." He glances at the window again. "But they're patient. They're also immortal; built to last forever. Any approach they take to anything is long, thought-out."

I turn my focus to the frosted window as well. "And what is their end goal? Are they the ones messing with the weather? I assume they're able to somehow control the System?" I ask.

"They might be able to control the weather…but I can't make sense of what their intent would be there. I believe their access to the System is limited."

"Limited?" I echo. on

He pauses. "I think they might want something far more sinister for the people of this city than death." My breath stops. Michael goes on. "I don't know if the System has decided to help them, but have you noticed there are far too many people being returned? No one has access to the cryotube room anymore – the System automated the organization of it and locked everyone else out. We have no way of knowing what's really happening to these people after they're returned." My heart seems to sink lower and lower with every word that leaves his mouth. More and more people are being taken off the streets everyday. Luke's face flashes through my mind. The memory of him being dragged away sends a shudder through my body.

"I think they want to convert this city entirely," says Michael.

"Why?" I ask.

"They want everyone to be like them because in their way, they're lonely, too," Michael replies. "That was my mistake. I gave them the ability to feel loneliness, because I wanted them to understand. But I also made them different…and the loneliness was too much. They're so alike to us, Astrid, but so different. Somewhere along the way, the logic in their thoughts changed."

"We can't let them change this city," I whisper.

"We'll save this city if it kills me."

It feels like someone's driven a knife into my chest. The thought is unbearable. "I thought you can't be killed," I say.

"Not easily."

"I don't know what I would do."

He squeezes my hand. "You'd survive, Astrid. Just like you always do. You're the woman who lives."

I hold tightly onto him, and never want to let go. "I wouldn't want to live without you."

"There's a whole other world beyond this city," he says. "Someone has to save it."

Another world. Yet, this city is so big it's hard to imagine anything beyond it. "What is it like out there?" I ask.

"Even I don't know anymore," says Michael. "All I've heard are rumors, whispers."

A chill runs down my spine. Too much is still unknown, and it scares me. Michael looks at me, then smiles. "It'll all be fine, Astrid." Finally, I've gotten all the transparency that I've wanted from him for *so* long. But I can't tell if I'm glad or not. All I ever wanted was for him to share himself with me, and now I know everything about him. Would it have been better to live in blissful ignorance? "Are you regretting this?" asks Michael.

"Regretting what?"

"Knowing this. *Us.* Everything."

He's close now. His face is inches away from mine, and I want to close the gap. "I don't regret it," I say.

"Any of it?"

My hand is on his wrist. I can feel his pulse, and it keeps getting faster. My thoughts are reeling but if he isn't real, then what is? I press my lips into his. I don't regret *any* of it.

CHAPTER 49

I've tried warming the window, just so I can see a little bit of what's going on outside. It does no good – and it's absolutely freezing in here. I tap the glass. It's like it's not just frosted over, but covered by a sheet of ice. Michael walks out of the bedroom and I turn my head. He's not dressed as warmly as I am, but he looks nice and comfortable, as if the cold doesn't affect him at all. Perhaps it doesn't.

"Are you leaving?" I ask.

He shoots me a sad smile. "I have to."

"Please be careful. I can't even see what it's like outside."

The smile disappears from his face as he looks at the window. "I'll be fine," he replies.

He walks over and gives me a quick kiss. I want it to last longer, like I always do. I grab his arms and don't ever want to let go, but he pulls away. "I'll see you later, Astrid. Stay in here if you can."

The door closes behind him. I turn back to the window. My heartbeat gets faster the longer I look at it. My med stats flash across my vision, followed by a suggestion to take deep breaths. But the worry is crushing me. *What is happening to the people in Lutum?*

My smart glass buzzes and knocks through my thoughts. I pull it out of my pocket, but there's no message notification. Strange. I put it back into my pocket. It buzzes again. I pull it out and stare at it. No new messages. I hold it, not sure what to do. Is it malfunctioning? I've never had problems with it before. I put it back into my pocket and it buzzes again. I sigh as I check it. Still no new messages.

My focus shifts back to the icy window. Is the OR calling me in? I know I shouldn't go outside, it's dangerous. But I'm curious. I grab an extra coat and scarf, then head out the door. The elevator seems to take forever to descend. Strange, creaky noises meet my ears. The lights flicker. I shudder. Finally, it reaches the lobby. I exit as quickly as I can when the doors open. There's no one there. It's strangely dark, the only light emitting from the welcome screen. I pull my collar up and wrap the scarf around the bottom half of my face before stepping into the street.

The cold bites into my eyes. The air freezes in my nostrils. There's little snow, but what there is of it is strange—just like the other day. It doesn't seem to be coming only from the sky, but also the ground, the walls of buildings, everywhere. I walk down the street. A thin layer of white ice covers everything, even some of the people. *The people.* All of them move slowly, as if their muscles are being frozen. My pace almost doubles everyone else's as I head to the OR. I hear the buzz of a Regulator's gun for every block I pass. So many are being returned.

But where are they being returned to? I stop and turn as I hear the Regulator's gun again. They're taking a man: young, attractive; just like most of this city's residents. Are they going to convert him? Could that really be what they're doing with everyone who's returned? I brace myself against the cold and continue walking.

I have the sickening feeling that what Michael said is true. I'm a block away from the OR now. The whole city seems darker today. The flurry of snow and frost can't distract from the fact that some of the buildings aren't lit. The streetlamps should be on in weather like this, even though it's the day. But none of them are.

The people around me seem to be moving less and less. A woman has come to a full stop. She's leaning against the side of a building: eyes closed, teeth chattering. Has everyone been outside longer than I have? I know it's cold, but I can't make sense of why they're this slow. They look *sick*.

The cold might be making my eyes tear up, but I'm still able to function better than they are.

I press the handle of the OR door. It doesn't open. I press again. The door still doesn't open. A sinking feeling fills the pit of my stomach. *Have I been banned?* Are they coming for me? I wish the exterior of the OR wasn't mirrored. I desperately wish I could see inside, but the OR is so frosted over I can't even see myself.

I feel a familiar grasp, then a warm voice in my ear. "Astrid, come with me." Alex slips my arm through his and leads me down the street. "Slow your pace," he says, quiet.

I do as he says. "Why?" I ask.

He takes a deep breath in before speaking. "The Curat that Michael gave you—the advanced formula—it permanently increases strength and regeneration far beyond the formula that everyone else is given. That's why you're better able to withstand this weather."

I steal a glance at him. "But you look fine, too."

"I know."

"He gave it to you, too?"

"He did indeed," mutters Alex, and he doesn't sound happy about it. The shock is on my face before I can stop it, but he doesn't look at me. Did Michael give Alex the advanced Curat out of admiration? Or necessity? I don't know how I feel about this...or what else to think.

We move so slowly for blocks, but everyone else is still slower. I squeeze Alex's arm. "Where are you taking me?"

"Home," he says.

"Yours?" I don't succeed at keeping the reluctance out of my voice.

Amusement creeps into his green eyes. "No, Astrid. *Yours.*"

"Oh," I breathe. "Thanks."

"I don't know why you're thanking me."

"You just seem to have a knack for showing up at the right time," I say.

He lets out a small, bitter laugh. "Just for you, Astrid."

Guilt fills my chest. Where would I be without Alex? I owe him so much, and yet, I've done *nothing* for him. "Was I banned from the OR?" I ask.

"No, I don't know what's going on with that."

"You can't get in either?"

"No one can get in," says Alex. His green eyes glaze over. He stares straight ahead of him, lost in thought.

"What is it?" I ask.

"Things are disappearing from the System," he says, voice hoarse. "We used to hack into the surveillance across this city. The System's eyes if you will. But things are going offline. The OR went offline today."

"What do you think it means?"

Alex shakes his head. "I don't know. But I know how it affects us. We're able to hack in and manipulate what's seen. But with each building that goes offline, so does that building's surveillance. That means there are surveillance gaps."

I turn his words over in my mind. "Is a new surveillance system being built that we don't know about?"

Alex's feet stop for a moment. "It's possible…"

We've turned a corner. I look around. I can see a couple figures in the distance. But besides that, the street is empty. Memories from the last time we were in the street together flood my mind. "The man and the woman who came after us. Do their kind have a name?"

Alex's brow furrows. Our gazes lock. Bitterness fills his eyes. "They go by the names of the people in whose image they were created. Lilah, Christian, Ezra…"

Images stir in my brain. *Fire.* Someone walking out of the fire. Suddenly, pain sears through my brain. My ears ring. My knees buckle and the world around me spins.

"Astrid!" cries Alex. Images race through my brain so fast that I can't see. "Astrid, look at me," Alex pleads.

But I can't. I see pain, hurt, death. *So much death.* Then, I see the flames. Everything is clearer now. I can see who's walking out of the fire. *It's me.* "No, no, no…" My voice drifts off. I can't stop.

Alex's hands press into my shoulders. "Astrid, calm down."

I can't. Because I'm remembering. I'm remembering *who I am*. And it hurts like hell. Tears run down my face. There are too many terrible images streaming through my mind. I hyperventilate. Now, I know. I killed in the past. The pain in my head stops, but it leaves behind something far worse in its place. The snow beneath me has turned red. I don't know why. Then, I realize my nose is bleeding, as are my eyes. I wipe the blood off my face, something that I've done countless times before. "Why didn't you tell me?!" I scream.

He stares at me, stunned. "You remember what you were," he says.

"This whole time you've known, and you didn't tell me."

He brings his face closer to mine. "I only remembered everything when I saw *you,* Astrid," he says. "The day I first saw you at the OR. Then everything made sense."

Blood is still trickling out of my nose. I wipe it with my sleeve. Words are tumbling out of my mouth before I realize. "You were there. You were running with me. And then they gave me this city, this country..."

My feet are backing up. I gaze at him: tall, dark, covered in snow and frost. He straightens his back. "I could've run against you and won on my own." Then, his expression softens. "But I loved you, Astrid."

And I remember that I loved him, too. *Loved.* Until I couldn't take it anymore. "This whole time, I thought I wasn't made to kill." His green eyes grow somber. "But I killed thousands with my choices," I say, hoarse.

Alex steps forward. "The world was a bad place. We needed a President who wasn't afraid of war."

I shake my head. "Not me."

"They called you a revolutionary. People sang your praises everywhere. The praises of 'The Best President.'"

"No," I say, voice not coming out any louder than a whisper. "Stop."

"Then you met *him*. And you decided you wanted to be different. He didn't just steal you from *me*. He stole you from the world." Confusion contorts his face. "I don't pretend to accept it," he says. "But I try to understand."

"Why were we even at war?"

"Multiple countries were locked into a technology race. It had permeated every aspect of our culture. For a moment, we forgot bombs. Countries tried to destabilize each other with perfectly-crafted lies instead. No one in the world knew what to see or believe anymore....but then, the weapons came. Far more advanced than anything had come before. And the race was longer than we thought."

He keeps walking toward me, and I keep backing away. "You were the world's savior at one time, Astrid. For every measure another country took, you went further. People were afraid of you...but that fear inspired so much respect." His words drive into me like a knife. What sort of monster was I where my success depended on fear? But there's something that doesn't make sense.

"If I was the world's savior, how did I end up stuck in this city?"

He pauses. "This city is what's left of our civilization."

"I don't believe you."

"What? You think there's something better out there?"

His voice is challenging but his eyes tell me that he wants to comfort me. He's reaching out, but I don't let him reach me. "Michael said there's a whole other world out there."

Alex pulls his hand back. "Did he paint it as some grand place?" asks Alex. "'Cause it's not." I don't say anything. He goes on. "If you can barely handle the terribleness of this city, then I advise you not to go beyond its limits."

"Why?" I ask. "What lies beyond?"

"The stuff of nightmares, Astrid." My pulse is racing. There's so much I don't know. "Do you remember the Infirmum?"

"Of course I remember it. It took everything from me."

"It took more from others," says Alex.

"That's not possible."

"But it is." We stand in silence for a while, gazes locked. There's a sinking feeling in my chest. "What do you think the Infirmum was?" he asks.

"It was a sickness that swept the Earth."

Alex's eyes narrow. "In a way, it *was* a sickness that swept the Earth. They released a biological weapon in our country." Pain sears through my head again. People crying in the streets. Fire, misery, death. "The people in this city are the ones who escaped."

"It took my *children*," I breathe. "And it took my ability to have any more. Escape? I didn't escape."

Alex rushes forward and grabs my shoulders. "But you're still *human*, Astrid."

My breath stops. "What are they?"

"I don't know what you would call them. They've devolved," Alex says. "Or maybe *evolved*. I guess it depends on the way you look at it."

More images flash through my head. *So much fear.* We were running away. "How did we escape?" I ask.

"We received intelligence that it was coming. It gave us just enough time to put a plan in place."

"*Us?*"

"We chose a city that was far from the capital, one that we were sure wouldn't be the main target. You'd originally visited this place a few times when campaigning. Then it became where you retreated with your family when you needed a break. 'Far away from everything,' you said it was. You suggested this city, and we began moving everyone in."

"Moving who?"

"Everyone we picked," says Alex. "Everyone was brought in for a reason. I personally escorted them in, the last one right as the weapon hit. Then, we sealed the city off." Alex's mouth straightens into a grim line. "But we didn't seal it off in time," he says. "All the children – and the oldest of us - started getting sick. We figured out that the weapon was meant to stay in the air for as long as possible with its effect on people increasing the longer they were exposed. We had an advanced air filtration system in place, but it didn't work fast enough."

And I remember. "Nothing can get in..."

"But no one can get out," finishes Alex.

Something stirs in the back of my mind. "Who launched the weapon?"

The color leaves Alex's face. "Vado Grayson."

I try to call to mind a face, a voice, anything. "I don't remember him." And I'm too stunned in this moment to hate.

"He wasn't even a politician," says Alex, voice hoarse. "That's what cuts. He wasn't like you or me. We weren't supposed to be at war with *him*."

"Who was he?"

"A successful businessman who made his fortune in tech and medicine. He was born here, but moved away when he was young and built his empire in another country."

My head spins with what feels like a million thoughts. "Why would he launch a weapon like that?"

"Money."

"From who?" I ask, disgusted.

"Everyone."

I stare at Alex and wait for him to explain, because my thoughts lead me nowhere.

He continues, reluctant. "Everyone wanted to take you down, Astrid. All of the world leaders, and other powerful people who were aligned with them."

"Was I so bad?" The wind goes out of my lungs.

"They all thought that you always went too far. In every respect."

"And did you think I did, too?"

"No," he says. "I supported all of the choices you – we – made. But…I wonder what exactly is out there now."

"You want to leave?" I ask.

"I want to *see*. We saved ourselves and left the rest to die. I want to know if there is a chance to fix what happened. We had drones circling after the blast— to see what the effects were—but they all stopped functioning three months later. Any connection we had to the rest of the world is long gone. I can only imagine."

My head starts to pound again. Memories are streaming through my mind. Faces appear in front of me; similar to mine, similar to Michael's— but young, innocent. They died. And I couldn't do anything except stand by and watch. But the others - the millions who put their faith in me and trusted me to make this country the best place it could be for them…

I left them to die while I saved myself.

I turn and start heading down the street. I need to get back home.

"Slow down!" cries Alex. But I'm running. There's ice flying into my eyes. I can hardly see. Alex catches up to me. "Astrid, I know what it's like. *Stop.*"

But I don't stop. I keep running. I need to get away from him. I need to go home. Alex keeps trying to grab me until I reach the apartment building. I rush into the lobby. My head has stopped hurting and my nose has stopped bleeding. I swipe for the elevator. It seems to take forever to come down. Alex is outside. I can feel him watching me through the glass. I don't want to look at him, but it's like I'm being pulled. I turn my head.

His green eyes pierce into mine. Chills run down my arms. Things are different now. I remember hurting him, and I remember my actions killed *millions.* Guilt wracks my chest. The longer I look at him, the more I feel his frustration, anger. The elevator doors open. I step in.

CHAPTER 50

"You remember everything?" Michael stares at me, blue eyes wide. We're on the way to the meeting. It's even colder than it was earlier in the day, if that's possible. Our breath freezes in the air in front of us. The streets are completely empty.

"I remember almost everything," I say. "I remember you, me, our children, Alex. I remember—" My voice catches in my throat. I take a deep breath. "I remember what I was." *How could Michael love me?* How could he love me after all I did?

"But that's not who you are now," he says.

"The choices I made killed so many."

Michael takes my hand. "You changed, Astrid."

"Did I?"

His grasp on me tightens. "Trust me, you did. First, you changed when you met me. You began backing off. Then you changed after we'd been in this city and…" The scars are there in his eyes again.

"Can people change that much?"

"I believe they can," he says.

"But what if I changed too late?"

A sad smile crosses his face. "I believe people can be redeemed, no matter how long it might take. That's why I have to do this." He lets go of my hand. We start walking again. "I didn't just bring you back because I love you, Astrid. I brought you back because you're a fighter."

He shoots me a glance. "And that's one of the most extraordinary things about you: your ability to fight. It's rare. I wish I had more of it. I wish I was more like you."

I shake my head. "I didn't fight when I was brought back, not like how Alex fought."

Michael stops again, I follow suit. Our eyes meet. "But you'll fight now, won't you?"

And I know I will. I straighten my back. "I'll fight with you to the end."

There's more sadness on Michael's face, despite the lasting smile. "I know you will." He starts walking again, faster. I match his pace. A notification flashes across my vision telling me that the temperature is dropping. But I feel fine. *I feel strong.* I'm dealing with the cold even better now than I was during the day. The snow is getting thicker, swirling everywhere, highlighted by the silver in the sky sometimes. But my eyes aren't tearing up, and my muscles are warm.

We're almost to the warehouse now. My heart is beating fast, but it's out of excitement. I push my way through the door and see Alex. He's in the middle of the room, hands in pockets. The guilt that I was feeling earlier in the day comes back. My breath pauses for a moment.

Michael steps around me. "Good to see you, Alex," he says.

But Alex's eyes stay on me. "It might take a little longer for Thomas and Noah to get here," he says. "With all of the snow on the streets."

Michael nods. "Of course."

So, we wait. But we wait too long. Alex begins to pace. My chest fills with worry. I turn to Michael. "What should we do?" I ask.

He and Alex exchange glances. Their faces are pale, brows furrowed with worry. "We could go look for them," says Michael.

Alex shakes his head. "No, I don't—"

The door clicks open. It's Thomas. He stumbles in shivering, covered in snow and ice...and blood.

"Thomas!" Alex rushes forward and grabs his shoulders. His green eyes scan the dark-haired man. "Michael, the Curat."

"I'm fine," gasps Thomas.

"No, you're not. What on earth happened?"

"They tried to return me. I fought them off, but they ..." His voice drifts off, like he has no energy left to speak.

Michael rushes over with bandages and a vial of Curat that's sky blue. Alex rubs Thomas' arms, trying to warm him up. I go to help. But it doesn't look like it does much good. Blood gushes out of a deep gash right beneath Thomas' chest, and a smaller one closer to his heart. Every movement he makes is stiff, as if he's slowly freezing. "Is Noah safe?" he asks.

Alex's gaze meets mine. I nod. I draw Thomas into me and try to stop the blood with the bandages as Michael injects the liquid into his veins. Alex steps back and pulls something out of his pocket. At first, it looks like a roll of paper. Then, I realize it isn't. It seems to be made of flexible, opaque glass.

He rolls it out and it lights up. He catches my stunned look. "Can't hack with regular smart glass," he says.

"Where did you get that?" I ask.

He says nothing. I was okay with not knowing who he works with, who helps him. But as I watch him, the fact I don't starts to irk me. I never met the rest of the fifteen. They're so important, and I have no idea who they are…or how many are left. Text is flowing across the thin screen. He's swiping on different things, working his way further into the System.

"Alex, who's working with you?" He doesn't reply. The color leaves his face. He looks up at me and Thomas. I feel my heart drop. "What is it?" I ask.

He hands me the screen, and I hold it up so both Thomas and I can see. Noah's face stares back at us. The whole description of his being crammed into as few, untrue words as possible. Now, I see why Alex has gone pale. A red notification is flashing above his photo. "Returned." There's a time stamp next to it, it was only a few minutes ago.

A quiet whine comes from Thomas. I hand the screen back to Alex just as Thomas' body starts to wrack with the most intense sobs his failing body can manage. We sink to the ground. I pull his head into my shoulder, and just let him cry. The Curat that Michael just gave him is not enough. Alex's gaze is glued to the ground, eyes wide and hands tearing at his hair.

Michael walks back over. The color has left his face as well. "The heat function isn't working."

Alex turns around and drives his fist into the wall. I think I hear something crack.

"Alex!" cries Michael.

"It was never supposed to be like this," hisses Alex. "This city was *not* created for people to end up like this."

Michael stares at him for a moment. His shoulders slump forward a bit like it's out of shame, guilt - but it's not his fault. He leans down next to us and studies Thomas. I can tell from the look on his face that there's not long left. Thomas' sobs are getting quieter and quieter.

"Michael," I whisper. "Give it to him." He looks at me for a minute, eyes shifting with hesitation. "Please, Michael."

Without a word, he gets up and runs out of the warehouse. Alex watches him go, then turns back to me. "Why did he leave?"

"He's gone to get the last vial of the advanced Curat."

Alex's jaw drops. "Then there'll be no more."

Thomas has gone silent. His eyes are half-open. I've completely enveloped him. Rubbing his arms, his back, just trying to keep some life in his bones. His blood has soaked through the bandages, dying my clothes and expanding into a puddle around us. "You don't think he's worth it?" I ask.

Alex kneels down. "Give him here." I gently lay the dying man in his arms. I know Alex will be more effective than me. Thomas is about the size of me; roughly half a foot shorter than Alex. "We'll save him," says Alex, but I can't tell if he thinks it's worth it.

We sit there, waiting for Michael to come back. The lights in the warehouse flicker. Alex's mouth straightens into a grim line. "This city is insane."

"The world was insane when this city was sealed off," I reply. "So it's no wonder."

Alex sighs. "Look, Astrid…there's honor in what you did."

I study his face, trying to figure out the motive behind his words. "Why do you say that?"

"Because I know you think there's no honor in killing," says Alex. "But there is honor in saving. And we saved as many as we could."

"Did we really?."

"We did. We had no other choice."

I rub my forehead. "But I can't get the blood—the *death* out of my mind that happened along the way. There was so much of it."

"Everything that happened wasn't your fault."

"But I *did* it, and so did you. We executed everything."

"We did what was necessary."

"Why didn't we try to find some other way?"

"We tried, Astrid. But we always did what we *had* to. There's no question about it." The memories flying through my mind are so sickening, I don't see how what he says could possibly be true.

Thomas is completely silent, except for the sound of his shallow breaths. I shift my focus to the warehouse door. My heart starts to pound in my ears. If Michael doesn't come back soon, Thomas will be dead.

"Astrid…"

"What?"

"He's stopped breathing."

I try to feel a pulse. But there's nothing. The door clicks open. I don't look up. I can't stop staring at the cold man in front of me, trying to search for any sign of life.

"He's gone," says Alex.

Michael kneels next to me. "There's a chance."

"A chance for what?" asks Alex.

"A chance the Curat could still work. But I don't know if there's enough of it."

Alex's eyes grow cold. "So it could be wasted."

I turn to Michael, my fingers digging desperately into his arm. *"Do it."*

He squeezes my shoulder and nods. Then, he pulls a box out of his pocket and opens it to reveal the last vial and a syringe. "Here we go," he mutters, piercing the cover with the needle. "Take off his coat and unbutton his shirt, Alex."

"There's no point, Michael," asks Alex.

"Do it now."

But Alex doesn't move. I pull off Thomas' coat and unbutton his shirt. Every inch of his skin feels ice cold. Michael presses the needle into the left side of his chest.

Alex's brows fold above his eyes. "What are you doing?" he asks.

Michael raises a hand to his lips. We sit, not saying anything, barely breathing. Just watching in hope. A minute passes with no visible change.

"It didn't work," says Alex. Michael leans forward and lays his fingers on the side of Thomas' neck. Alex scoffs. "He's dead, Michael. He's *gone.*"

"Wait."

I'm not sure how long we wait in silence. But Thomas' chest starts moving, however slightly.

"It's working," breathes Michael.

I take Thomas' hand in mine. He opens his eyes.

CHAPTER 51

This is it. The night where we try to redeem as much of our souls as we have left. Everything's gone dark. No one is walking in the streets. The cold has become too much for them. The air is dead quiet. The only sound that meets my ears is our feet pressing into the snow. The only illumination is something that falls like moonlight, broken now and then by the harsh silver light. The last time it hit, it nearly sprawled across the entire sky. The eerie vacancy of the streets sends chills down my spine.

We're just outside of Lutum. Just Michael, Alex, Thomas, and me. Treading through this place that was supposed to offer salvation to those encased within. But what has it done for us? This city has killed everyone, in some way. But I'll be damned if I ever let it kill *anyone* again. Everyone deserves to live life in its beautiful, terrible entirety.

Michael slips his warm hand through mine. I hold on tight. We've reached Lutum. It's a different place compared to the last time I was here. *Havoc* came to mind when I passed through it before. Now, it's quiet and empty. *It's dead.*

Fear wracks my chest. Is there anyone left to save here? Michael's hand slips away. I want to pull him back. He scans the walls of the buildings, the side streets, the alleys. He's searching for something. Alex and Thomas come up to me, one on either side. Both have hardly said anything on our walk here.

Alex nudges me. "You ready, Astrid?"

"Yeah," I breathe.

Thomas clears his throat. "I want to say something."

"What is it?" I ask.

Thomas pauses. We all stop for a moment. "Thank you," he says.

"For what?" asks Alex.

Thomas nervously shifts his weight from foot to foot. "For everything."

We stand there, silent. My heart is beating faster. Guilt crosses Alex's face as I lay a hand on Thomas' shoulder.

"Almost there," Michael calls out. He's far ahead. I run to catch up.

We're nearing the center of Lutum. I scan the area around me. The trash everywhere is grotesque. It covers the sidewalks, the sides of the buildings, the middle of the street. "I don't understand. Everything in this city is so carefully monitored, planned. How did we end up with an area as terrible as Lutum?"

"It's protective," says Michael. "Intentional. No one wants to come here. It keeps people away so the entrance can't be discovered. And Lutum used to be beautiful...until *they* got to it."

The faces of the man and woman fly through my head. A pang of rage flies through my chest though at the end, I was worse than them. "They intentionally drove everyone here mad?"

"The people here are not mad, Astrid. They just never fit this city...and because they were different, they were easy to exploit. Being able to access the System and people's heads in the way we're about to is granting too much power. The gods in this city would never allow anyone that."

Michael stops in front of an alley sandwiched between two rundown buildings. Both are dark, with broken windows. It looks like neither have been used for anything for a while. He points to a faded white mark on the side of one. It's smeared but it looks like a circle divided into six parts like a wheel. "This is it." His voice quivers. I want to bring him into me, but he walks into the shadows. Alex and Thomas come up behind us. The further we go into the alley, the darker it gets. Michael stops in the middle and looks down at the ground. Trash is mixed with the ice and snow in a blurry mess. "Help me clear this away," he says.

We all kneel down and start pushing everything to the side. We clear a strip in the middle of the alley, about fifteen feet wide. But all we've revealed is cement. "What are we looking for?" I ask.

"It's here," says Michael. He kicks the ground with his foot. The cement beneath us vibrates. Michael walks to the side of the alley and starts running his hands along the wall.

Thomas walks over. "Tell me what to look for," he says.

"There should be a circular part of this building about one foot in diameter that's slightly raised."

Alex's green eyes are piercing into me. I can feel his gaze, even in the dark.

"What?" I ask.

I can hear him breathing. His chest is rapidly rising and falling. But he shakes his head.

"Nothing."

I want to ask him what's wrong, because I know *something* is, but Michael's voice interrupts. "It's not working."

I come up behind him. There's a circular panel in the wall, barely distinguishable from the rest of the building if it wasn't raised by less than a centimeter.

"What do you mean it's not working?" asks Alex.

"I programmed this," huffs Michael. "I should still be able to access it. But it's not responding." He presses his hand into the panel.

Alex scoffs. "Great," he mutters.

I lean forward to get a better look, running my fingers along the edge of the panel. There's something about the smooth outline that feels familiar. I lay my hand in the center.

Suddenly, a green light glows around its edges. The panel begins to turn. The ground beneath our feet rumbles. Michael pulls me to the side. He's staring at me, eyes wide.

I stare back. "I don't know," I say.

A square section of cement in the center of the alley has separated from the rest of the ground and gone down. Thomas looks at me, brow furrowed. "How did you do that?"

"I don't know."

Alex lets out a small, sarcastic laugh. "Well," he says. "Glad we got that sorted."

We all rush forward to see what has been revealed. All I can see is darkness. Michael reaches into his back pocket and hands me three silver ovals, all about the size of a pebble. "Hand those out," he says.

I give one to Alex, the other to Thomas. I run my finger over the smooth surface, then squeeze. It glows with a bright light, the strength of which seems impossible for such a tiny thing. I shine the light down and see the ladder. It stretches down for about thirty feet before hitting the ground. Michael lowers himself in and starts climbing down. I follow. Everything seems to echo in this place. My breath seems more than twice as loud, and my heartbeat as well.

Alex climbs down behind me. Unease fills my chest. "You're leaving Thomas alone up there after everything he's been through tonight?"

"I care more about you," Alex shoots back, and my unease only grows. I reach the bottom and step onto the metal floor. I pull my smart glass out of my pocket to check if it's still working. It is. I wonder why it's still alright when everything else in this city is dying.

I flash my light around me. Hallways spread out all round. Then down the hallways, more offshoots, more hallways. *It's like a maze.*

"Damn," mutters Alex, as he steps down next to me.

Michael waves us down the hallway directly in front of us. "This way."

Alex and I follow. Michael leads us down the hallway, then turns onto another, turns onto another, and another. "How do you remember where to go?" I ask.

"The AI implants," says Michael. Then, he stops and looks back at me as if to check if he's said the wrong thing. Alex sighs. Michael's eyes narrow. "I remember everything."

Everything. I wonder if that's a burden. I haven't even regained the fullness of my memory. But I remember who I am—who I *was*—and that's almost too much.

Michael turns and starts going down the hall again. Everything feels familiar. A mild pain fills my temples. No memories, no images flash through my brain. But it can't feel familiar if I've never been here before. Chills run underneath my skin.

"You alright?" asks Alex.

We've been treading along in silence for so long, the sound of his voice makes me jump. "Yeah, I'm fine." He shines his light in my face. I push it away. "What are you doing?!"

"Just checking," he smirks.

Michael stops again and turns back to me. "Are you alright?" he asks.

There's *something* in his blue eyes, too. I don't know what it is. My chest tightens more with anxiety the longer he looks at me. "Yeah," I repeat. "I'm fine."

He stares at me for a little longer before starting down the hall again. A notification flashes across my vision from the Spora, telling me to take deep breaths. *I'm fine.* We keep turning down new hallways. I lose count of how many we've gone down. Occasionally, there are doors. But none of them seem to interest Michael.

Alex sighs. "We've probably passed it already, haven't we, Michael?" Anytime he speaks it sounds flippant. I remember he always did this, though, whenever we had to make a decision in war. He's scared, but he doesn't want anyone to know.

"We're almost there," says Michael. He turns down another hallway and his pace quickens. Then he stops at a door in the middle. It looks like all of the other doors we've seen: thick metal, screen to the side of it, small window in the middle.

"This is it?" asks Alex.

Michael nods. "This is it." He sets his hand on the screen. A minute passes before anything happens. My heart pounds in my ears. Then, the door clicks.

Michael pulls it open. It creaks so loud that it seems to echo throughout the whole maze.

"Jeeze," mutters Alex.

The stale air inside of the room filters out. I flash my light around, so does Alex. This room doesn't feel familiar to me. The equipment is rudimentary. I'm sure we had this technology far before I went under. The other side of the room is covered with a large screen. Beneath it, there's a large keyboard and two panels of switches.

Michael leans over, scanning the switches. He reaches out to slide a red switch, then pauses. "Are you two ready?"

"Yes," I say.

Alex lets out a long, slow breath. "Do it."

Michael flips the switch. A quiet whirring sound emanates from the walls. The room lights up. "System Access" flashes on the screen. Michael's hands fly across the keyboard and a list of options starts flowing across the monitor. "That's strange," he whispers.

"What is?" I ask.

"It's giving me options of information to access."

"Isn't that what it's supposed to do?"

"This control room was specifically designed to only give me access to the Spora. There's a menu here with everything from surveillance to weather. The programming changed."

"Who changed it?"

He shoots me a glance, eyes wide. "I don't know."

"Look, this is all great," says Alex. "But let's hurry up."

"Just a minute," mutters Michael, scrolling back through the options.

"We don't have a minute," hisses Alex. "And this is too easy, Michael. I don't like it."

Michael clicks on the weather option. A list of icons and statistics fill the screen. He studies the screen for a moment in silence "This doesn't make sense."

Every muscle in my body tenses. "What do you mean?"

"It doesn't make sense because it says that the weather is supposed to be 80 degrees and sunny right now." His fingers flit over the keyboard. "Unless…"

Michael navigates back to the menu and scrolls down to an option titled, "Security." He clicks it and the screen fills with blaring red text.

"Seal Compromised."

My body feels like it's floating. Michael types away, accessing further details. Alex stands, frozen next to me.

"Cause: External. End of Life: 6 months max."

"End of life?" I echo.

Michael looks over his shoulder, with no surprise in his eyes. "The seal will be gone in six months at most."

"Gone?" Suddenly, I'm too warm. My face feels like it's on fire. "How can it be gone?"

"It's been weakened by whatever's on the outside," says Michael. "It's going to collapse and either it hasn't been able to control the weather because it's weak…or the outside has actually been coming in."

I try to breathe. "Has someone been trying to break through the seal or is that the way the world is? Is that what the weather is like out there?"

"I would tell you if I could, Astrid," Michael replies.

"And we can't fix the seal?"

"Structurally, it's already too weak and we don't have the resources to fix it. The people who could have done something are long gone."

The light. His face when he looked up in the street.

"You knew when you saw it," I gasp. "I remember how you looked, Michael."

"I didn't know," he corrects me in a voice that's too calm. "I had suspicions because of tests that were run on the seal material before it was constructed. It's supposed to emit that light occasionally when it's reconfiguring the weather, but it also used to react like that as an injury response when we were trying to see if anything could break it. But I had no way of knowing for sure."

"You could've asked Alex for help to hack in, to try and find out what was going on. Right, Alex?"

But the green-eyed man says nothing with his voice or face. Now, I'm sinking. I have a hundred questions I want to ask, but will anyone in this room answer?

"Michael, take care of what we came here for," Alex orders, voice low.

Michael scrolls through the options again. The pain in my temples is getting worse. I grab Alex's arm. "We have to do something. Come up with a plan…"

I look at his face and now, I see nothing but helplessness. He shoots me a quick glance and I can't tell if he's more unsettled by us facing the end of this world we created…or the fact that he has no idea what to do about it.

The sound of my heartbeat in my ears becomes deafening. I need space to think. I stumble out of the room. There's no air here. There's nothing but dust, steel, and cement. I keel over, trying to catch my breath.

Alex is out with me. "Astrid…"

"What have I done?" I gasp. Because this is nothing but my fault. I drove the world to want to end us. I left so many behind that were in my care and kept myself – and the people I *chose* – alive. Still, I failed. The children are gone, so many have died…

I was brought back to kill.

The seal is breaking.

Does a future even lie ahead?

I slide to the ground and clutch my pounding head. I've done nothing but fail over and over. Alex is grabbing my arm, saying something, but I can't hear him…

Suddenly, the pounding stops and everything I hear is muddy, like I'm underwater. *It can't feel familiar if I've never been here before.* I grab the light out of my pocket and shine it down the hall.

I've been here before. I know it well.

A strange energy snaps across my nerves, making me walk down the hall. I'm being pulled, like there's a rope attached to the middle of my chest and someone's trying to lead me away. I go down the hall to the right. *Something* is calling to me. If I go this way, I'll find it.

My feet keep moving. Alex's voice is a distant echo behind me. "Astrid!"

I don't stop. I turn another corner and there's a door, but it's not like the others, and this isn't a hallway anymore. It's an open space, with a ceiling that stretches up about forty feet. The door reaches until right below the ceiling. It's about twice as wide as all the other doors I've passed down here.

I hear Alex's footsteps stop behind me. Why do I know this place? I walk up to the door. It's made of thick steel and there's a huge screen next to it, far larger than any entry screens I've seen in this city.

Alex comes up next to me. I shoot him a glance. His eyes are wide, face lined with fear. But there's nothing to be afraid of here. I walk over to the screen. There's a green light circling its perimeter, like it's been waiting for me. I raise my hand, but Alex grabs it before I can touch the screen.

"I don't think we should be here."

"Why not?"

"There's something inside we don't want to see."

"What is it?" I ask.

He hesitates, grasp on my hand growing tighter. "I can't remember…"

We stand there for a minute, gazes locked in silence. Then a low rumble echoes through the maze and the floor shakes beneath us.

Michael. I take off running. It feels like my heels have been set alight. I know where I'm going, but I didn't realize how far I'd gone.

Alex follows me. He could run ahead, but he wouldn't know where to go. These hallways and doors all look the same, but a map of this maze is now seared into my head. The ground beneath our feet begins to shake more violently as we reach the control room.

"Michael!" I stumble in.

He gets up from the keyboard. Everything in this room is vibrating so fast I'm surprised it hasn't burst into flames. *"Connected"* flashes across the screen in red.

I take his hands in mine. "What's happened?"

He fixes me with his blue eyes, and I've never seen him like this. He looks…resigned. I freeze.

"What's happened?" I repeat.

"I couldn't change the settings of the Spora," he replies, quiet. "I'm sorry. I failed, and now it's exactly like last time."

I stare at the screen. "Why does it still say *connected*?" Alex asks behind me.

I grab Michael's hands so tightly that my nails dig into his skin. "Michael, what are you doing?"

The *"Connected"* melts into *"Destruct."*

"You won't forgive me," says Michael. "But this is the only way. This is how you and I designed it. To make a choice of this magnitude, something has to be sacrificed…and we can't let everyone continue being the way they are. That's no life, Astrid. That's not why this city was created."

I tear my gaze from the screen, unable to make sense of what he's saying. There's a smile on his face but it's so sad. Alex rushes over to the keyboard, typing and flipping switches in vain.

"Oh my god," he shudders. "What have you done?"

But Michael doesn't even look at him. He brings his hands up to my face and cradles it gently. "Just remember that I love you."

Then, his beautiful hands close around my throat. I claw to try and make him stop, try to get free. But he's so strong and his hold is so tight. My feet are off the ground and I'm being moved across the room. Everything blurs together. Alex is shouting something, but I can't hear anything.

My back hits the wall outside of the room and the last bit of air is knocked out of my lungs. Alex rushes toward me, still shouting something that I can't hear.

The door to the control room closes. I see Michael turn away through the window.

"Astrid, can you hear me?"

I hear creaks, sparks—like things are falling apart and catching fire. My breath comes back to me. "Help me up," I tell Alex.

Alex stares at me, bewildered, as I get up and cross to the door. It's locked. I keep pressing down on the handle, and it's not giving away. I pound on the door. "Michael!"

I can see him through the window, typing away on the keyboard. The switch panel has burst into flames. *"Destruct"* keeps blaring in red.

Then, he turns and looks at me. I can see something light up in the corner of my eye.

Alex lays a hand on my shoulder. "Astrid…" It's the screen next to the door.

"Now you can try again," is emblazoned across the screen but I'm too confused – too angry – to understand.

I look back through the window. "Open the door!" I scream. But all Michael does is turn away and no matter how many times I pound on the door, he won't look at me. I need to get to him. I ram my shoulder into the door. Alex pulls me back. "I'll do it," he says.

He rams his shoulder into the door, then kicks it again and again. But it doesn't give way. It's thick metal, why would it? My heart is beating the fastest it's ever beat. I press my hand on the screen, trying to access some controls. I can't navigate away from *"Now you can try again."*

Try again? Try *what* again? I don't want to do anything again if Michael isn't there.

Then the text melts into something else. *"Take care of each other."*

I want to scream, but my voice is gone. The walls are shaking now. I rush to the window. Everything in the room has lit up. I pound on the door. I just want Michael to turn around so I can see his face. Alex hasn't given up on opening the door. His knuckles have gone white from wrenching the handle. But I know it'll do no good.

"Michael!" I cry.

He doesn't look at me. I keep screaming his name, keep pounding on the door. *"Destruct"* keeps flashing across the screen. I kick the door. A loud bang meets my ears. I look through the window; the room is all but engulfed by flames.

Michael turns around. My heart stops when our eyes meet. *"Get out now,"* I mutter under my breath.

Michael walks toward the door, his eyes never leaving mine. He looks so calm, so resigned. He's not going to open this door and come out. Flames wrap around his arms and I see the metal that lies beneath his skin. I ram my fist into the door. I scream his name. This is not how it's supposed to be. Then, all I see is fire. But it's like every fiber of my being has been frozen. I don't know how long I stare at the billowing flames before Alex pulls me back. It could've been seconds, minutes. When he touches me, it's like I wake up. I run back to the door and try to open it.

The heat sears through the door and burns my hand. But I keep going. I keep trying to turn the handle, kick the door, scream Michael's name. Alex's arms envelope me. I try to push him off. I try to fight him. *I have to get Michael out.* But the door won't open and all it does is burn me.

Alex pins my arms in front of me and pulls me into him. "You can't go in there, Astrid!"

I've burned my hands and arms trying to open the door. But I don't feel any pain from that. The pain that I feel is much worse and it's torn through every part of me. My chest feels like it's caving in. Tears stream down my face. *Is Michael gone?* He can't be. He fought too hard for us to have this future. He couldn't have just given up like that.

I lift my face to look at Alex. "We have to get in the room. We have to open the door. We have to—"

"No, Astrid."

I push him away, hardly knowing what I'm doing. "He's still in there!" I yell. The corners of Alex's mouth have turned down. His eyes are wide and filled with pity. He doesn't understand. "He's still in there, Alex!"

"No one—*nothing*—could have survived that."

I shake my head. "You're wrong," I say. "He's not like us."

"Look at the flames, Astrid! Look and tell me you think he's still alive. That room is sealed off. We can't get in, and it's too late..." His voice drifts off when he sees the message left on the screen.

I keep shaking my head until my body wracks with sobs. My knees buckle. Alex catches me right before I hit the ground. "He's not gone," I whimper.

Alex pulls me in and lets me bury my face in his chest. "I'm sorry," he says. "I really am."

I sit there, body shuddering in pain. Alex strokes my hair. I push him away and crawl toward the door. Nothing is escaping around the edges. There has to be a way to open it. There has to be a way to get Michael out. I reach for the handle again.

"Astrid, stop it. He's dead. And so is everyone else." Alex's hands are pressing into my shoulders. His face is inches away from mine, green eyes piercing into mine. I realize he's right. Michael's gone...and we failed everyone again. I'm not sobbing anymore, but the tears keep streaming down my face. Alex's hands slip to the back of my neck. He rests his forehead against mine and we stay like that for a while. Notifications from the Spora keep flashing across my vision. I try to steady my breathing and heartbeat so the implant stops. I close my eyes. I need some sort of calm. I need to be able to understand what just happened.

Finally, Alex speaks. "Thomas must've felt something. Or he's noticed - "

He stops. I open my eyes. We're beneath a city of death and Thomas is all alone up there...

But then I feel it again. The pull. The rope that's tugging at the middle of my chest. I turn my head. It's like it's calling to me.

Alex squeezes my arm. "Astrid, what is it?"

I get up and start walking. Every corner I turn, every hall I go through, every move I make is driven by some other energy that's possessed me. Alex follows me, silent. Soon, we reach the open space. The door stretches up, begging me to open it. Green light flies around the edge of the screen. I raise my hand and set it in the center. The door clicks, and a loud creak resounds. I pull on the handle; it opens a few inches. "Help me," I gasp.

Alex grabs the handle with both hands. We pull back. The door slowly opens. The sound that fills the air makes me think it hasn't been opened in a long time. Finally, we open it enough to get in. I slip past the door, Alex follows. Row upon row of lights on the ceiling begin to illuminate. The room is vast with thick, metal shelves spread out as far as I can see.

All the shelves are lined with cryotubes.

My jaw drops. Is this where everyone goes when they're returned? A powerful voice knocks into my thoughts. "Welcome!"

I nearly jump out of my skin, and so does Alex. "Jeeze, where'd that come from?" he mutters.

There's a metal structure straight ahead of us, taller than Alex and shaped like a bullet. The top of it spins to reveal a screen with "Welcome" flashing across it in bright blue.

I walk to the welcome screen, footsteps echoing. Alex follows. Lasers reach out from a panel right below the screen to scan me.

"What's going on?" asks Alex.

He sounds scared. If I knew, I would tell him. The lasers disappear. "Identification accepted. Welcome, Astrid Rayner," the voice booms. "You have unlimited access." Chills run down my spine. I shoot a glance at Alex. He's frozen, a thousand thoughts running behind his eyes.

"Alex?"

"We should leave." He grabs my shoulder and starts pulling me back toward the door.

I push him away. "What are you doing?"

"This place is not for us!" His voice climbs into something near a scream. I've never seen so much fear in him before.

"Then why did it welcome me?" I ask. "Tell me I have unlimited access?"

"Let's leave," he begs.

"There's nowhere to go."

The fear on his face becomes too much as he realizes that I'm right. Now, he looks like he's holding back tears.

"It was of our own making."

"What was?"

"This nightmare, Astrid."

I follow his gaze to a plain gray plaque further down the metal, but we've strayed so far that I can't read it from here. My footsteps echo as I near it and bend down. The words burn into my brain as I read them.

"The System. Created 2120. Modeled after the consciousness of Astrid Rayner."

There's another inscription right below.

"Dedicated to Astrid Rayner by the Creator of the Life2 Initiative, Alex Azar."

I fall back onto the ground, trembling, thoughts on fire in my head. I don't know how long passes before Alex sits down next to me, and I don't know how long goes by before he speaks.

"The System knows that the seal's breaking."

"So?" I wipe away the fresh tears running down my cheeks, hot with shame.

"So maybe bringing everyone back into the cryotubes here was its way of preparing to keep everyone safe."

"Maybe," I reply. It hadn't occurred to me. "That still doesn't fix any of the terrible things that have happened."

"It doesn't. But it gives us some hope," he replies.

"Does it?" I gasp and I can't believe him, because this feels so hopeless. "What do we even do now?"

"There's only one way forward."

I look over at Alex. "Which way is that?"

He laces his fingers through mine; the fear on his face has been replaced with determination. A bittersweet smile bends his lips – and I catch my breath.

"Are you ready for the world, Astrid?"

ABOUT THE AUTHOR

Aisha Tritle is an award-winning entertainment analyst and strategist, novelist, playwright, and actress. Spending her childhood in Arizona, she was active in the performing arts—which led to her moving to Los Angeles to pursue a career in entertainment. She has studied with famed acting coach John Kirby and at the Royal Academy of Dramatic Art in London. Turning her hand to plays, she completed two One-Act Comedies in 2016: both of which have been published and performed in the U.K.

Aisha recently relocated to the U.K. where she spends her days as a consultant for major film studios and fulfilling her passion of writing novels.

NOTE FROM THE AUTHOR

Word-of-mouth is crucial for any author to succeed. If you enjoyed *Noumena*, please leave a review online—anywhere you are able. Even if it's just a sentence or two. It would make all the difference and would be very much appreciated.

Thanks!
Aisha Tritle

We hope you enjoyed reading this title from:

BLACK ROSE
writing™

www.blackrosewriting.com

Subscribe to our mailing list – *The Rosevine* – and receive **FREE** books, daily deals, and stay current with news about upcoming releases and our hottest authors.
Scan the QR code below to sign up.

Already a subscriber? Please accept a sincere thank you for being a fan of Black Rose Writing authors.

View other Black Rose Writing titles at www.blackrosewriting.com/books and use promo code **PRINT** to receive a **20% discount** when purchasing.

www.ingramcontent.com/pod-product-compliance
Lightning Source LLC
Chambersburg PA
CBHW010515100726
47903CB00009B/2764